Urban Tigers

A novel by

Kathy Chisholm

Ailurophile Publishing

Library and Archives Canada Cataloguing in Publication

Chisholm, Kathy, 1955-
Urban tigers : tales of a cat vet / Kathy Chisholm.

Issued also in electronic format.
ISBN 978-0-9868301-0-5

I. Title.

PS8605.H585U72 2011 C813'.6 C2011-901597-8

Copyright © 2011 Kathy Chisholm
All rights reserved.

Ailurophile Publishing
3650 Hammonds Plains Road
Unit 14, Suite 225
Upper Tantallon, Nova Scotia, Canada B3Z 4R3

Follow Kathy on Facebook: www.facebook.com
Twitter @UrbanTigersBook
Blog: www.kathychisholm.ca

Editors: Elizabeth Peirce, Robbie Beaver
Cover photos: Ron Illingsworth, Robert George Young, Getty Images
Author photo: Hugh Chisholm
Graphic design: Margaret Issenman

Cover photo of Patrick O'Neil, esq. appears courtesy of Atlantic Cat Hospital. Patrick was born to a feral mom at the hospital on St. Patrick's Day, 2008. His quirky ear, the result of a harmless birth defect, only adds to his charm. For more information on Patrick, his buddies, and the real-life Ocean View Cat Hospital, go to www.atlanticcathospital.ca.

Urban Tigers, Tales of a Cat Vet is a work of fiction. Names and characters are products of the author's imagination or are used fictitiously. Any resemblance to persons living or dead is entirely coincidental.

Saving one animal won't change the world,
but surely the world will change for that one animal.

– Quote above the door
of an SPCA shelter in Bathurst, New Brunswick

For Sully

Foreword

WHEN MY WIFE, Kathy, asked me to write the foreword for *Urban Tigers*, I was honoured but horror-stricken. She is the writer, after all. I'm the veterinarian. My writing is limited to prescriptions, illegible notes on patient charts, and thank-you letters to clients at Christmas. Of course, I didn't mention this shortcoming to my wife, and mumbled meekly, "Yes, dear."

If you're like me, you never read the foreword because you want to go straight to the story. Please feel free to do so, but I warn you, you'll miss some really important stuff about this extraordinary book.

Urban Tigers is a work of fiction. Well, sort of. Before you ask for a refund because you were expecting a memoir, let me fill you in on a few details. In 1987 Kathy and I established the first, and still the only, feline practice east of Quebec. Atlantic Cat Hospital grew from a staff of two, one resident cat and seven hundred square feet, to a staff of ten, five resident cats and two thousand square feet. In the early days, Kathy was not only co-owner but also the manager, receptionist, technician, accountant, grief counsellor, kennel attendant, and custodian. As the hospital grew, her job description gradually changed, but her love for the cats and their owners never wavered. She laughed with them, cried with them, consoled them, and celebrated when they returned with a new kitten to begin another journey.

This is the book I would love to have written if I wasn't draining abscesses, trimming ingrown claws, and neutering reluctant patients. It is a tapestry of stories woven from our experiences running a busy cat hospital for more than two decades. Although some of the stories may seem too incredible to be true, most are based on actual events. I know. I was there.

I promise *Urban Tigers* will make you laugh out loud and, once in a while, sob like a child. Such is life in a veterinary hospital. But ultimately, this is a book about hope; a book that celebrates the human–animal bond through the keen eye of a gifted writer. Read it, enjoy it, be moved by it. Then go and cuddle your cat.

Dr. Hugh Chisholm
Feline practitioner and co-founder of Atlantic Cat Hospital
Halifax, Nova Scotia

March 2011

Acknowledgements

Urban Tigers has been twelve years in the making. Thanks to help from many people along the way, it has grown from a helpless infant and unruly teenager into a sensible adult. Without my husband of thirty-two years, it would never have been born. He was the one who, during one of my mid-life crisis rants, said, "Well, why don't you write?" And then he filled the next twelve years with inspiration, patience, and gentle guidance.

Although my grandmother, my parents, and my brother did not live to see this book published, they are no less an important part of my life. I am grateful for their love. The values that they instilled and nurtured have made my life better and *Urban Tigers* possible.

My sister Judy has always been my biggest, albeit biased, fan. She faithfully read every chapter, analyzed every story line, and always made me feel like I was a genius, even when my work belonged in the sewer. I am blessed to have that kind of unconditional love and support.

Susan Kerslake, author, co-guinea pig enthusiast and friend, has always been one of my most ardent supporters. "When's that book coming out, Kathy? I want to buy a bunch for my friends!"

I would like to thank Elizabeth Peirce for her insightful comments and copy-editing, Robbie Beaver for additional copy-edits, Peggy Issenman for the fantastic cover design and layout, Ron Illingsworth for the photo of Atlantic Cat Hospital's Patrick

O'Neill esq. which appears on the front cover, and Robert George Young for his professional photographic expertise.

Thanks to my musical buddies who keep me sane. "Flutes rule!"

To the staff and clients of Atlantic Cat Hospital, I owe a huge debt of gratitude. It has been a privilege to be a part of your lives through these remarkable little beings we call cats.

For those who have gone before: Bootsie, Chippy, Eddy, Mickey, Spike, Wilbur, Emily, Jessie, Foster, Carter, Tina Louise and Sullivan. Your memory lights my way.

And last, but by no means least, I would especially like to thank those individuals and groups all over the world who are working tirelessly to preserve animal life and wild habitats.

Urban Tigers

Tales of a Cat Vet

Chapter 1

"Hymie has never spent the night away from home! Can't you just give him a shot of something?" Mrs. O'Malley peered anxiously at me over the rims of her bifocals.

I would have loved to give Hymie an injection of antibiotics and send the pair on their way. With the arrival of Mrs. O'Malley and the belligerent Hymie, movement in and out of my exam room had stalled. As reception filled with waiting clients, the occasional throat-clearing had progressed to a lively chorus of coughs, wailing babies, and scraping chairs. Unfortunately, Hymie had a whopping abscess on his rear end, probably the result of being a Jewish cat in a Catholic neighbourhood. His attempt to trespass through the backyard of a little female tabby with an axe to grind had resulted in a swat to the backside. The wound would need to be surgically lanced and drained under anesthetic.

"Anesthetic? Oh, dear God." Mrs. O'Malley clasped her hands and rolled her eyes heavenward. A faint sheen of perspiration glistened on her forehead and upper lip like sap oozing from a heated log. Leaning against the wall, she shifted her considerable bulk from one swollen foot to the other and, grabbing my copy of *Emergency Veterinary Medicine,* began to fan herself. Waves of mind-numbing perfume rolled my way. Mrs. O'Malley glanced at Hymie and wiggled her index finger, beckoning me closer.

"Dr. McBride," she confided in a whisper, stealing a peek at Hymie, "sometimes doctors give too much anesthetic. It was on

Oprah." Assured the cat wasn't listening, she continued, "Perhaps we should check with Dr. Doucette and see what he thinks. He just loves Hymie."

After working two months for Dr. Hughie Doucette in a feline-only practice, I decided he had chosen his profession well. Ninety percent of our patients had female owners and Dr. Doucette loved them both. Among his loyal clientele he was the Cat Messiah. I suspected he was hovering around forty. Scattered threads of grey wove their way along his temples and made random appearances throughout the rest of his thick wavy hair. He had a lean build, a quick smile, and existed in a state of perpetual motion.

In a brisk voice, I explained that Dr. Doucette wasn't at work today, but I was sure he would agree with my diagnosis.

Mrs. O'Malley stared blankly at me.

"In fact," I added, "the longer we wait, the worse Hymie will feel. Trapped bacteria can spread through his bloodstream, causing all kinds of other problems." I paused for effect. In the silence, Mrs. O'Malley's eyelids fluttered wildly and her lower lip began to tremble. This was followed in short order by the rest of her body. I watched in horror as she dissolved into a quivering mass of lime green polyester. Sobbing, she wrapped billowy arms around an ungrateful Hymie and howled. Ears scrunched flat against his skull, Hymie howled right along with her. His tail slashed the air with single-minded intensity and his eyes narrowed to tiny slits as he considered his next move. Mrs. O'Malley reached into her pocket for a tissue. Hymie seized the opportunity, launching himself off the exam table into the air. The plum-sized abscess ruptured, releasing a stream of foul-smelling, creamy-coloured goo. I was directly in its wake.

Dr. Doucette's receptionist, Althea, chose this moment to knock politely on the gateway to hell. I opened the door a crack.

"Oooh, Dr. McBride," she whispered, fascinated by the string of slime that dangled from my glasses and clung to my hair. The pungent mix of perfume and pus forced her to take a step back.

"Oooh, Dr. McBride," she repeated in awe.

I squinted in her direction. "Yes?"

Peeking over my shoulder, Althea stammered and cleared her throat. "Uh…you have a pregnant cat coming in that's been locked in a suitcase for five hours."

"What! How did that happen?" Sighing, I glanced at the armada of cat carriers in the reception area and then at my watch. "Is the cat going into labour?"

Althea hesitated. "Well, the owner wasn't very clear."

I sighed again. This was one of those rare days when I wished I had chosen another career. Telephone psychic, maybe. I could sleep till ten, hang out in my pyjamas, and avoid pus altogether.

"See if you can reach Dr. Doucette." I turned back to Mrs. O'Malley, who had collapsed in a chair, and handed her a box of fresh tissues. An unconcerned Hymie lay sprawled on the floor, washing his face.

"Thank you, dear," she sniffed, hauling several out of the box and blowing vigorously.

"Mrs. O'Malley?" I pulled up a chair and sat down beside her.

"Yes, dear?" she hiccupped.

"I have a possible emergency coming in. Susan, our head technician, is going to look after you and Hymie. And I'll be in touch as soon as I can."

Hands folded around the crumpled carcass of a tissue, Mrs. O'Malley nodded. "My late husband, Bertram, God rest his soul," she sighed, placing a hand over her ample bosom. "He was so much better at this sort of thing. The man was a saint. Mind you," she added after a moment, "a saint that always left the toilet seat up. And did he wash a dish one day in his life? No!" Mrs. O'Malley ripped another tissue from the box and dabbed her eyes.

I patted her hand then eased myself out the back door of the exam room. High above me on a decorative border, Sylvester chased Tweety Bird *ad infinitum*. Secretly, I sympathized with Sylvester who never seemed able to catch up with the sanctimonious little yellow bird.

I hated to call Dr. Doucette. I didn't want him to think I couldn't handle the pace. But the waiting room was full and half the surgical ward held patients waiting for surgery, recovering from surgery, or plotting revenge. In isolation, an introspective Siamese named Belafonte stared at the stainless steel wall. One claw pinned the head of his favourite toy, a catnip-filled veterinarian, to the floor. His owners thought the toy hilarious but a headache had been gnawing at me all day. Feline voodoo? I shuddered.

Tossing my soiled lab coat into the laundry basket, I grabbed a fresh one off the shelf. Hilary, one of the veterinary technicians, looked up as I rushed past. She and Tanya were drawing blood from Eugene, an obese black and white diabetic. In reception, I could hear Althea's calm voice as she offered coffee and donuts to the waiting clients. A reverent hush fell over the crowd when she added that Dr. Doucette would be arriving shortly.

I had just entered the bathroom, a female oasis of scented candles and Chatelaines, when Althea burst through the treatment room door.

"Dr. McBride, the pregnant cat is here!" she announced breathlessly.

Ripping a piece of toilet paper off the roll, I cleaned my glasses then hurried to the exam room. A young woman in tight jeans cast a long, sour look my way, then a long, sour look at her four-year-old daughter. Bleached blonde hair stuck out from her head like dried hay stubble.

"Hi, Mrs. Martell," I began. "I'm Dr. McBride."

Unimpressed, Mrs. Martell stared at me. "It's *Ms*. Martell."

"Oh, sorry." I felt myself shrivelling under her caustic glare.

"You're a real doctor, right? I mean, you're not a…student, or something?" Ms. Martell grimaced.

"Actually I graduated three years ago."

Ms. Martell folded her arms across her chest. Bored, her little girl had begun opening and closing the door with annoying precision.

"So…," I began, "Jenny's having some trouble, is she?"

"Yeah, thanks to this one!" She nodded at her daughter, who had stopped to look at us and pick her nose. "Jill, what did I tell you about boogers?"

I looked down at my notes. "She's pregnant and was locked in a suitcase for five hours?"

"That's right." Ms. Martell glared defiantly at me.

"Do you know when she was bred?"

"No! How would *I* know?" Ms. Martell was incredulous. "She didn't rush home to tell me when she got knocked up!"

I paused. Among my clients who loved to "talk cats," Ms. Martell was a tight-lipped maverick.

"Okay," I said, rubbing my hands together and grinning foolishly. "Let's have a peek at Jenny."

Ms. Martell bent down to pick up the sturdy pink kennel.

"I can do it!" Jill's chubby hand grabbed the handle of the carrier.

"Go sit down," her mother ordered. "Now!"

Pouting, the little girl retreated to the chair in the corner. She watched in silence as her mother lifted the gaily decorated kennel onto the exam table and unhooked the latch. Scrawled above the door in childish letters was the warning "Jenny's Place. No Boys Allowed." I stifled a smile as a petite Himalayan with an enormous belly waddled through the entrance. Someone had clearly not read the sign.

Ms. Martell leaned closer. Cigarette smoke clung to her clothes like cellophane wrap on yesterday's leftovers. Ignoring her daughter, who was busy vandalizing my exam room, she gently kissed Jenny's forehead. Uncomfortable, but trying her best to be friendly, the gracious little cat began to purr.

I checked her vital signs and palpated her swollen belly. Her sides rippled as the kittens twisted and wriggled, anxious to meet mama face to face. Under Ms. Martell's vigilant scowl, I lifted Jenny's tail. A small bit of blood-tinged fluid oozed from her vulva. Using sterile lubricant, I inserted a gloved baby finger and probed gently.

Jenny glanced back at me in concern. Her memories of mating weren't preceded by an expensive dinner and flowers, nor did they include whispered endearments and a leisurely cigarette in bed afterwards. Around a female in heat, the male cat has but one thought. In addition, the male cat's erect penis is armed with barbs to stimulate ovulation in the female. No doubt if the human male was so equipped, world overpopulation wouldn't be an issue.

Ms. Martell had remained silent during the physical exam. Now her chilling, green eyes wanted answers. I peeled off the glove and cleared my throat.

"Well," I began, "Jenny's ready to give birth right now, but she can't."

"Why not? Can't you just induce her like they do with people?" Ms. Martell demanded.

"Normally, that's exactly what we would do. But her cervix isn't dilated. I'd like to do X-rays but there just isn't time. We need to do a C-section right away. The longer we wait, the greater the risk to the kittens."

Ms. Martell regarded me for a moment then began rummaging through her bag. I had visions of her pulling out a pearl-handled automatic with a comfortable grip. Instead she withdrew a tube of lipstick. Disgusted, she tossed it back like a fish that was too small and continued her frantic search. Her hand finally closed upon a slender container. Opening it, she removed a single cigarette and raised it to her lips.

"Mommy!" Jill declared. "You're supposed to be quitting!"

"There's a no-smoking policy in the hospital," I added, siding with Jill.

Without a word, Ms. Martell slowly lowered the cigarette with her right hand. The red-capped fingers of her left pounded a jagged rhythm on the table. Jill had grabbed the edges of her seat and kicking her legs into the air, hammered the chair against the wall. Delighted, she repeated the procedure several times until, inevitably, both child and chair crashed to the floor. My thoughts drifted to the locked drug cabinet. I wanted to slap a narcotic patch on both mother and offspring.

"Fine!" Ms. Martell finally sputtered as she tried to comfort her howling daughter. "Just do whatever you have to. That cat's worth a lot of money." She turned to her daughter. "Jill, get your coat on. We have to go."

I scooped Jenny into my arms. Still sniffling, Jill grabbed her coat and stormed out of the exam room. At the door, her mother paused. The cat clock on the wall marked each long second with a slow blink and a mechanical click of its tail. Ms. Martell looked at me. Her body sagged, softening the hard edges.

"Take good care of her," she whispered. Then she was gone.

In anticipation of a C-section, Hilary had laid out the autoclaved surgical pack, gown, and drape as well as the prep solutions. She checked the anesthesia and oxygen levels and prepared the gas induction box. Rather than the usual pre-op sedative followed by barbiturate and then gas anesthesia, the safest approach for Jenny and her kittens was gas induction. She would wake up quickly and be able to look after her family.

I placed Jenny on a blanket inside the plexiglass box and closed the lid. As the oxygen and isoflurane mix flowed into the box, she sank lower and lower until she was asleep. I lifted her out and slipped an endotracheal tube down her throat.

"You start an IV line," I instructed Hilary, reconnecting the anesthetic line. "That'll keep her blood pressure up and her fluid levels good."

Hilary nodded. Her fingers, long and slender, worked together like a well-coached team. Within minutes, Jenny lay on her back in the V-shaped surgical trough. Overhead, an IV line dripped silently into her vein at four-second intervals. The rebreathing bag attached to the endotracheal tube swelled and contracted in the relaxed pattern of normal respiration. In the background, the heart monitor beeped with comforting regularity. These were the rhythms of life in an operating room.

While Hilary shaved and prepped Jenny's abdomen, I stepped outside to prepare for surgery.

"Vegetables or teddy bears?" Tanya asked, holding up two surgical caps. Dr. Doucette had charmed a new drug rep into leaving an assortment of designer surgical caps along with the usual pens and glossy brochures.

I tucked my hair under a swarm of smiling chili peppers then began the six minute, self-inflicted torture known as scrubbing. This always left my hands in prickly, red ruins and the results had once cut a promising date short. I slipped into the autoclaved surgical gown and snapped on a pair of sterile gloves while Tanya tied the gown in back. Hands held above my waist and face mask in place, I entered surgery.

"Vitals are good," Hilary reported. I double-checked all the monitors and listened to Jenny's heart as Hilary held the stethoscope to my ears.

During Jenny's physical exam, I could feel three kittens so Susan was standing by in the adjacent dental area which had hastily been converted into a nursery ICU. C-sections were rare in cats and this was my first. Scalpel poised, I pictured the colour-coded photos in my surgery text that made a C-section look like a Paint By Number kit any child could master. In the textbook photo, a happy veterinarian assisted by a happy technician performed surgery on a happy patient.

Humming along with Strauss' Blue Danube, I made a long incision in her belly. The Y-shaped uterus, normally the thickness of a knitting needle, swells to the diameter of a broom handle during pregnancy. The kittens, each developing in its own amniotic sac, look like beads in a giant's necklace. I quickly uncovered the huge organ and eased it onto the surgical drape. Then I froze.

"Oh my God!" Hilary breathed, her eyes wide above her face mask.

Together we stared at the accommodating uterus which sheltered not three, not four, but six kittens! Where had they all come from? Through the protective membranes, I could see a kaleidoscope of colours and patterns in the wet fur. Jenny had certainly made the most of her night on the town.

"Have you ever done a C-section where there were so many kittens?" Hilary's voice seemed distant. "Dr. McBride?"

"Dr. McBride?" she repeated when I didn't answer.

"Turn off the music," I snapped, deciding to ignore Hilary's question. "And tell Susan she's going to need help."

With six kittens, time became the critical factor affecting their survival. I made an incision in the main body of the uterus and removed the first kitten. Using a piece of gauze, I wiped away the placental membranes around his face, then clamped the umbilical cord. He was a beautiful mackerel tabby, with white toes and a white bib. As with all newborn kittens, his ears were flat against the side of his head, his eyes closed. One day he would be a big, strong boy but at this moment he was completely helpless. As I held the tiny body in my hand, he took his first breath. To be present at this moment of transformation, when a tiny being exists for the first time outside the shelter of its mother's womb, always takes my own breath away. But I had little time to celebrate.

In the nursery, Susan began a gentle but vigorous towel massage, imitating the mother's tongue. Puffs of hot air from a blow dryer warmed his damp body. The shivering ceased. Hilary held up six fingers and I heard Susan holler for back-up.

In the meantime, I "milked" the second kitten along the uterine horn to the same place where I had removed the first. With just one incision, Jenny would heal faster and feel less discomfort. I eased the tiny calico into the world and repeated the same procedure I had followed with her brother. Even so, her breathing was sporadic at best.

"We've got to get the fluid out of her lungs," I told Hilary as she wrapped the fragile life in a warm cocoon of flannel. Nodding, she darted into the nursery.

I turned my attention to the next closest kitten. Only ten minutes had passed since we began, but this little fellow seemed quite sluggish. He was breathing, but his heartbeat was weak.

The surgery door opened. "We can't seem to get her going." Hilary's voice was low and urgent.

"Here," I said, handing her the third kitten. Although I had given them a brief rundown before surgery, none of the current staff had ever been involved in a C-section either. Hilary waited for direction, cradling the kitten close for warmth. In her silence, I heard the desperate appeal. Babies weren't supposed to die before they lived.

"Did you try the respiratory stimulant?"

Hilary's head bobbed up and down.

I reached for a pair of hemostats and knocked the suture material onto the floor. "Damn!"

Three kittens were still trapped inside Jenny, and every minute that passed reduced their chances for survival. Time was an enemy, not a healer. In frustration, I barked, "Try swinging her like I showed you!"

Outside my window, a crowd had gathered and I caught

glimpses of their feverish attempts to revive the first three kittens. A waitress from Tim Hortons had taken over the hair dryer and I spied the parking lot attendant running with towels. I saw Susan sandwich one of the kittens firmly but tenderly between her hands, head facing outwards. Then she raised the kitten above her head and swung her in an arc. The centrifugal motion would help expel fluid from the lungs and stimulate breathing; too much could cause blood vessels in the brain to hemorrhage.

Sorry that I had snapped at Hilary, I shouted to be heard in the ICU. "Hilary. Hilary!"

Hilary poked an anxious head back through the surgery door.

"Just remember, the kittens are anesthetized so it's going to take them awhile to come round," I explained as I clamped an oozing blood vessel.

"Right." Hilary turned to leave.

"Reviving newborns can sometimes seem hopeless," I continued in a rush. "The thing is...," I looked up and, lowering my voice, added quietly, "the thing is don't give up."

Hilary's nod was slight, almost imperceptible. A surgical mask and cap obscured most of her face. But her eyes, large and brown, held my own for a heartbeat of time. That was all we could spare.

I delivered the fourth and fifth kittens. They were orange tabbies, perfectly formed with miniature claws visible on their tiny toes. Neither was breathing.

The last kitten to leave her mother was the smallest. A miniature version of Jenny, she lay limply in my gloved hand, lost in its vastness. I strained to hear a heartbeat, willing myself to feel the faintest shudder as I began chest compressions. But there was nothing. Taking the kitten, Hilary left for the last time, leaving me alone to close the incision.

Jenny was doing well, oblivious to the chaos created by her promiscuity. I gave her an injection of pain-killer then mechanically began stitching, two layers for the uterus and three more layers through the body wall. The final layer of stitches I secured underneath the skin so nursing kittens wouldn't harm the incision.

Stripping off my gloves, I reached for the switch, cutting the intense glare of the surgical lamp. The room dissolved into the grey pallor of stainless steel. The only sound was Jenny's peaceful, regular respiration echoing against unyielding walls. In the wake of emergency surgery, bloodied gauze, ECG tracings and dirtied surgical instruments littered the room, washed up like flotsam after the storm. I turned off the anesthetic and waited for Jenny to wake up.

Activity in the ICU had slowed down. As Jenny began to shiver and paw the air, I removed the endotracheal tube. I listened to her chest once more, then wrapped her in a blanket and carried her to the recovery ward.

There I was met by an odd assortment of staff, clients, and employees from other businesses in the strip mall. Quietly proud, each member of the team held a mewling kitten. Ms. Martell and her daughter were nestled together in a chair. Under her mother's hawk-like supervision, Jill gently massaged the last kitten to be born. It squawked in healthy protest.

"I was late for work anyway," Ms. Martell shrugged.

Later that evening, I slipped back to check on my in-patients. The surgery ward at night was a peaceful haven, lit only by the warm blush of a table lamp. With satisfaction, I noticed Jenny had eaten a small meal. Her dozing family, nestled in the shelter of Jenny's love, rose and fell rhythmically with each breath their mother took. Smiling, I gazed at the celebration of life in kennel number seven. This was why I had become a veterinarian.

The moment was shattered by a familiar, throaty growl and a bar-rattling lunge at the kennel door by my knees. Hymie O'Malley! His wound had been treated and a Penrose drain was in place. Silently, I blessed Dr. Doucette and turned to leave, tripping over a cat carrier in the dim light.

A primeval chorus of grunts followed by an authoritative snort rose from the far corner of the room. Head back, mouth open, Mrs. O'Malley was sprawled in an armchair with her knitting. Startled, I hurried out of the recovery ward and down the darkened hallway where a beam of light pooled at the far end.

Inside the office, Dr. Doucette slouched lazily in a reclining chair, legs stretched across his desk. In one arm he cradled a cat, in the other a textbook. A bag of jelly beans lay within easy reach.

"I'm going to wake her when I finish this article," he grinned, seeing the look on my face. "Apparently she had an extra glass of sherry after supper to calm her nerves." Then he nodded at the filing cabinet. An envelope addressed to Ocean View Cat Hospital was propped against a bottle of wine. The card inside said simply "Thank you" and was signed "Helen and Jill Martell." Underneath, a child had drawn one large pink heart surrounded by six small ones.

As I held the card in my hand, Hughie reached for the bag of jelly beans. "Help yourself, Em. I always buy extra. You never know when one of your staff is going to pull off a miracle."

Chapter 2

It was my mother who found the job posting on the Internet.

Two years ago, my sister-in-law, regional sales rep for a large computer chain, had converted my old bedroom into the high-tech heart of Mom's two-story Dutch colonial. While most seniors creaked out of bed at the crack of dawn and swallowed a dozen pills before settling in front of the TV, Mom slept like a rock till ten. After checking her e-mail, she put in her teeth, got dressed, and played a round of gin rummy with the octogenarian next door. Then she cruised the Internet for a couple of hours. Mom could discuss bitmaps, Booleans, and browsers with computer nerds half her age.

At 6:00 a.m., the shrill ring of the phone strafed my apartment. I had been in bed for only three hours thanks to Mike Ludofsky's prize sow Eva who had a nasty cut on her flank. Eva had fourteen piglets, an evil disposition, and a body the size and shape of a Volkswagen Beetle. Dimly aware that I smelled like a pigsty, I reached for the phone.

"Emily! It's your mother!" Mom had no respect for the four time zones that separated Nova Scotia from Vancouver Island. "Are you listening?"

"Uh huh." I closed my eyes and started to drift.

"I've found the perfect job for you! Just listen, 'Ocean View Cat Hospital requires veterinarian for progressive feline-only practice,'" Mom read. "'Established 1987. Excellent support staff, loyal clientele, good working conditions. Must love cats.' You love cats," Mom pointed out. "And it's here in Halifax!"

My mother's children had drifted like dandelion puffs across the continent, putting down roots in such exotic locations as Big Tickle, Newfoundland, and Athens, Ohio. Mom would be delighted if at least one of her offspring returned home to Nova Scotia prior to what she termed "the great fire." Mom refused to take up hermetically-sealed space in a graveyard when she could be burnt to a crisp and her ashes tossed to the wind.

"Emily! Are you there?"

"Yeah," I mumbled, rifling through a pile of clothes. "I'm looking for something to write with."

"I don't know why you don't get a computer," Mom sighed.

"Here it is." I pried a pencil out of a pair of muddy overalls.

Like most displaced Maritimers, I longed to return home. After three years in a mixed practice on Vancouver Island, I had abandoned any notion of becoming a female James Herriott. As a child, I had fallen in love with his wonderful memoirs about life as a rural vet in England's Yorkshire Dales where he treated all manner of animals. But the dramatic advances in veterinary medicine over the last fifty years made specializing more practical. Cats remained my first love but these days, in the mid-nineties, there were few feline practices.

"I ran into Benjamin Mombourquette the other day," Mom added in a conversational tone.

"Yeah. You told me, Mom."

"He's still not married. Good-looking boy like that. Can you imagine?"

"It's hard to believe."

"I think he's a plumber. Plumbers make good money, you know, Emily."

I didn't care if Benny Mombourquette was prime minister. To me, he would always be the boy idiot next door who, at six, hid in the pine tree that towered over the Mombourquettes' front yard and peed on my doll's tea party. Mr. Mombourquette cut the tree down after Mrs. Parks, collecting donations for a church fund-raiser, also fell victim to Benny's yellow reign of terror.

"That tree was rotten anyway," Mom declared.

I sighed. Mom wouldn't rest until the youngest of her children was safely married and reproducing. Although any decent men I had met in British Columbia were already married, gay, pig farmers, or a combination thereof, Mom was not discouraged. There were risks associated with moving 7200 kilometres closer to such a determined matchmaker.

Even so, I found myself sitting in the reception room of Ocean View Cat Hospital on a humid, overcast day in mid-August. For the third time in an hour, my bladder reminded me who was really in charge. This organ always took control of the pack in stressful situations and my noon-hour interview with Dr. Doucette was bound to be stressful. Cold sweat dribbled down my arms.

I settled into a rocking chair and looked around. Except for the computer terminals on the reception counter, I felt like I had entered someone's home. Classical music floated from speakers high above me. In the centre of the room, a coffee table overflowing with cat books rested on top of a colourful braided rug. A simple chandelier cast a warm glow on the papered walls.

Most of the chairs were occupied by dozing cats. On one wall, an aquarium labelled "Feline Therapy Centre" pulsed with life as giddy tropical fish darted among castles and scuba divers, unaware of the daily parade of would-be predators just beyond the glass. French doors led into the Cat Nap Inn, a lush indoor courtyard with a fountain and terra cotta tiles. Nestled among the greenery, twelve luxurious suites contained cats who were boarding while their owners were away.

I wondered where the bathroom was and had just gathered up enough courage to ask the busy receptionist when I felt eyes boring into me. I looked around but everyone seemed preoccupied with their own affairs. Then I glanced at the floor by my feet. A white cat with orange spots and intense orange eyes stared back at me unblinking. The tip of his tail twitched ever so slightly and his mouth opened in a silent meow. I patted my lap encouragingly.

The receptionist looked up from her telephone conversation and clamping a hand over the mouthpiece, whispered, "Dr. McBride? You're in Carter's chair."

"Oh. Sorry," I apologized to Carter and retreated to a tiny chair beside an equally tiny table strewn with crayons and plastic farm animals. As I struggled to keep my legs together in a ladylike fashion while balancing on one cheek, Carter reclaimed the ample rocker. He spent several impassioned moments readjusting the blanket. Then, with a dramatic sigh, he curled into a tight ball and closed his eyes.

I heard laughing as the door to Dr. Doucette's exam room opened. A sleek, well-bred Oriental shorthair emerged followed by a sleek, well-bred woman in her early thirties. Dr. Doucette watched the pair appreciatively as they strolled to the reception counter. Then, turning to me, he smiled.

"Emily, is it?" he asked, extending a hand. "Good to meet you."

I jumped up, sending the little chair on its heels. Mounds of comatose cats awoke, assured themselves no one was heading to the refrigerator, and resumed their snooze.

"Look. I'm running a bit late," he explained over his shoulder as I struggled to keep up. "Let's grab a bite to eat before your interview. Pub food okay?"

I nodded breathlessly as Dr. Doucette sprinted through the hospital, adjusting an IV line and trimming an ingrown toenail en route. Halfway out the back door, he was still shouting a few last-minute instructions to one of the technicians.

Waiting at the curb was a mud-spattered Jeep. Where dirt had somehow miraculously failed to find a foothold, diseased orange blotches and peeling paint were exposed. The thing had leprosy. I glanced up at the dark, foreboding sky.

"Hop in. It's not locked," Dr. Doucette announced as he clambered over a stack of journals and settled behind the wheel.

I grabbed hold of the dented passenger door, but it refused to budge. Leaning sideways, Dr. Doucette beat it into submission with his right foot. I lifted a piece of soggy rawhide from my seat, climbed inside, and secured the seatbelt. Yellow foam padding oozed from wounds in the faded vinyl upholstery.

"Hold on!" Dr. Doucette shouted, peeling away from the curb.

A brown apple core appeared out of nowhere and rolled back and forth between my feet as we careened down city streets. Blasts of rain-laden air sliced through the interior from unseen cracks and crevices. By the time we reached the pub, I felt like I had been flogged with wet laundry.

The pub's exterior did little to inspire confidence. Built before the retreat of the last ice age, it rubbed arthritic shoulders with an adult video store and pawn shop. Inside, however, the pub oozed old-fashioned charm. A stone fireplace nestled in one corner and beside it, a pool table. Prints from another era decorated the walls.

"Hughie!" A rotund little man greeted my companion warmly. "How's she hangin', b'y?"

"Doin' great, Cecil," Dr. Doucette answered. "I'd like you to meet Emily."

I stepped forward from the shadows. The bartender's face turned as red as the Bloody Mary he was mixing. Beside Cecil, an equally rotund woman shook her head in disgust and swatted him with a dishrag. His eyes followed her adoringly as she continued down the counter wiping out ashtrays.

As Cecil's embarrassment gave way to curiosity, a healthy shade of pink returned to his chubby cheeks. His hand, smelling vaguely of curry and beer, grabbed mine. "Pleased to meet you, dear! Are you two…?" Cecil waggled his bushy eyebrows up and down.

"Emily's a vet. She's come all the way from Nanaimo for an interview," Hughie explained.

"Nanaimo, eh?" Cecil winked at me. "I was stationed there once. That's where me and Viv hooked up."

Hearing her name, Viv looked up from the counter and wiggled her fingers in greeting. I wiggled back. We followed Cecil to a window table.

"What'll it be?" he asked, hands on his hips. No menus were forthcoming.

"I think I'd like a spinach salad, please. No onions. Light on the dressing. But lots of mozzarella and just a sprinkle of bacon."

Cecil stared at me.

"And can you add some of those little mandarin orange segments?" I added.

In the silence that followed, Hughie said helpfully, "I'm having the special."

"Oh." I looked from Hughie to Cecil. "You know what? That sounds good. Can I change my order?"

Cecil beamed. "Two specials!" he hollered. When there was no response from the kitchen, he thrust his head through the doors.

"Henry! Git off yer arse! Two specials."

I caught a glimpse of Henry and his nose ring perched on a large, plastic drum. Eyes closed, his body pulsed to the silent beat from a pair of headphones. His white chef's apron was stained with what was likely today's special.

"The wife's nephew," Cecil shrugged apologetically then stormed into the kitchen. Pots and pans clanged in his wake.

"Do you come here often?" I asked, turning back to Hughie.

"Every Friday," he smiled, reaching for a handful of peanuts. I followed suit. The mound of peanut shells grew as we waited for lunch.

"So, Emily," Hughie leaned back in his chair and crossed his arms. "why did you become a vet?"

"Well. . . ." Someone hollered for a fly swatter from the kitchen.

Hughie took a sip of his root beer and nodded encouragingly.

I had never been considered a talker unless the subject was animals. For this my elementary school teachers were grateful, although Mrs. Higgins once wondered if I was "all there." I was, however, on a first-name basis with all the dogs and cats in the neighbourhood and regularly cared for a scarlet macaw named Julian while his owner was at sea. My parrot-sitting days ended abruptly when Julian locked heads with my mother over his refusal to be silent during bridge group. When Mom threw a towel over his cage, he unleashed a string of curses that made even my father blanch.

Hughie laughed. He was a good listener and I found myself chatting happily about Veronica, the seventh-grade hamster who got pregnant during the national anthem when Archie, the eighth-grade hamster, chewed his way into her half of the duplex. The results had sparked my fledgling interest in veterinary medicine. I told him about my dad, who nurtured my love of nature, and about my Aunt Rebecca, aged 82 and still substitute teaching in an inner-city school in Baltimore. When I thought I wasn't good enough to get into vet school, they inspired me to try.

Cecil plunked two steaming plates in front of us then hovered anxiously as we took our first mouthfuls of baked haddock.

"Mmmmm." Hughie closed his eyes.

"Delicious," I added. Whatever other shortcomings he had, Henry was a gifted short-order cook.

Cecil beamed. "Prison was good for him."

We devoured the delicately seasoned fish along with mashed potatoes and mixed vegetables. Hughie leaned back and, patting his belly, sighed in contentment. Swallowing the last morsel of fish, I laid my knife and fork across the plate.

"Emily! Do you play pool?" Hughie bolted upright.

I glanced over my shoulder at the brightly-lit pool table that loomed in the corner. Memories of Friday night at Stompin' Tom's flashed through my mind. For the class of '91, Stompin' Tom's was the weekly antidote to bowel torsions, parasitology, and a grueling schedule. In that smoky potato farmer's bar, where pictures of the queen and Anne of Green Gables graced the walls, I learned to play pool. Well.

"I've played a little. Sure."

Hughie jumped up. "We've got time for one round."

Six slender cue sticks lined the wall, like young girls waiting for an invitation to dance. Hughie looked them over and, selecting the most promising, rubbed the tip with blue chalk.

"You break," he offered generously, racking the balls.

I centred the cue ball on the golf-green surface and with a hard, quick jab sent it crashing into the triangle of colour at the opposite end of the table. The solid blue ball rolled into the nearest pocket. Hughie stared at the table and cleared his throat.

"Nice break, Dr. McBride."

I sank my next four shots. Hughie's grip on the cue stick tightened with each ball that disappeared. When a shot I banked off the side of the table missed its mark, Hughie murmured sympathetically, then sprang into action. He circled the herd of striped balls then selected an easy victim.

Number five lay directly in front of a corner pocket, the cue ball three feet away with nothing in between. Hughie leaned over until his face was almost level with the table. With his left hand, he formed a bridge for the cue stick. The fingers of his right curled around the shaft. Elbows bent, shoulders square, he pumped several times before gently tapping the cue ball towards its target. It rolled gracefully along the edge of the table and with a gentle kiss, sent number five down the hole. Hughie's smile faded, however, when the cue ball teetered at the edge of the abyss, then toppled over.

"Not again!" Cecil clucked sympathetically as he waddled past.

"I don't need your pity, Cecil," Hughie called after him.

Aware that beating my prospective boss at pool might not have helped my cause, I insisted on paying for lunch as he headed to the men's room. My bulging purse had been crafted by an elderly aunt and for reasons unknown to me, and probably my aunt as well, opened at both ends. Chatting absently with Cecil, I opened both of them. When Hughie returned, I was wallowing in coin, gum wrappers, used Kleenex, and keys. He bent down to help and picked up my wallet photos.

"Is this you?" he asked, studying a faded black and white photo. A toothless six-year-old cradling a tiny kitten squinted at the camera.

I stopped foraging on the floor and smiled. Although every year of school brought a revised edition of his daughter, this was the snapshot in time my father had always carried with him.

Hughie gingerly turned the picture over and read Dad's simple scrawl – "Best Friends." In 1968, I had begged, whined, and howled my way into pet ownership. My mother, not a cat enthusiast, was descended from a long line of like-minded individuals. My father loved animals but deferred to my mother who preferred a fur-free home. It was our next-door neighbour, Horace Birch, Ph.D., who suggested a pet might bring me out of my shell. Bootsie, as she became known, would enrich my life for twenty-one years, my dad one year beyond that.

I took the photos from Hughie's outstretched hand and tucked them safely inside my wallet. Back in the Jeep, I braced myself for the ride to the hospital. Hughie inserted his key in the ignition, then changed his mind.

"Emily," he declared, turning to face me. "I think you belong here. Do you still want the job?"

"Well, I. . . ."

"Wonderful!" Hughie cried. He slapped the steering wheel in delight, then turned the key. The Jeep chugged to life.

"Hold on!" he shouted.

Chapter 3

In 1492, with three small ships and more balls than brains (according to family members), Christopher Columbus discovered the New World. In 1967, James T. Kirk and the starship *Enterprise* boldly went where no man had gone before. In 1994, Emily McBride and her aging Volvo, Bill, crossed Canada with three cats and a guinea pig.

After I accepted Dr. Doucette's offer, the task of getting us safely to Halifax fell on Bill's shoulders. My intrepid auto was named after Bill Carr, the comedian, whose namesake had his own special brand of humour, usually reserved for steep hills or cold mornings. My twenty-two-year-old unemployed neighbour, a self-proclaimed car expert, had helped me pick Bill over a hundred other used vehicles. To be fair, my consumer guidebook described Volvos as "a beacon of reliability in a fog of frivolous pleasure vehicles." The salesman assured us, as he undoubtedly assured everyone, that the car's previous owner had been a senior citizen. Bill had spent a comfortable youth in relative luxury with few demands placed upon him.

However, once the ninety-day warranty had expired, Bill began to exhibit erratic mood swings and mysterious ailments that thinned my wallet and raised my mechanically-inclined neighbour to a new tax bracket. Even so, I learned to accept Bill's idiosyncrasies. I had a few of my own.

At least he had a big trunk. I finished loading the last of the boxes and green garbage bags that held three years' worth of accumulated wealth. This was pretty much limited to clothes, hiking gear, boxes of books, and the scattered remains of Corelle Livingware. Contrary to the ad campaign, Corelle was destructible and I was the woman who could prove it.

Three large cat carriers took up the entire back seat and what was likely an illegal portion of the rear window. Securely buckled into the passenger seat, Florence, my guinea pig, rooted happily in the fresh wood chips of her traveling cage. So long as her bowl was full, Flo's happiness knew no bounds. I was more worried about the cats, whose leisurely existence in Nanaimo hadn't prepared them for a cross-country marathon.

When I turned the key in the ignition, Bill's coughs aroused a few tentative meows. By the time we reached the highway, each cat was convinced I had lost my mind. They howled for mercy. The long, lonely road snaked 7,200 kilometres before me. In desperation, I sang to them, I played classical music, I told jokes. Finally, I slapped on my headphones while Bill's arthritic wipers tried to keep the grey October drizzle at bay. The ferry ride to the mainland was a short reprieve which ended when I resumed my place behind the wheel. This time they didn't even wait for the ignition.

We were ten kilometres closer to Halifax when a familiar odour grabbed me from behind.

Yanking a turtleneck over my nose, I scanned the road ahead for a place to pull off. With rain pouring down in barrels rather than buckets, opening the window was not an option. Spying an abandoned building, I guided Bill through the remains of a parking lot. Where black holes hadn't gobbled up the pavement, weeds prospered. Wrenching my seatbelt loose, I straddled the stick shift and scowled at the three suspects. Now that the car had stopped, they purred and rubbed against the kennel doors.

As a group, veterinarians have a soft spot for society's leftovers. Our pets tend to be the crippled, the abandoned, the unhinged. Mine were no exception. Lionel, for example, was a neurotic, wool-sucking Siamese who hated men; they were loud and insensitive to his needs, a sentiment often voiced among my female friends. Instead of support groups, however, Lionel turned to violence. When my client adopted him from a shelter, she was single. Two boyfriends later and a Chinese restaurant that refused to deliver, she was desperate. Behaviour modification and drug therapy failed to weaken Lionel's resolve. With no men in my life except the national news anchor, I adopted Lionel. In the company of women and children, he oozed charm. And he adored my ten-year-old cat, Mickey.

Mickey came into my life when someone tried to drown his pregnant mother. At the time, I was volunteering in a veterinary hospital and adopted Mickey, the only kitten to survive. By the time he was five, an aggressive herpes infection forced the surgical removal of one eye. But Mickey never considered the loss of his eye a disability. He could sweet-talk voles out of their tunnels and into his waiting jaws. And at ten, his tail was still a constant source of surprise and delight. The eternal optimist, Mickey saw the food bowl of life half full.

I shifted my gaze to the third carrier, where Melody blinked in wide-eyed innocence. A towel mounded in the back of her carrier looked suspicious. When I opened the kennel to examine its contents, she squeezed past and leapt onto the back seat, scratching luxuriously.

That she could move at all was a miracle. At four months of age she had been attacked by a large dog and was near death when she was brought to the hospital. Her owners were unwilling to proceed with expensive medical care so the hospital assumed responsibility. The tiny waif endured seven surgeries in six months to repair broken legs and internal injuries. In the evenings, I took her home. She followed me stiffly on her metal splints, like a miniature robot. The constant song of joy which earned her the name Melody evolved into a deep rumble when she nestled in my duvet at night. More than once, I cried for her. But Melody never cried for herself.

A careful search revealed a bowel movement that had started well but deteriorated towards the end. I deposited the entire towel in a forgotten garbage can at the end of the parking lot. When I returned, Melody was sprawled in the back window basking in a few rays that managed to slip through the sky's grey armour.

"Do you guys want out too?" I asked, opening the two remaining kennel doors.

Mickey and Lionel extended cautious heads and looked around. Deciding that I had apparently slain the car monster, Lionel hopped up front and introduced himself to Flo. In Nanaimo, her fleshy body was out of sight in another room, and he could only fantasize about her.

With everyone occupied, I started the engine. The half-hearted protests faded as each cat explored new freedoms. Mickey, who loved to cuddle, soon discovered that a human driving a car was an opportunity. Drooling contentedly, he snuggled into my lap.

The new arrangement seemed to work well. The cats dozed as we wound our way through the craggy sentinels which guarded a vanishing wilderness. The highest peaks were white with snow year round, but in the mountain passes, only a light powder lay sprinkled like icing sugar against the dark needles of the evergreens. I loved my native province, but the mountains of the Canadian West were an elixir. I had logged many hours hiking through forests to lakes that lay like turquoise gems against her rocky throat. There was peace here in this place where time unravelled, peace born of a land untouched by man, where life began and ended and began again as it had for millennia.

Towards the end of the second day, we passed through the last of the mountain ranges. With mixed feelings, I watched them recede in my rear-view mirror. Ahead lay the prairies. No curves. No bear warnings. Just put the car in cruise control and watch for prairie dogs. I could feel Bill gaining confidence.

Yet the prairies are far from the boring, flat land described by road-weary travelers. Their mercurial spirit is at once inviting and ruthless. I was forced into a roadside diner when the blue sky that stretched to infinity suddenly turned black. A restless wind in advance of torrential rain churned up clouds of dust. As Bill valiantly battled the rain and spears of lightning that pierced the wheat fields, I wedged him into a space between two transport trucks. The parking lot was packed with license plates from across the nation. I thought, not for the first time, that the strength of this country lies in the diversity of her land and her people.

Or as my dinner companion "Buzz" Henshaw so eloquently described the chain-smoking, beer-guzzling group near us, "Takes a lot of different turds to make the rest of us smell good."

The diner overflowed with burly truckers who looked up when I entered. I was grateful that the elderly Mr. Henshaw offered me a seat at his table. When he learned I was single, unattached, and a veterinarian, Mr. Henshaw produced photos of his dour-looking son, an unmarried hog producer. I dutifully admired the unusual mix of genes that resulted from the Henshaw union.

"You know, he's had opportunities," Mr. Henshaw assured me. "Thelma Stewart for one. Betsy Richards for another. If she'd got rid of that big mole I think he'd of had her...but a vitnery! Now he'd like that."

Mr. Henshaw, Sr., also a hog devotee, was shocked to discover I was leaving a mixed practice to become a cat veterinarian. To a rural farmer, a cat's lifespan was based on its ability to eat rodents. Shaking his head, Mr. Henshaw returned the photos to his wallet and finished his pumpkin pie in silence.

After leaving the prairies behind, Bill twisted for three days on the windy, pot-holed roads of Ontario. I planned to drive through Quebec in one day. My anemic French was the result of six years with the mythical Desjarnac family created by the Nova Scotia Department of Education. Years of conjugating verbs had not prepared me for real-life francophones.

It was, of course, in Quebec where Bill broke down.

Normally, I pump my own gas. Like taking out the garbage or fixing the toilet, I feel a sense of independence in doing a "man's job." But just outside Rivière-du-Loup, as Bill choked on the last remaining gas fumes, I was forced into a full serve station. The teenage attendant motioned for me to roll down my window. I pointed to the hissing Lionel and declined. The young man wisely selected a pump at random. His gaze remained fixed on Lionel who skirted around to the back window for a better view.

When the tank was full, I rolled my window down just enough to extend the credit card. Lionel thrust out a long, white leg. His finely honed claws glinted in the sunlight as they slashed the air in vain. Grabbing my card, the attendant sprinted back to the office while I fiddled with the radio. When I looked up, a small crowd had gathered in the door of the gas station. They were staring at my car and pointing excitedly. The door opened and unseen arms propelled the sacrificial lamb forward.

The attendant walked slowly towards the car, gripping a pair of pliers. Lionel watched his approach with narrowed eyes. Standing as far from the car as possible, the teenager poked my credit card through the window using the pliers. His audience applauded from behind a plate glass window.

"Merci! Merci!" I babbled and waved goodbye. Surely Lionel and I had strained the francophone-anglophone connection enough for one day.

We hadn't gone more than fifty metres when Bill lurched. I felt a sickening thud in the front of the car after which we leaned to the right. Ignoring the complaints, I stuffed everybody back into a carrier, then scrambled out to survey the damage.

"Qu'est-ce que c'est?" a gruff voice asked.

Suddenly, I was back in grade seven with my first French teacher, Mrs. Gonzales. For half a century, she had opened her French classes with a series of "Qu'est-ce que c'est?" as her demonic pointer crashed down on some unsuspecting noun. Generations of students were moulded by her unique vision of the French language. Rumours circulated that she had never actually been born but created instead in a biological weapons lab and tested on junior high students.

Rather than risk a misunderstanding, I resorted to the universal language of a woman in need. I wrung my hands, I shrugged my shoulders, I pointed under the car and threw my hands into the air. I pouted.

The intrigued mechanic crawled under Bill for a better view. Incoherent muttering in French was followed by a long, drawn-out whistle. "Mon Dieu!" he sputtered. After a moment, he snaked out from underneath the car and standing up, batted away the dust and grime of the ground. He looked at me sympathetically and sighed.

"Ah, mademoiselle," he said sadly, shaking his head. He held up an index finger. "Un? Non." Holding up two fingers, he continued, "Deux? Non." Holding up three fingers and quivering in excitement now that he had reached the climax of the story, he announced, "Trois? Oui!"

By now, the crowd had relocated. They circled Bill, peering in the windows at Lionel and poking under the hood. Their congenial head-bobbing and muffled conversation seemed to confirm some awful truth. I waited, shivering in the crisp air.

All heads turned my way as the first mechanic waved me over. Everyone fell silent, parting like the Red Sea as I approached.

"Mademoiselle?" he began, then paused thoughtfully. He sniffed, scratched his head, picked at his dirty fingernails and pursed his lips. Then he sighed. I sighed too.

"Votre...engine?" he said at last, pointing to a big part of Bill's innards that were grazing the ground.

"Oui?" I prompted.

"Paul. Paul. Ici." One of the men retrieved a stubby pencil from behind his ear. Another produced a crumpled invoice stained with coffee rings.

My interpreter smoothed the piece of paper against the side of the car and began sketching. Bill, with his unmistakable tilt, soon materialized. This was followed by a pussycat with dripping fangs in the window. Paul's buddies chuckled in approval. Next he drew a close-up of the engine showing four supports. Tapping my hand at this critical moment, he made a bold stroke through three of the four supports. Then looking at me he symbolically slashed his throat.

An expectant hush fell over the crowd.

"Can you fix it?" I asked to a circle of blank stares. "Uh... reparez?" Mrs. Gonzales would have been proud.

"Oh, oui! Oui!" Heads nodded emphatically. An animated discussion followed, none of which I understood. I followed the group back up the hill as preparations got underway. Paul donated his office to my traveling companions. Only somewhat larger than a coffin, it boasted a desk and a well-worn calendar. Miss October smiled sweetly as she gripped a teddy bear in an imaginative pose. I piled the three carriers on top of each other, put Flo's cage on the desk, then returned out front.

Someone had produced a tired yellow chair, still clinging to life through the miracle of duct tape. Wedged between a pyramid of windshield washer fluid and a nut dispenser, I waited for Bill. Overcome by the lure of cashews, I rummaged through my purse for coin. The four quarters I unearthed netted me six nuts.

Looking up, I was startled to find one of the mechanics looming over me. He held a Walkman in one hand and a wrench in the other. Intricate tattoos snaked over his muscled forearms and disappeared under the folds of his T-shirt. His head had been recently shaved although hair was making a prickly comeback. Wordlessly, he lowered a pair of headphones over my ears. I cringed, expecting the maniacal outbursts of a heavy metal group. He grinned at my surprise as the haunting tones of Celine Dion rose above the din of sweaty men at work.

Throughout the afternoon, I nibbled on nuts and listened to music. A few locals popped in to chat with Paul and catch a glimpse of the unfortunate anglophone and her entourage.

Word had spread quickly. The bilingual bank manager managed a mid-afternoon break to discuss mutual funds and his award-winning turnips. Even the owner of the Bowl-A-Drome in L'Isle-Verte dropped by with a coupon for ladies' night.

By the time Bill was ready to go, I had amassed a jar of home-made jam along with a basket of rolls from Paul's wife Florence, several turnips, and fresh cream for the cats. Amid goodbyes, I loaded everyone back into the car. Paul produced a slice of apple for Florence. He thought it hilarious that my guinea pig and his staunchly anti-rodent wife had the same name.

I arrived in Halifax late the next evening. The cats were thrilled with Mom's large, two-storey home. George and Gracie, Mom's pair of eccentric budgies, were horrified. They screeched dire warnings well into the night and gnawed on their toes. Sometime soon, I would need to find my own place, but for now, I was content to let Mom fuss over me and the four-legged grandchildren. Safe in the home where I grew up, I drifted to sleep listening to Celine Dion. The tape was a gift from my tall, tattooed mechanic so I wouldn't forget Rivière-du-Loup.

Chapter 4

The initial excitement of a new job in a feline-only practice began to fade as the weeks fell into a dismal pattern. Dr. Doucette was immersed in a swirling whirlpool of cats, clients, and castrations. Occasionally he surfaced for a gulp of lunch or bathroom break. I busied myself reading journal articles and tidying the office. No one wanted to try the unknown Dr. Emily McBride from the other end of the country. Although the staff tried to steer new patients my way, Dr. Doucette's appointment sheets overflowed while mine were marked by the occasional drug rep or the staff's doodlings.

One day as I alternately watched my fingernails grow and catalogued some reference materials for Dr. Doucette, Althea tapped on the door. "Dr. McBride, will you do a house call for a guinea pig? The owner is a Mr. Frank McWhirtle."

I would have treated the ingrown toenail of a gorilla. I had come 7,200 kilometers to work in a cat practice and so far had vaccinated a handful of cats, performed two spays, and supervised one of the technicians during dentistry.

Estelle Parsons, esthetician and disciple of Dr. Doucette's, had voluntarily suggested I wear my hair up and pluck my eyebrows. "You have a raw kind of beauty," she explained, handing me a business card. "A makeover might give you more professional credibility."

The unsuspecting Mr. McWhirtle had only requested a vet. If Dr. Doucette was too busy, then I, the raw and unplucked Emily

McBride, would gratefully answer the call and raise the level of guinea pig medicine to dizzying new heights.

Mr. McWhirtle lived in Halifax's south end near Point Pleasant Park. In a well-groomed cul-de-sac where no weed survived infancy, a trio of stately homes eyed my approach. As I wandered up the cobblestone walk to number 6720, a regal-looking woman in a pale rose cashmere suit appeared at the door.

"You must be Dr. McBride. I'm Theodora, Frank's sister-in-law. Do come in." With a sweeping gesture, she ushered me into the marble foyer. "I must say your firm provides very quick service."

"We do our best," I acknowledged humbly, removing my coat. Cat hair, a hazard of my profession, clung to the black wool.

Theodora held it at arm's length and smiled politely. We continued to smile at each other for a few moments.

"Well, I guess I should have a look at the patient," I said at last.

"Yes, of course. It's just down the hall." Theodora hesitated. Glancing at my feet, she made an odd little sound in her throat.

I looked down. "Oh, sorry!" I slipped out of my shoes, a comfortable, well-worn pair of loafers.

"The cleaning girl won't be back till next Wednesday," Theodora explained. Bending down, she gingerly picked up my shoes and deposited both them and my jacket in the utility closet. We continued down the hallway to a pair of French doors.

"Frank?" Theodora tapped on the doors. "Is it safe?" Opening the door a crack, she poked her head through and scanned the room. I waited as she cupped a hand to her ear, listening. Apparently satisfied, she thrust the door wide open and motioned me inside.

A thin man sitting in a chair looked up with a smile.

"Frank, this is Dr.......aaagh!" Theodora stifled a scream as a fat, brown sausage with legs scooted by, squealing in delight.

"Dr. McBride," I finished, shaking his hand while Theodora clambered aboard the nearest chair.

"Nice to meet you. This is Peter," he added, pointing to the docile Abyssinian guinea pig in his lap. With his whorls and ridges of spiky hair, Peter was the rodent version of a punk rocker. "And Robert's gone behind the bookcase over there."

"No! He's coming out! I can see him!" Theodora shrieked from her vantage point high above us.

"And you've met Theodora?" Frank winked.

"Of course we've met!" Theodora snapped. "Can someone please grab that creature?"

As Robert waddled past on his second lap, I scooped him up and placed him back in the cage. Theodora exhaled slowly and began her descent. Back on the floor, she smoothed her skirt and tucked a few wayward strands of hair back into their French roll.

"I asked you to keep those things locked up," Theodora glared at Frank. "They're disgusting!"

"Aw, now Dorie. That cage is pretty small."

Theodora turned to me. "They were a gift from his niece," she explained in a tone that made it clear she would never have made such a choice.

"I've grown rather fond of the little fellas," Frank said softly, his gnarled hand stroking the contented Peter. "But this gentleman seems to be putting on a lot of weight. I'm a little worried about him. And they both need nail trims, I'm afraid. I can't seem to do it and my niece is back in university."

"Well, don't worry about a thing," I assured Frank. "We're well-trained in the area of lab animal medicine."

Snapping open the briefcase, I removed a lab coat folded neatly on top. "In fact," I added, donning the sparkling white garment, "we now refer to these little guys like guinea pigs, hamsters and gerbils as pocket pets. They really are becoming quite popular. I have a guinea pig at home named Florence."

Frank nodded in approval at Theodora, who scowled back at him from her seat near the door.

With a professional flourish, I draped the stethoscope around my neck. "May I?" I asked, pointing to the coffee table.

The McWhirtles watched in awed silence as, one by one, I removed the contents of the briefcase. Althea's portable Weight Watchers food scale was first. This was placed in the centre of the coffee table. I then carefully laid out two pairs of toenail scissors, disposable latex gloves, needles, blood collection tubes, a digital thermometer, a file for overgrown teeth and, last but not least, The Eye. This impressive piece of equipment was worn over the head and held in place by an adjustable band. A large magnifying lens could be lowered over the eyes like a visor. Knobs on the side of the band controlled the amount of light and the angle of the lens. It was not usually used to examine guinea pigs.

"My goodness," Frank said at last, staring at the coffee table.

"Yes," I replied, my mood expansive. "Veterinary medicine has come a long way from the days of James Herriott."

Each pig sat motionless on Althea's scale as I recorded their weight. I palpated their internal organs and, using The Eye, examined their mouths, ears, feet, and skin. After listening myself, I held the stethoscope so Frank could hear their rapid-fire heartbeats. Peter sat still in wide-eyed disbelief when I inserted the rectal thermometer but Robert made a run for it. Theodora quickly swung her legs into the air but Robert didn't get far dragging a thermometer. Frank then cradled each animal as I trimmed their nails, four on the front feet, three on the back.

I finished making detailed notes in each patient's medical chart, only half-listening as Frank chatted about his days as a farmhand in the forties.

Theodora cleared her throat.

Taking the hint, I started packing my repertoire back in the briefcase. "Well," I began, "you have two healthy guinea pigs. They're in excellent condition."

"There. I told you they were fine, Frank." Glancing at her watch, Theodora rose to her feet.

"But Peter is pregnant."

"Oh...My...God!" Theodora gasped, her limp body collapsing back into the chair. "What are we going to do?"

Frank's broad smile split his face in two. "Well, now, isn't that exciting!"

"Dr. McBride, you've got to do something!" Theodora clutched my sleeve, the blood draining from her face. "You don't understand. I can't have these things in my house. They carry disease. And they smell. They're rodents, for God's sake! And they eat their own...," she lowered her voice, "excrement."

"Actually, it's quite normal," I assured her, "and very clever. For most mammals, stool's just a waste product but in guinea pigs, some stool sits for awhile in a special part of the intestine called the cecum."

Theodora stared blankly at me.

"The stool ferments there," I continued, warming to my topic. "It becomes more digestible. The guinea pigs seem to know which ones are special and take advantage of the extra nutrition when it finally pops out." Theodora's hands rose to cover her face.

"It really is wonderful recycling," I added, pleased with my explanation.

Theodora peeked at me through her fingers. "What about… what about an abortion?" she whispered.

"Oh no, she's much too far along for that," I replied. "Besides, you should be able to find homes for them quickly. Guinea pigs are born fully-furred and start eating solid food almost right away. But I think we should neuter Robert as soon as possible before he can strike again."

"I couldn't agree more!" Theodora glared at Robert, who was back in his cage and sitting in the food bowl. When I left the house, she was still muttering and wringing her hands while Frank planned an addition to the guinea pig homestead.

Frank called about two weeks later to tell me Petunia, formerly Peter, had given birth to three healthy guinea pigs. Although guinea pigs have only two teats, Petunia made sure the whole family was well-fed. Robert revelled in his role as father now that his role as lover had been surgically altered. Fortunately, all three offspring were female so no further surgery was necessary.

After the triplets were born, I began making regular house calls to trim toenails and check on the herd's overall health. The sitting room was evolving. In November, the French provincial loveseat was replaced by a padded rocking chair. By December, a luxurious new wing on the main cage had been completed. During January and February, plastic guinea pig tunnels began to appear and lengthen with every passing week. Theodora might have been less supportive if she knew that the tunnels which wove behind her sofa and under the end tables were actually sewer pipes. Plants flourished in the windows. Here in the domain of Persian rugs and Tiffany lamps, Frank McWhirtle was creating a new biosphere.

Once I remembered to bring the appropriate footwear, Theodora thawed considerably. While she couldn't bring herself to actually hold a guinea pig, she talked to them and rubbed their ears.

When she thought Frank was asleep in the rocker, she offered them treats and smiled at their antics.

"At least they don't have tails," she confided.

One busy Saturday morning, she called the hospital in an uncustomary panic. Theodora was a discriminating shopper who rarely patronized large, price-conscious department stores. However, when her specialty pet shop was unexpectedly closed, she was forced into mainstream shopping at the local big-box store. In the pet section, a horde of listless guinea pigs shared a filthy cage with an overturned water dish.

"They were feeding them birdseed!" she cried. "Birdseed! Can you imagine! Do they look like birds?" The phone grew hot in my hand. After six months of sharing her world with guinea pigs, Theodora had become an expert in their care.

Unable to rouse the provincial SPCA on a weekend, she had marched into the store manager's office and demanded the release of the guinea pigs into her custody. I pictured the manager cowering behind his desk while a very rich, very angry guinea pig activist threatened legal action and store closure.

So, Theodora now had eighteen sick guinea pigs in shoeboxes and Tupperware containers lolling about in the back seat of her Mercedes. Could I see them right away?

Thus began the parade of guinea pigs into Ocean View Cat Hospital. Theodora breathlessly apologized to everyone in the reception room that this was a rodent mass emergency and I was the only one who could help these poor creatures. Somehow this did little to improve my status among the waiting cat owners, who were already disappointed that Dr. Doucette was not available.

We examined the little creatures one by one. Most hadn't been in the department store too long. With the appropriate medical care and a well-balanced diet, they would be fine. I was most concerned about an adult guinea pig that was completely unable to move. Malnourished and dehydrated, he was probably suffering from scurvy. Guinea pigs require daily vitamin C because their bodies are unable to store it. Even vitamin C in commercial guinea pig food degrades over time. While Theodora cradled the despondent animal, I injected vitamin C and fluids. Although his prognosis was poor, she insisted on home nursing care, claiming he would never recover surrounded by predators.

With promises to keep me informed, Theodora strode purposefully to her car. She was an elegant figure, with her snow-white hair, flawless complexion, and designer clothes. As she walked, she chatted with the Tupperware container tucked under her arm.

Almost a month passed before I saw the McWhirtles again. No one had heard from them, although I left repeated messages on their answering machine. One Saturday in April, as I was racing through Point Pleasant Park with Dr. Doucette's endlessly enthusiastic Jack Russell terrier, I decided to pay them a visit.

The day was a rare and glorious gift, a promise of things to come. The sun was just beginning to awaken after only sporadic appearances during a long, slushy Halifax winter. The rays reached everywhere, kissing life into embers that had been smouldering all season. In another month, the trees would begin to bud and I would need to think about buying a new bathing suit, hopefully one that hid the defects.

Theodora greeted me warmly without even a glance at my shoes. "Oh, Dr. McBride. Come see! "

As I gazed about the guinea pig room I thought how sweet life was for these south end rodents who dined on only the freshest produce and grains. Without warning, Theodora suddenly threw back her head, pursed her perfectly lined lips and squealed. The sound electrified the entire troop who stood at noisy attention while she doled out sprigs of parsley.

But the *pig de resistance* was Colonel Ernie, so-named for his solidly white coat. At rest, guinea pigs are inert lumps. When motivated, they are streamlined torpedoes. The Colonel was the largest torpedo I had ever seen as he raced on tippy-toes around the perimeter of his suite, pink ears flapping wildly. Sometimes overwhelmed by his own excitement, he would jump straight into the air and reverse direction. Gone was the pathetic creature I had treated four weeks ago.

"You've done a wonderful job," I exclaimed in amazement. "Where's Frank? He must be thrilled!"

Theodora turned away from me and stared out the window. A young couple strolled past, smiling as they pushed a baby carriage ahead of them. Somewhere a dog barked.

"Frank's not well," she said at last, twisting the rings on her finger. "Cancer of the pancreas. Same as his brother."

In the silent minutes that followed, I searched for something to say.

"Would you like to see him?" Theodora asked suddenly. "I know he'd enjoy a visit."

She led me into Frank's room, which was lit only by the thin veins of light filtering through the Venetian blinds. Occasionally, the spring breeze lifted the barrier of metal slats, and the fleeting pools of light which gained entry drifted across his gaunt face. I glanced at the army of pill vials on the night table, a broken, ragged line which could no longer hold back the cancerous advance.

"Frank," Theodora whispered, running her hand tenderly along his cheek, "Dr. McBride is here." His eyes fluttered open at her soft touch. "Why don't you two have a chat? I'm just going to make some tea." She hesitated in the doorway, then disappeared down the hallway.

"Ah, Emily," Frank breathed softly. I stared at the emaciated arm which struggled to rise from the bed in greeting. It belonged to the same person, who, in another time, could throw a man out at home from centre field, who loved to play the banjo, who had held his wife close on the porch swing as they listened to the summer crickets. I reached for his hand and his fingers clasped mine tightly. I told him how wonderful the guinea pigs looked, especially Colonel Ernie. Frank smiled. "That was Theodora's doing."

Closing his eyes, he whispered, "She was a tough nut to crack, Emily…but we finally did it."

Chapter 5

"WHADDYA MEAN, he's got no balls?"

Cecil's voice bounced off the exam room walls and into reception where Miss Pratt, retired schoolteacher-librarian, visibly stiffened.

"Are you sure?" he asked, clinging to the faint hope that I had somehow missed two marble-sized testicles. "He's pretty furry!"

"Check for yourself, Cecil." I held the obliging cat while Cecil raised his tail and peered anxiously.

"Aw, for God's sake. Nothin'," he sighed, after a thorough inspection.

I first met P.C. (Puss-Cat) at Cecil's pub several weeks ago. Hughie and I ate lunch there on Fridays to review the week's cases and shoot some pool. On this particular Friday, a ragged, black and white cat was sprawled on the pool table, surrounded by empty bowls. He had appeared earlier that morning along with the regular breakfast crowd and had refused to leave, despite Cecil's best efforts. Now, three weeks later, Mrs. Cecil had declared him family and insisted it was time for a visit to the vet. All had gone well until I pointed out P.C.'s truant testicles.

"All I wanted was a mouser," Cecil moaned as he stroked the little cat and rubbed his cheeks. P.C.'s small body trembled with a soft purr. "Aw, he even purrs like a sissy. What kind of mouser is he gonna be with no balls?" Cecil shook his head miserably.

"Well," I began, "it's not that he doesn't have any…balls. It's just that they haven't come down."

"Down? Down from where?" Cecil was clearly puzzled.

I explained how testicles begin their development inside the abdomen of male mammals. A few never seem to get the message to descend to the outer world. "He may be sterile but he still has testosterone," I added. "That means he might spray to mark his territory."

"Spray his territory? With what?" Cecil took a minute to digest this information. "Whoa, Doc. You mean pee? In my pub?"

"Think of it as graffiti. It's a normal feline method of expression."

Cecil cast me a pitying glance. "You don't get out much, do you, Doc?"

I grinned. "Don't worry. We can do an exploratory surgery, find the testicles and remove them. And P.C. can still be a great mouser."

Cecil looked doubtful. Growing up with a pack of sports-crazed, risk-taking, womanizing brothers, I understood the prestige men attached to that particular piece of the anatomy. Cecil's spirits needed boosting.

"You know, Cecil, this is a fairly uncommon surgery. I've seen only one other case." I leafed through *The Atlas of the Cat* until I came to a glossy 8½" x 11" of the uro-genital system. All the important parts were highlighted in user-friendly colours: fuchsia, lime-green, yellow and blue. As I pointed out the various features, Cecil nodded wisely.

"A cat with P.C.'s developmental problems is called cryptorchid," I explained. Cecil seemed pleased that the condition was important enough to have a fancy name.

I finished the physical exam, then vaccinated P.C. Cecil waddled out to the reception area where he spied Evelyn Pratt, who was doing her best to ignore him. He began pleasantly enough. "What's your cat here for, dear?" But bursting with his new knowledge, he couldn't wait for her answer.

"Mine's cryptorchid. No balls!" he winked.

Miss Pratt glared at him and resumed reading her magazine.

His good humour restored, Cecil paid his bill and scheduled P.C.'s surgery for the end of the month.

Over the next few weeks, P.C. gained some weight and established himself as a small but influential business partner. He rose at noon, roused by the lunch specials, and slipped downstairs to take advantage of the paying customers. "Cryptorchid" became the pub's new buzzword. Patrons who barely knew the name of their favourite beer tossed it around with confidence. As P.C.'s popularity grew, so did Cecil's creative streak. A jar had been set up at the bar. For fifty cents, you could guess how long it would take Doc McBride to find the missing testicles. The Wednesday special had been renamed "The Cryptorchid" – spaghetti minus the meatballs – and cost one dollar more. Henry couldn't keep up with the demand.

Even so, Cecil maintained his vigil and called me regularly with updates. When the little cat caught a mouse in the basement, he was convinced P.C.'s testicles were making a move. I explained that it was unlikely P.C.'s testicles were going anywhere without the help of a surgeon. Cecil sighed, then called me two days later when he felt a lump in P.C.'s belly.

"Balls?" he asked hopefully.

"More likely stool," I answered.

On the Friday before P.C.'s surgery, Cecil hovered politely in the background until Hughie and I finished lunch. Then beckoning me with an air of great secrecy, he produced P.C. for inspection.

"Any sign of 'em, Doc?" he whispered.

I shook my head.

Cecil lifted P.C. onto his shoulders and scratched his ears. "Well," he said in the voice of a man resigned to his fate, "next week it is, Doc."

Cecil once told me he was descended from a long line of pirates and rumrunners. On the night before P.C.'s surgery, I had a restless sleep and dreamed of a dimly-lit warehouse on the waterfront. Inside, a large cauldron of stew simmered over an open hearth. Harsh laughter mixed with violent curses erupted from a seedy bunch near me with eye patches and wooden tibias. Others sprawled on benches, their mugs of golden ale raised in respect as an unrecognizable song of glory filled the air. A buxom waitress cheerfully manoeuvred the roaming hands.

A knock on the door abruptly silenced the fun-loving group. Tension propelled the proprietor, a tattooed Pillsbury doughboy, towards the heavy oak door. Clambering onto a stool, he slid open a small window near the top.

"Password!" he demanded of the rotting teeth before him.

"Cryptorchid!" came back the throaty growl. The crowd sighed in relief. Music and drink flowed once again. I woke up eyeball-to-eyeball with Mickey, who was sprawled on top of me and my full bladder.

Apparently, Cecil hadn't slept well either. He met me at the door of the hospital, unshaven and clinging to a cup of coffee. Dark half-moons hung from his eyes.

"Doc, I'm a wreck."

"Don't worry, Cecil." I put an arm around his shoulder. "I'm sure P.C. will be fine."

I picked up the carrier. "Well, why don't you go home, have some breakfast, and I'll call you as soon as we're done?"

Cecil took a deep breath, then exhaled. In a husky voice, he told P.C. to be a good boy. "You won't forget to call, right, Doc?"

"I won't forget."

I waved goodbye to Cecil then settled P.C. in the surgery ward. Intimidated by his new surroundings and fellow patients, P.C. stopped howling and adopted what Hughie referred to as "the meatloaf." He lowered himself onto the blanket, tucked his front feet under his chest, and curled his tail tightly around himself. In this position, a cat can observe the world and simultaneously prepare for Armageddon while maintaining an air of apathy.

Armageddon arrived at 9:17 A.M. while I was on the phone with Mrs. Greenough. Her obese black and white cat, Baby, had developed an annoying habit of peeing around the house. Mrs. Greenough, admittedly incontinent herself, was sympathetic. Fortunately, as it turned out, she was also hard of hearing. Several meaningful screams followed by the crash of stainless steel against ceramic flooring echoed throughout the hospital.

I looked up to see Carter streak past the office door with P.C. in hot pursuit. Dr. Doucette's Jack Russell terrier Sullivan, always up for a good time, leapt out of his bed and joined the fray. A breathless Tanya brought up the rear.

"What happened?" I asked, joining the end of the line.

"Carter strolled by just as we were giving P.C. his pre-med," Tanya gasped. "It stung a bit and P.C. flipped. I think he blames Carter."

By the time we reached reception, P.C. had Carter cornered on top of the aquarium. The panicked occupants darted about in a mad frenzy as tidal waves pounded the glass walls. The remaining member of the posse had been diverted by the smell of an Egg McMuffin and hash browns. Unable to leave P.C. alone to face surgery, Cecil had returned with breakfast in tow. Sullivan sat drooling at his feet.

"I'm so sorry, Cecil!" I bent down to pat P.C. and soothe his frayed nerves before picking him up. "He jumped off the table when the staff was giving him his sedative."

Cecil waved aside my apology. "He sure put the boots to that big orange and white fella. Pretty good for a little guy with no balls, huh, Doc?"

"Very impressive." I was grateful that Cecil could see the bright side.

"So, Doc. Is it always this exciting around here?" Cecil asked, padding behind me as I carried P.C. back to the surgery ward. "Hughie never talks about stuff like this."

I smiled to myself, thinking there were lots of things Hughie never discussed with Cecil. Still, I was concerned that P.C. had been needlessly stressed. I wanted Cecil to know we had an excellent facility with a well-trained, dedicated staff.

"Cecil, would you like to actually watch the surgery?"

"Whoa, doc. You mean go right in with you, help out?"

"No, no," I laughed. "You could watch through the window."

Cecil was delighted. While he called Mrs. Cecil with an update, we gave P.C. an injection of pentothal barbiturate and shaved his belly. By the time Cecil returned, P.C. lay in a trough on his back, legs splayed. We inserted an endotracheal tube so he was breathing a mixture of isoflurane anesthetic and oxygen. Hilary prepped the shaved area which I then covered with a blue surgical drape. Using scissors from a sterile kit, I cut a hole in the drape to expose the surgical site. We were ready.

I turned to Cecil, who was perched on a stool, hands clasped in his lap. He reminded me of a placid little Buddha, rolls of fat cascading over each other. Grinning, he thrust an arm into the air and gave me an enthusiastic thumbs up.

On the physical exam, I had located one testicle in the lower groin and began my incision there. Within a few minutes I had tied off the vas deferens with the testicle's blood supply, making a natural knot. Patsy Cline crooned softly in the background about lost love.

Although I couldn't feel the second testicle, they were usually in the groin. To reduce P.C.'s anesthetic time and impress Cecil with my efficiency, I made an incision on the opposite side. After ten minutes, I realized it was the wrong move in this hide-and-seek game. Sweat began collecting around the rim of my surgical mask. Generally, I enjoy the quiet isolation of surgery, but this wayward testicle was frustrating. If I didn't find and remove it, P.C. could still develop habits frowned upon by even the most feline-friendly homeowner.

I decided to leave the groin and make an abdominal incision. Gently pushing aside the intestines and spleen, I uncovered the pulsing aorta. The body's incredible network of arteries and veins is like a roadmap. If I could find the blood supply for the testicle, I could follow it to my destination. Where a small blood vessel branched off the aorta, I took a left. The snaking route led me to a kidney and nestled beside it was the golden nugget. Closing my eyes, I took a deep breath of relief then unceremoniously removed P.C.'s last vestige of tomcathood.

Grabbing its mate from the instrument tray, I raised a gloved hand in triumph and turned to Cecil. A pair of testicles dangled between my thumb and forefinger.

Cecil was nowhere to be seen. Trophies in hand, I stepped closer to the window and looked around but only the stool remained. Puzzled, I finished closing, then left Hilary to monitor P.C.'s post-op recovery while I looked for Cecil. I found him in reception, sprawled in the rocker. His head was firmly wedged between his knees and a cold pack draped over his neck.

"Doc!" he groaned, addressing my shoes. "I don't know how you do that for a livin'."

I heard an odd little sound and looked up to see a familiar client smiling behind a large book about diseases of the cat. Whoever was in charge of fate had arranged for Evelyn Pratt to run out of cat food on the same day P.C. had his surgery. As Cecil held his stomach and moaned softly, she began to hum.

As the saying goes, one man's sorrow is another man's joy.

Chapter 6

We were strolling hand in hand along the deserted beach. High above us, the plaintive shrieks of a few straggling gulls were scattered by a restless wind. I pressed comfortably into his warm body, feeling his breath on my neck. As the last slivers of sunlight stretched across an inky sea and burst against the cliffs, he became more insistent. He pawed at me, his breath a torrent of desire. A light spattering of raindrops sizzled against my skin.

A brilliant probe of light followed by a thunder clap splintered my fantasy and I awoke to find myself eyeball to eyeball with Dr. Doucette's Jack Russell terrier. Saliva flew in every direction from a tongue that was out of control. The thunder and lightning storm that gripped the county had convinced Sullivan the end of the world was nigh.

I had agreed to look after my boss' house and its four-legged inhabitants while he attended a feline conference in Santa Fe. With the nearest neighbours a couple of acres away, Hughie's place was a welcome retreat from city living. A narrow driveway, carved through the trees, wound its way to a small cedar home at the edge of a lake. I had spent a quiet, uneventful evening with Humphrey Bogart, Ingrid Bergman, and Chinese take-out. I went to bed at eleven and slept soundly until the sky was ripped apart three hours later.

The cats were sprawled in the bedroom, idly watching Sullivan's nervous breakdown. As former victims of abuse and neglect, they were hardened to the natural elements. But life had not prepared Sullivan for the wrath of Mother Nature. His conception was a carefully planned event, his birth heralded with much enthusiasm. Sired by Winchester's Pride of Oakglen and suckled by Oakglen's Annabelle Lee, he led a charmed existence.

I lifted the duvet. "C'mon, Sul. C'mon underneath with Auntie Emmy." It was an invitation usually reserved for very close friends.

Panting so hard the bed shook, Sullivan chose instead to stand on the pillow. Drool streamed from his mouth.

Sighing, I got up and looked under the bed. It was a wasteland of half-chewed rawhide bones and tennis balls. I found Sul's squeaky toy and, with as much enthusiasm as I could muster given the hour, I squeezed the plush giraffe a few times then flung it across the room.

"Go get it, Sul!" I cheered, trying to coax him out of his fit of anxiety.

Sully ignored his favourite toy as well as the cat that had given chase and was now boldly sniffing it. In desperation, he clawed at my legs, begging to be picked up. Only one option remained. I scooped the little dog into my arms, and grabbing my pillow, descended to the bowels of the house.

A checkered sofa, its glory days long past, was propped against the concrete wall beside the furnace. On previous trips to scoop cat litter, I had thought it out of place in this male bastion of power tools, paint cans, and spare parts. Now, as we entered the abyss where no natural light or sound penetrated, I understood. Sully leapt out of my arms and onto the sofa. After circling a few times, he flopped with a contented sigh on the middle cushion. I arranged myself around him and closed my eyes, waiting for sleep. Instead, I tossed and turned, mindful of every spring on its thinly upholstered skeleton. Somewhere in the black void, a clock marked the passage of my sleepless night with annoying regularity.

I finally fell asleep just as the rest of the time zone was waking up. Had it not been for my dependable bladder, I would have been late for my 9:00 A.M. appointment with Anne Cummings. As it was, I had to forego breakfast and a shower although I did manage a cup of coffee.

Anne was one of my favourite clients. A spirited seventy-two-year-old spinster, she wore a T-shirt identifying herself as an "Unclaimed Treasure." It had been a present from one of Anne's nephews at her seventieth birthday party. She drove a '57 blue-and-white antique Chevy with whitewall tires and miles of chrome. Last year, she water skied for the first time and this year spent three days straddling a mule in the Grand Canyon. On the downside, she owned a large, evil cat named Claude.

The eighteen-pound Claude was cursed with spare toes, like many Maritime cats. Left unchecked, the extra nails could curl right around into his footpads and cause an abscess. Anne hauled him into the hospital every three months for a manicure. Claude, on the other hand, preferred his nails long and lethal, and vigorously resisted our efforts. His visits to the vet were always followed by a conciliatory basket of goodies from Anne.

I had unwittingly inherited Claude from Dr. Doucette because Anne preferred my French pronunciation of his name. My Cape Breton colleague referred to the orange apocalypse as "Clod." While this was acceptable for a stray, Anne had recently adopted the neighbourhood terror and was trying to improve his image. Under her care he had acquired six pounds and a rhinestone-studded collar.

"Good morning!" Anne greeted me with a bright smile that quickly faded as she noticed the dark circles under my eyes.

"Oh, goodness dear. You look exhausted."

"Late night," I acknowledged. "Early morning."

"Ohhh...," Anne winked. "Say no more. Unless, of course, you want to," she added eagerly.

Beside me, Hilary snickered. The staff were always trying to fix me up with someone and took a keen interest in my personal life. Their latest attempt was a referral via Hilary's brother's girlfriend's best friend who just happened to know the managing editor of a local-interest magazine. She had just hired a great guy, recently divorced, with a super personality and was sure we would be a match.

We met for coffee. Once. Darren passed three of the fifty or so criteria on my list, a list my mother felt was far too restrictive.

"If I had been that judgmental, Emily, you would never have been born," she was fond of saying. "And then where would you be?" It was a question that defied an answer.

"So," I began, turning everyone's attention back to Claude. "How's my boy?"

A low, sustained growl rattled the carrier.

"Oh, Claudie," Anne scolded. "Be a nice boy."

"Did he get his pill?" I asked dubiously.

"Oh yes, dear. Every bit. I mushed it up in some tuna juice." The hospital supplied Anne with a little vial of orange pills, free of charge, so that she could sedate Claude before each visit.

Feeling more like the leader of a commando assault than a veterinarian, I looked around.

"So...is everyone ready? Here we go."

As I tipped Claude's carrier, gravity drew him to the front

where all four feet firmly straddled the opening. Just behind me Hilary dangled a thick beach towel, ready to restrain the patient when he landed. She worked out three times a week and was the key to our success. Beside her, Susan waited with the canvas muzzle.

Claude struggled to maintain his balance in the now upright carrier but one hind leg slipped through the gaping hole. Pressing my advantage, I wiggled the carrier and a second leg appeared. In desperation, Claude gripped the inside edge of the door while his hind legs scrambled for a foothold in mid-air.

"Here he comes!" I cried, just as my arms were about to dissolve.

The newly acquired six pounds proved to be Claude's undoing. Unable to hold on any longer, he released his grip and descended onto the hell of the veterinarian's examining table. The team sprang into action while Claude gnashed his teeth and howled death threats.

"Now Claude...tut-tut," Anne chided.

Claude beat the table with his tail and managed to force one dripping yellow fang through the muzzle. Like a barnacle attached to a rock, it waited for whatever drifted too close.

I gripped Claude's front leg. Only a thin sliver of canvas separated our faces. Pushing down on each toe to extend the nail, I managed to reduce his arsenal by three before he decided to disembowel the towel. Twisting sideways, he hooked his hind nails in the terry cloth fabric and kicked to kill.

"I'm losing him!" Hilary exclaimed as gaping holes appeared in the towel.

Throwing on the Kevlar gloves, Susan grabbed his back legs. I held onto Claude's front leg and kicked a footstool over to Hilary.

She clambered on, the extra leverage allowing her to gain the upper hand once again. Claude snorted like a raging bull through the muzzle as he gathered strength for his next act of defiance. My fingers a blur, I snipped the remaining nails on his front feet.

"What's that smell?" Anne asked, wrinkling her nose.

"That would be his anal glands," I grimaced.

Cats have a small gland on each side of the anus, used for scent-marking. Under stress, they sometimes squirt a pungent drop or two, the feline equivalent of biological warfare.

Holding a monogrammed hanky to her nose, Anne excused herself and left the room. Even Claude seemed overwhelmed by his own creation. Although he continued to hurl insults, he relaxed enough for me to trim the remaining nails on his hind feet without any bloodshed.

"We're done," I announced at last, my knees creaking as I straightened up.

The room emptied quickly. Claude jumped off the table and stalked to the door. His caustic glare sent the resident cats scurrying. I sighed. I always aged during these visits but today, I felt prehistoric.

"Thank you, everyone," Anne gushed. "I don't know what Claude and I would do without you girls." Grabbing my hand, she whispered, "Men! Who needs 'em? I find a good Harlequin romance and a glass of sherry work wonders!"

Despite my exhaustion, Anne made me laugh. Nevertheless, after she left, I trudged back to the office, tracked down some Tylenol and washed them down with stale coffee.

Althea handed me the next patient's chart.

"Wow! You look terrible," she added. "Are you all right?"

I grunted as I reached for the chart.

"Sammy. Eight weeks old," Althea added helpfully. "It's his first visit."

"Okay, thanks," I sighed, grabbing a fresh lab coat from the closet. Althea followed me to the door of the exam room.

"Did you want to freshen up a bit? He's really cute," she whispered.

"All kittens are cute," I answered, turning the doorknob.

Too late, I realized she was referring to the client. Inside the exam room, a ruggedly handsome man rose to greet me. Underneath his casual, loose-fitting clothes lurked a body type I would like to spend more time with. He cradled a tiny kitten to his chest with one arm and shook my hand with the other. I wished I had taken Althea's advice. This was not a good time to look like a rotting corpse.

"Hi. This is Sam…or Samantha," he grinned. "I'm not sure which."

I held his hand and pumped vigorously. "So…this is your first visit?" I asked, tucking a sweat-soaked strand of hair behind my ear.

"For both of us. I've never had a cat before."

"Oh," I managed.

"I just want to do everything right, you know? Vaccinations, food, kitty litter.…I heard from a reliable source this was the best place to come," he added with a smile.

"Uh-huh," I nodded, still shaking his hand. His eyes were so dark it was hard to see his pupils.

The kitten, bored by the conversation, climbed up to the man's shoulder. "So…um…do you want to check him out?" the man asked.

"Oh, yes!" I released my grip and watched, mesmerized, as

he struggled to unhook Sam/Samantha from his shoulder. The kitten had dug in all eighteen toenails in order to enjoy the new vantage point safely.

"Um…can you?" he gestured helplessly.

"Yes. Of course." I sprang into action and gently freed the little toenails while lingering over the scent of freshly-laundered clothes.

"How long have you had…," I peeked under the kitten's tail, "her?"

"It's a little girl? Oh, good," he smiled. "The kids chipped in and bought her a pink collar so that's perfect."

"You have kids?" I asked, vaguely disappointed.

"Yeah," he chuckled. "Thirty-two of 'em. I teach Grade Five."

"That's great!" I bobbed my head up and down in support of his career choice.

"Yeah, I love it," he continued as I began my examination. "I used to have my own business but I sold it and went back to school for my B. Ed. One of my students found this little one wandering alone in the parking lot and brought her to class. I bet a hundred kids came to my room that day and promised me that their mom said it was OK for them to take the kitten home."

I laughed. "Yeah, I used to be one of those kids."

What a wonderful man. A saint, really. He loved animals, was great with kids, and clearly kept in good shape. Judging by his tanned face and worn hiking jacket, he was an outdoorsy type. And he smelled really good. He had already surpassed the half-way mark on my list and I'd only known him for five minutes. True, I was a modern woman and did not need a man to complete me, but they came in handy sometimes. I smiled my biggest and brightest smile.

"Sorry," he said after a moment, "I don't usually chat so much. My students' main goal is to get me talking. Anything to avoid fractions," he grinned. "The boys want to know about my favourite teams, what kind of car I drive. The girls want to know what music I like, who I'm dating."

I had to confess a certain interest in the latter as well but wisely hauled out my stethoscope instead. "Come here, sweetheart," I cooed, only partially addressing the kitten. The little grey tabby purred as I listened to her lungs and chest. When I was done, Samantha curled up in her owner's lap and played with a frayed edge on his jacket.

"Well, she's in good health," I began. "She's got a slight heart murmur which will hopefully disappear as she gets older. We'll check it next visit but for now, I don't think it's anything to worry about. I'm going to give her the first deworming treatment today, but you should pick up some more at the front desk. They'll also show you some products for flea control."

Most of my clients liked to poke their head right beside mine when I examined their cat but Samantha's owner had remained at the far end of the table during the visit. Occasionally, he turned his head to cough or clear his throat. I hoped he wasn't ill.

"We should just take a bit of blood for a combo test," I continued. "Since she was a stray, she could have picked up feline leukemia or the feline AIDS virus. It'll just take a minute."

"Sure. Whatever you think is best," he agreed.

I whisked Samantha back to the treatment area. The room had been buzzing with conversation that ended abruptly when I entered.

"Can you take some blood from Samantha for a combo test?" I asked, looking from Althea to Tanya to Hilary. They smiled idiotically at me.

"Well?" Althea asked.

"Well, what?"

"He's nice, eh?"

"Yeah, he's nice," I agreed, handing Samantha to Hilary. "So's Mother Theresa."

"Dr. McBride, let's take stock." Althea began counting on her fingers. "You're thirty…something. You're not married. You don't have a boyfriend. You live with three cats and a guinea pig. You spend Friday night with your mother."

"We play poker and drink," I added defensively.

Althea stopped counting. "What's that smell?"

I tried a few tentative sniffs. "I don't smell anything."

"It's right around here." Althea was relentless.

"Check the garbage," Tanya suggested. "Cuddles had diarrhea this morning."

"No, it's…." Horrified, Althea turned to me. "Dr. McBride, it's you."

"What?"

"Did you go into your appointment smelling like that?"

"Smelling like what?" Then I remembered Claude and his God-forsaken anal glands. Apparently, not all of it had landed on the examining table. No wonder my client had stayed at the far end of the room.

"It's too late now!" Althea shook her head in mock despair. "The damage is done."

"It's not your fault, Dr. McBride," Susan said kindly. "You just probably couldn't smell yourself after awhile."

At thirty-five, Susan was married with a toddler and a six-month old. She was accustomed to sleepless nights and bad smells.

The good news was that Samantha tested negative for both viruses. I buttoned my lab coat tightly over the telltale brown smudge on my blouse and carried her back to the exam room where her owner waited anxiously. He held out his arms. Tired from her ordeal, Samantha nestled against his chest and began to purr.

"I always knew you'd be a vet," he smiled, looking up at me.

Puzzled, I looked up from my notes.

"You don't know who I am, do you, Em?"

Uh oh. Another social blunder.

I shook my head. "Gosh, I'm sorry. I had a really late night, and today's been so hectic...."

"It's me, Benny. Benny Mombourquette."

My mouth opened and stayed open until I thought to cover the gaping hole with my hand. I flipped the medical chart over. Under client information, Althea had written "MOMBOURQUETTE, Benjamin" in clear, bold letters. In my haste, I hadn't even looked at the owner's name.

"Oh my God! Benny? I never would have recognized you. You look so...different!"

"You haven't changed a bit," Benny grinned. "I'd have known you anywhere."

I smiled politely. I'm sure he meant well.

"Why didn't you say something sooner?" I asked.

"I guess I just wanted to see if you'd know me. Your mom told me you worked here. It's been what...twenty years?"

"Yeah, about that," I nodded. "You guys moved away when I was in Grade Six, I think. But Mom said you were a plumber. How long have you been teaching?"

"Just a couple of years. I did have a small plumbing company. One of the guys who used to work for me bought it. I always wanted to teach so I went back to school part time and got my degree. Sold the company."

"Wow! Good for you, Benny. That's not easy."

"It's not so bad if it's what you really want to do," he smiled.

"Yup. True enough."

"So, Em," Benny added enthusiastically, "we should get together sometime and catch up over coffee."

"That would be fun," I agreed. The day was improving. I found myself wondering when Benny Mombourquette had turned into a good-looking, nice guy.

He put on a ball cap and rose to his feet.

"So I'll see you in a few weeks with Sammy here. Thanks again." Shrugging his shoulders, Benny added with a rueful grin, "Sure hope my girlfriend doesn't mind a cat in the house. She doesn't know yet."

Girlfriend? I stared at his retreating back.

"Hey, Em?" Benny called out when he reached the reception counter. "Do you still sleep with your baseball glove?"

"Hey Benny!" I shot back. "Do you still pee from trees?"

He laughed and waved goodbye.

When I got home that night, I threw my soiled blouse in the laundry basket. Taking Anne's advice, I curled up on the sofa with one of Mom's favourite Harlequins and a glass of wine. Tonight I would ride the wild English moors with the darkly mysterious Roger von Syberg, who did not have a girlfriend.

Chapter 7

A CLUSTER OF PINT-SIZED HUMANS gathered around my boss.

"Hello," Hughie began. "My name is Dr. Doucette. I'm a cat doctor."

No one seemed particularly impressed. A few stared at Hughie, waiting to see if things got any better. The rest of the crowd began to disperse. A couple of girls found the rack of neon-coloured cat collars and began trying them on.

"Look! A cat!" someone cried. The crowd set off in pursuit. Carter had been discovered and he spent a frantic few minutes trying to avoid his admirers until Susan opened the door to the treatment room. There was a disappointed groan when he disappeared through the crack.

"Children, children...," Hughie called desperately.

A freckle-faced redhead, identified earlier as Geoffrey when he tried to eat some cat food, pointed at a much taller classmate and pouted.

"Mister, she just called me Geoffrey the Peffrey!"

"I'm sure she didn't mean it," Hughie replied.

"We're not supposed to call each other names," one little boy declared. Folding his arms across his chest, he shook his head, shocked by the behaviour of his fellow six-year-olds.

Inspired, Geoffrey's nearest neighbour poked him in the ribs. "Hey," he giggled, pointing at my boss. "Dr. Doo-Doo." The group found this hilarious, and Dr. Doucette became the focus of their attention.

"Do you have any little children?"

"Are you married?"

"Do you know my brother? He's in high school."

"I hope you don't smoke. Smoking kills."

My boss smiled benignly through the barrage until a small boy, clutching himself with one hand, tugged on Hughie's pant leg with the other.

"I have to pee," he announced.

Alarmed, Hughie looked around at the group. "Does anyone else have to pee?"

Eight heads nodded. In single file, they trooped to the bathroom behind their fearless leader, Dr. Doo-Doo.

Rejuvenated after the conference in Santa Fe, Hughie had made feverish plans to plunge us into the twenty-first century. Management experts predicted that survival of the small veterinary practice depended not only on a high level of service and medical care but also on increased community involvement. Hughie had decided we should host open houses, offer free seminars on cat care, and give tours to school children. Five minutes into his first tour, Dr. Doucette was pale and sweating profusely.

"Emily, Emily!" he hissed. "What should I do with them? Their teacher had to leave. One of the kids got sick."

"Use your charm," I smirked.

Hughie nodded absently then grabbed my arm. "Em, you're a woman. Women are good with kids. You could...."

"Nope," I pointed to the exam room. "Patient waiting."

As I hurried up the hallway, I could hear Hughie's plaintive voice. "But you can't have to pee again. You just went!"

I opened the door to the exam room where Brenda Picker, her four children, and Leonardo da Vinci were waiting. The children had common enough names but their parents had splurged when naming the cats. Leonardo, an affable Siamese, shared the house with Socrates, Aphrodite, and Horatio. Leonardo was a gadabout who enjoyed nothing more than sharing afternoon tea and a bit of gossip with the neighbours. As a result, his belly was most un-Siamese-like.

"He doesn't seem any better," Brenda sighed, brushing a strand of limp hair from her face. "And he won't eat anything."

Two days ago, Brenda had accidentally captured Leo in a live-trap intended for an unneutered stray. She was hoping to catch the stray, fix him up, and find him a permanent home. Instead, she had found Leo sprawled on his back in a catnip and shrimp-induced euphoria, the stray nowhere in sight. Leo had vomited several times that night but otherwise seemed fine. Brenda had assumed he was merely paying the price of gluttony.

Today a very depressed Leo refused to leave the comfort of the laundry basket, so he had arrived via Rubbermaid on a pile of clean towels. A single hair out of place normally sent Leo into a grooming frenzy, but now he showed no interest in his surroundings or himself. His vacant eyes stared into space as he withdrew into a private world of pain. The four Picker children crowding the room looked as mournful as their cat.

"He's really sick, isn't he?" the older girl asked.

"Yes, he is, sweetheart, but we're going to try and help him," I answered.

Brenda and I knew each other from an aerobics class at the community recreation centre. Sometimes after class, we dragged ourselves to the local watering hole to replace the calories we had paid the city fifty dollars to burn. Over a pitcher of draft and a plate of wings, Brenda confessed she and her husband of fifteen years had recently separated. Although they cared for each other and loved their children, it wasn't enough.

Addressing me formally in front of the children, she asked, "What do you think's wrong, Dr. McBride?"

"I'm not sure, yet," I answered. "I'd like to do bloodwork and take some X-rays. He's quite dehydrated so we should put him on IV fluids too."

"Will Leonardo have to stay?" one of the boys asked. "Mommy said he might have to stay."

I gazed at the halo of anxious faces surrounding Leo. When I nodded yes, the children solemnly produced Leo's overnight bag. Inside were his favourite toys, his personal dishes, and a picture of the family.

"In case he gets lonely," Stephen confided.

"We'll take good care of him," I promised, lifting Leo out of the basket.

Brenda shifted a youngster on her hip. "I'll be at home if you need to reach me."

"Mommy's going to sell Mary Kay," the little girl explained. "She might win a pink car!"

"Shh, Jenna," her older sister warned. Silenced, the little girl thrust a thumb into her mouth.

I wondered how this little family would manage in the months and years to come. I hoped that at least I would be able to help Leo. I leaned over and whispered to Jenna, "Pink's my favourite colour."

"C'mon, kids. Say goodbye to Leo. Stephen, Gary, you two carry the laundry basket."

Brenda ushered the little flock out the door. Jenna, holding onto her mother's shoulder with one hand, turned to wave a shy goodbye. They left quietly, the excited babble of children around animals absent. By contrast, another group of children in another part of the hospital were having the tour of their lives.

I poked my head into surgery, where Dr. Doucette was feverishly directing a team of midgets. Everyone wore a surgical mask except the patient, who was stretched out, shoeless, on the surgery table. An empty IV bag dangled above him and a surgical drape covered his belly. The patient began chatting with one of the nurses.

"Mr. Lippman!" cautioned a stern voice. "You are in a coma! No talking!" Mr. Lippman closed his eyes and giggled.

"Nurse!" Hughie ordered, "Ze syringe, if you please!"

"Yes, Doctor!" A pixie in pigtails handed Hughie a 3 cc syringe. He paused, hand raised dramatically in mid-air.

"Wait! I zink we need to take out ze brain." Hughie rubbed his hands together in his best mad scientist impersonation and laughed maniacally. "I have a collection in ze basement! We can pick out a new one and stick it in ze hole left by ze old one!" There was an excited buzz among the consulting physicians. Mr. Lippman bolted upright.

Eight voices groaned in unison. "Mr. Lippman!"

Hughie handed rubber tubing to the nearest child. "Dr. Smeltzer, could you suck out ze brain please?"

Dr. Smeltzer nodded agreeably and patted his patient on the arm. "You won't feel a thing, son," he announced in a deep voice then, turning to Hughie, whispered, "This is going to be tricky."

"You can do zis, Dr. Smeltzer. If you can colour between ze lines and count to one hundred, you can suck out a brain. All your training at ze daycare has prepared you for zis moment!"

Dr. Smeltzer looked up at Hughie. "I've only been there since the baby-sitter quit," he confessed.

Hughie's hand rested on the switch for the dental machine. "Are ve ready?"

Dr. Smeltzer took a deep breath. "Okay."

"Ze lights, Dr. McBride!"

As bidden, I flicked off the overhead lights. While most of the room faded into obscure shadows, the halo of light from the surgical lamp illuminated the stage.

"I am turning on ze brain-sucking machine!" Hughie declared in his best mad-scientist voice. Lights flashed on the console of the dental machine as it started to hum. Dr. Smeltzer added his own slurping noises and the crowd clapped appreciatively.

Susan tapped me on the shoulder. "We're ready."

While the ground-breaking surgery continued in the OR, I slipped outside to study Leo's X-rays. His intestinal tract was empty and his belly was distended. My eyes were drawn to a white, circular object that glowed like a full moon in the darkness of Leo's stomach.

"Well," I mused out loud, "that certainly doesn't belong there."

"A coin, do you think?" Susan asked.

"Maybe. Might be a marble. Or a button." I shook my head. "Guess I'll go call Brenda. Can you tell the brain surgeons in there to tidy up? We're going to need the surgery."

Leo's bloodwork had shown abnormal levels of electrolytes but this was likely due to vomiting. Except for his tendency to devour anything remotely edible, he appeared to be an otherwise healthy cat.

"There are always risks associated with anesthesia and surgery," I explained to Brenda, who answered on the first ring. "Since he's almost twelve we'll take extra steps to reduce that risk.

But I'm anticipating that he'll do fine."

"Thank God it's something you can fix," Brenda breathed. "But why would he swallow something like that in the first place? I mean, he has bowls of food all over the neighbourhood."

Why indeed? In my short career, I had retrieved many tourists from inside cats' bellies: elastic bands, a plastic farm animal, sponge earplugs, the cord from a Butterball turkey, sewing needles, and several calcified mysteries. Dogs get a bum rap; cats can be just as indiscriminate as their arch-enemies.

I passed Dr. Doucette and the Lilliputians in the hallway.

"Impressive brain surgery," I murmured. "I've never seen that technique before. How are you holding out?"

"Actually, Em," he whispered, "this isn't too bad. I'm kind of having fun."

"Leo Picker's X-rays are still up," I added. "The kids might want to see them."

Hughie's eyes lit up. "Oh, good idea!"

By the time I finished my sterile scrub and entered surgery, Leo was intubated and lay flat on his back in the metal trough. Stubby limbs stuck out from his plump body like afterthoughts. Susan prepped his shaved belly then mercifully covered the view with a surgical drape. As Leo dozed, I began cutting through jiggling layers of fat until finally his pale swollen stomach lay glistening in front of me.

Picking up a sterile needle from the instrument tray, I placed a single stitch at opposite ends of his stomach. Instead of cutting the suture material, I left a long thread at each end. Susan was then able to hold his stomach upright by grasping a thread in each hand. If any fluid from Leo's stomach spilled into his abdomen, he could develop a serious infection.

Susan's hands were steady, her brow wrinkled in concentration as I made a small incision through the tough outer layers of the stomach. Picking up a pair of forceps, I probed gently for the source of Leo's misery. It wasn't brain surgery but it was nonetheless rewarding as my forceps locked onto something hard. The crowd "oohed" and "aahed" as I pulled a penny out of Mr. da Vinci and flourished it in the air. From Hughie, I had developed a flair for the dramatic. It was a 1988 model. Elizabeth II's serene profile showed no hint of her recent ordeal. I popped the penny into a pill vial. I doubted this penny would ever rejoin its kind in the busy world of commerce. Most people liked to save the stuff I pulled out of their pets. Even the lowly, disposable earplug was elevated to the status of cherished keepsake after spending a few days in the digestive system. One of my clients had a necklace made from her cat's extracted teeth.

We stitched Leo back up, minus one penny and a few gobs of fat. Back in the recovery ward, he was wrapped in a warm afghan. Hilary heated a Magic Bag and pressed it against his back. The IV line that had been started before surgery continued to drip slowly. I hoped to keep it in place at least twenty-four hours but my patients often had other plans.

While Susan monitored Leo's recovery, I began outpatient clinic. The afternoon was packed with vaccinations, runny eyes, skin problems, and a geriatric cat that refused to use his litter box anymore. About three o'clock I went to check on Leo before grabbing some lunch. Through the window I could see Brad, Brenda's estranged husband, sitting on the floor. His shirt sleeves were rolled up and his suit jacket flung carelessly over a chair. Snoopy dogs danced across his loosened tie. He had opened Leo's door and was gently stroking the cat.

Hilary stopped me on her way to the laundry room. "One of the kids called him at work," she whispered, her arms laden with towels. "He came up right away. Paid the whole bill, too."

I hesitated, my hand on the doorknob. Just then Brad looked up and, recognizing me, smiled. I opened the door.

"Hi, Brad. Nice tie," I grinned.

"Oh," he smiled, looking down at his chest. "A gift from the kids last Father's Day." The smile slowly faded as he continued to stare at the tie.

"Leo's doing great," I added quickly, kneeling down beside Brad to check the cat. "We'll probably be sending him home in a couple of days."

"Good!" he declared, his face brightening. "That's good. The kids really miss him." He continued to stroke Leo as the silence stretched between us. I got up to go.

"We got Leo just before Brenda found out she was pregnant," he said quietly. "I dropped out of school and got a job. But we had fun, you know. We were living in this crappy little basement apartment. It flooded every time it rained. We'd have these romantic dinners with candlelight and Kraft Dinner. We were like two kids...." His voice trailed off as he struggled to reconcile the past with the present.

I waited for him to say more but he continued to pat Leo, lost in his own thoughts. I made an excuse about neglected paperwork and left the room. In the office, Sully was sprawled in his bed, his feet occasionally twitching as they ran through gopher-filled fields. I watched him as he slept the peaceful sleep of a dog who is loved and is secure in that knowledge. As he gradually became aware that someone was in the room, his eyes opened and his little stump of a tail began to vibrate in excitement. Dogs never wake up in a bad mood. I leaned over and began to absently rub his tummy, lost in my own thoughts.

"Em!" Hughie poked his head through the door less than five minutes later. "I've been redecorating. Come see."

I followed him to the exam room, where colourful six-year-old interpretations of life in a cat practice lined one wall.

"They're great," I managed.

"Yup," Hughie nodded, folding his arms across his chest as he surveyed the wall. "There's even one of you here, Em." He pointed to a smiling stick figure wielding a large knife. A cat twice her size with a large circle in his tummy stood on two legs beside her. The cat was smiling too.

I stared absently at the pictures. "Do you ever wish you and Michele'd had kids?" Michele was Hughie's ex-wife.

Hughie hesitated. "Sometimes," he said at last. "You make choices, you know?"

"Yeah."

Hughie was quiet. "Em?" he asked suddenly. "Do you remember playing hide-and-seek outdoors until it got dark?"

"What?" Sometimes it was hard to follow Hughie's train of thought.

"When you were a kid," he explained. "Drinking Kool-Aid all summer instead of beer? When anyone over twenty was old?"

I hesitated. There were lots of good times in our family but as I got older, I remembered my parents fighting a lot. And in the egocentric way of children, I assumed it was my fault.

"The music of the ice cream truck," I smiled at last, remembering. "Every Friday night." A parade of kids, some walking, some riding bicycles, followed the driver along his route. Fathers had finished their work week and moms had just tidied up after supper. Everyone was always happy on ice cream day.

Hughie grinned. “Water balloons!”

“Bee stings. Playing catch with Dad in the backyard,” I cried, warming up to my subject.

“Tobogganing down the big hill so long you got frostbite! Making out with Anna Polanski behind the school.”

“Peter Newton,” I sighed.

“Life was simple, wasn’t it?” Hughie said, studying the pictures. “You made choices with your heart.”

I looked at my boss.

“C’mon,” he smiled, picking up his jacket. “Let’s go get something to eat. I’ll tell you about the time some little kids took me on a tour of a cat hospital.”

Chapter 8

"Who is this?" the crisp voice on the other end of the phone demanded.

I paused for a moment. At 4:00 a.m., even the simplest questions require considerable thought. "Dr. McBride. Can I help you?"

"Where's Dr. Doucette?"

A number of possibilities came to mind. "He's not on call," I answered carefully. "Is this an emergency?"

"Well, *yes*, of course!" the voice replied in a tone which suggested I must be the village idiot. "But I'd rather speak with Dr. Doucette. It's Bethany Carmichael." She waited. "Bethany MARIE Carmichael?"

Standing in a thin nightshirt, I shivered in the cold night air and pondered the best way to get back into bed. The cats were nestled in my new duvet, a gift from Mom. She was worried that after three years on Vancouver Island, I had been spoiled by the temperate west coast weather. In her words, east coast winters were "colder than an unpaid whore's heart." My mother's father had been a sea-going man with a colourful vocabulary.

"I'm sure you've heard Dr. Doucette mention Marcel and Francois, my Persians?" Ms. Carmichael continued. "Marcel just won three ribbons including Best of Breed at the Atlantic Championships this year."

Marcel might be fluent in Chinese and able to solve Rubik's cube, but I had never heard Dr. Doucette mention him or his owner.

There was a deep and meaningful sigh as Ms. Carmichael considered her options. "Well," she said at last, "I guess we'll have to see you. Marcel is squatting everywhere and trying to pee but nothing's coming out."

I was instantly alert. A male cat straining to urinate is a serious situation. "How long has this been going on?" I asked.

"Well, I've just noticed it in the last few hours."

Once I went to bed, whoever threw up the fur ball in the bathtub, ate the leftovers on the counter, or shredded the spider plant remained unsolved mysteries of the night. Yet, many of my clients could rattle off at great length the nocturnal habits of their cats and, indeed, made notes.

I recommended that we meet at the hospital as soon as possible. I wanted to check the size of Marcel's bladder. Cats can suffer from a urinary tract disease in which small crystals actually clog the urethra and prevent the bladder from emptying. If the crystals aren't removed and the flow of urine restored, the kidneys eventually shut down, causing death.

I threw on a pair of sweatpants and guzzled some mouthwash. I avoided the bathroom mirror. It would only have added to my stress. When I arrived at the hospital fifteen minutes later, a tall woman wrapped in fur stepped out of a limousine. Waves of chestnut hair swirled around her flawlessly made up face. No one should look and smell that good at four in the morning.

I unlocked the hospital and turned on the lights. Ms. Carmichael's high heels clicked efficiently behind me as we proceeded to the treatment area. Marcel had buried himself under the blanket in his carrier, assuming that if he couldn't see me I couldn't see him. While his owner hovered anxiously, I lifted the entire contents of the carrier onto the treatment table. When

I peeled back the blanket, Marcel's bulbous yellow eyes blinked sadly at me from an otherwise flat face. Persians are the pugs of the cat world.

"What's wrong with him?" Ms. Carmichael demanded.

Without answering her, I began my physical exam. Marcel clung to the edge of the table with his front feet and howled mournfully.

"Oh, Marcel! My poor baby! Is the doctor hurting you?" Straightening up, she looked at me accusingly. "He doesn't act like this with Dr. Doucette!"

I bit my lip and gently palpated Marcel's bladder. Although it was now the size of a grapefruit, no urine trickled out. I explained that he would need to be anesthetized and a catheter inserted into his penis to flush the urethra and bladder. Marcel followed our exchange with growing dread. Drool flowed from each side of his mouth like twin waterfalls. When I finished my examination, he crawled into his mother's arms and refused to look at me.

I reached for a consent form in the drawer and gave Ms. Carmichael a pen. She signed with a flourish, not even glancing at the costs. Laying down the pen, she kissed Marcel and rocked him in her arms.

"What's that mark on your neck?" she asked suddenly.

I had been born with a dusky-pink patch of skin in the shape of Nova Scotia on my neck. I liked the idea that wherever I traveled, this symbol of home was always with me. It was a free spirit, a barometer of my emotions. Nourished by the ungodly hour and a cranky client, it was now probably the colour of cooked lobster.

"Oh...," I stumbled over my answer. Most people were too

polite to ask. “It’s just a birthmark.”

“H’mm. You can get those things removed, you know.”

“H’mm,” I replied with a smile. “I don’t want to.”

Prying Marcel from her coat, Ms. Carmichael kissed him on the forehead one last time. “Tell Dr. Doucette to call me in the morning,” she added, sweeping past me into the night. I quickly locked the doors behind her.

“Your mother is nasty,” I told Marcel as I carried him back to surgery. His bug eyes blinked at me in silent disapproval.

I placed him on a blanket inside the Plexiglas gas induction box. After closing the lid, I turned on both the anesthetic and the oxygen tanks. These two gases flowed into the box at one end and a scavenging system removed them from the other. Marcel hid under the blanket in denial until sleep overtook him. I lifted him onto the treatment table and slid an endotracheal tube down his airway. Then I reconnected the hose to the tube so he was once again breathing the anesthetic/oxygen mix.

Exposing the male cat’s penis is an elusive goal at any time, let alone at four in the morning. It leads a quiet, sheltered life unless summoned by the sinewy Siamese down the street or a single-minded veterinarian. I fiddled and prodded until a tiny organ no bigger than a cooked grain of rice finally popped into view. Patiently, I threaded an olive-tipped catheter inside and began flushing his urethra with sterile saline. The backwash that trickled into the sink was filled with sharp, sand-like crystals. I had once overheard Hughie explaining this painful condition to a middle-aged male client who was reluctant to part with his cash for no good reason.

“It’s like peeing razor blades, man!” he had finally cried in desperation.

Mr. Philpott, who himself had a persnickety prostate, had quickly authorized treatment.

Once Marcel's urethra cleared, I removed the first catheter and inserted a larger catheter aptly named the Tomcat. To the end, I attached a syringe and began the process of draining and flushing. I could only imagine the smile of relief on Marcel's face when he woke up. Anyone who has been stuck in rush hour traffic after several cups of coffee knows the agony of a full bladder.

When Marcel was awake and stable, I called Ms. Carmichael. After five rings, soft music and a surprisingly seductive, mellow voice advised me that Bethany Marie wasn't available to take my call at the moment. If I left my name and number, she would be delighted to return my call. Relieved, I was in the process of doing what I was told when a more familiar voice cut in.

"Dr. McBride. How is he doing?"

Damn.

"Oh, hi." I answered. "I was just leaving you a message."

"Yes, I know," she replied impatiently. The approaching dawn had not improved her mood.

"Well, he looks good right now. I flushed and drained his bladder, but I'd like to keep him here for a few days. He'll need medication and we'll want to watch his urine output closely. And he'll be on a special diet as well. It'll help dissolve those crystals and prevent new ones from forming."

"Thank you," she said grudgingly.

"Do you have any questions?" I asked.

"Just have Dr. Doucette call me in the morning."

I would be delighted to have Dr. Doucette call her in the morning. Sighing, I hung up the phone. The hospital would be open in a few short hours so I decided to stretch out on the sofa in the recovery ward. Marcel and I dozed fitfully until the morning staff began trickling in.

"Dr. McBride, what are you doing here?" Susan asked, flicking on the lights.

"Bethany Carmichael," I yawned, sitting up. "Bethany MARIE Carmichael?"

Puzzled, Susan shrugged her shoulders.

"Huh! You don't know her either," I announced triumphantly.

Squinting against the brightness of the overhead lights, I poured a cup of coffee and stumbled to the bathroom. Adjusting the shower head to its full potential, I stood underneath and let the water/coffee combination work its magic. By the time I emerged, the hospital was well into its day. The kennels were starting to fill with day patients, and in reception I could hear the hum of conversations. I found Hughie in the office, rifling through his briefcase.

"Morning," I said as I stood there, clutching a second cup of coffee.

"Morning," Hughie replied absently. "You're here early."

"Yeah, I had an emergency this morning so I just decided to stay."

Hughie gave up on the briefcase and began ransacking the In/Out tray.

"Uh…Hughie?" I began, as papers flew across the room

"Uh-huh."

"I know we're supposed to follow up on our own cases, but I think maybe you should deal with this one."

"Have you seen the bill from the electrician?

I shook my head.

"Well, it was on the desk yesterday," he added, implying that I must have had something to do with its disappearance.

I tried another approach. "It's Bethany Marie," I breathed in my sexiest, come-hither voice. "You remember my...Persians?"

Hughie looked up. "Em, are you getting a cold?"

"No!" I sighed in frustration. "Bethany Marie Carmichael? My emergency? She's got two Persians. Marcel, the black one, just won the big hurrah at a cat show."

"Good! Here it is!" Debris boiled over the edge of the desk as Hughie grabbed the wayward bill and stuffed it into a pocket. "Now Em, what were you saying?"

I took a deep breath. "Marcel came in last night blocked. Ms. Carmichael was really upset that *I* was on call and wanted *you* to see Marcel. Anyway, he's doing fine and I know we're supposed to follow through on our own cases, but I was hoping you'd take over this one."

"Sure, not a problem," Hughie grinned as he slipped into a lab coat. "She's a terrific person. I took her to a fund-raiser last year for the Shubenacadie wolves. Dinner-dance thing."

I stared at Hughie. "We *are* talking about the same woman? Bethany Marie Carmichael, owns two Persians, dark hair, pretty?"

"Very pretty!" Hughie winked. Before I could ask any questions, he grabbed his stethoscope and was gone.

By late afternoon, Marcel had not yet peed. Although his bladder was getting larger, he didn't seem distressed. The Valium given to relax his urethra had relaxed his inhibitions as well. Sprawled on his back, he kneaded the air, his tail dangling through the bars into the kennel below. Its occupant, recovering from a territorial dispute with the cat across the street, eyed it warily. From his upside-down vantage point, Marcel's bug eyes followed Susan adoringly as she prepared supper for the inpatients.

"I was just about to try Bethany again," Hughie said when he saw me. "Are you sure this is the right number? I've tried it a couple of times but there's no answer."

I glanced at the file. "Yup. That's the one I called this morning. She has an answering machine. Maybe you need to let it ring longer."

"I was wondering if she moved. She told me that the other condo owners found out she had two cats and they were trying to get rid of her."

I grinned. "Bethany Marie homeless? My heart bleeds." I put a hand over my chest in mock despair. "Hey, maybe she could move in with you."

"Worse things could happen," Hughie grinned. Picking up the phone, he dialed Bethany's number. After a long pause, he gave me the thumbs up and began speaking into her answering machine.

"Hi, Bethany. It's Hughie Doucette. I tried to reach you earlier but there was no answer. I just wanted to let you know that Marcel is doing well. He's a lovely boy and never complains. I'd like to keep him a bit longer, maybe overnight, to see how he performs. Please call me as soon as possible. Thanks."

Hughie hung up the phone. "See how easy that was, Em? Communication. That's the key to a successful veterinarian–client bond. It's something we veterinarians must always keep in mind. In fact," he added, "a good bedside manner is just as important as practicing good medicine." Whistling cheerfully, he disappeared down the hall.

I rolled my eyes and squeezed past the ailing washing machine that Hughie had hauled into the treatment area for either repair or dismemberment. Picking up the chart for my next patient, I knocked on the door of the exam room.

"Hi, Mr. Lawlor. How's Belle?"

"Eh?" An elderly man in a rumpled suit wheezed and cupped a hand to his ear.

"How's Belle?" I shouted.

"Belle," he nodded and smiled. A chubby calico chirped and thrust her head into Mr. Lawlor's outstretched hand.

"How is she?" I screamed.

"Oh…good, good. I'm a little deaf today," he added. "Forgot my hearing aid."

I smiled and lifted Belle onto the examining table. By his own admission, Mr. Lawlor had been a grumpy, retired civil servant until he found a tiny kitten abandoned in a dumpster ten years ago. He nursed her back to health and in the process, rediscovered the colours in each new day. Belle became the mistress of the house. She made sure Mr. Lawlor was up by 6:00 A.M. to feed her, dress himself, and eat breakfast, in that order. She also introduced him to Libby Halliday, the cat-loving, pie-baking widow who lived on the next street.

Holding Belle steady with my left hand, I inserted a rectal thermometer with my right. Although Belle continued to knead happily, several high-pitched squeaks pierced the air. Peering around Belle's behind, I stole a peek at Mr. Lawlor, who was busy grinding his jaws from side to side. The sound appeared to be coming from him. As I watched, he hauled out his false teeth and glared at them. With a sigh, he re-installed first the uppers then the lowers. For the moment, they were subdued.

Ten-year-old Belle appeared to be in good health. Last month, as part of a preventive health care program, we had performed a geriatric work-up. The variety of diagnostic tests would allow us to detect health problems early or prevent them from developing. If a cat was healthy, these tests provided an invaluable baseline of normal data that could be compared to any abnormal results obtained in the future. Belle was an important part of Mr. Lawlor's life, and we wanted to keep the two together as long as possible.

"Why is she here today, Mr. Lawlor?" I asked.

"Oh, yes. It's a beautiful day," he smiled. "But what about Belle's cars?"

"What's wrong with her ears?" I shouted.

"Eh?"

I moved closer.

"No. That's my bad side." He shifted in his chair to allow me access to what was presumably the good side.

Gathering a deep breath, I spoke directly to the omnipotent right ear. It was old and wrinkled and filled with little hairs.

"What's wrong with her ears?" I hollered. I was a little too close. Mr. Lawlor jumped back in his chair.

"Oops! Sorry," I apologized.

Mr. Lawlor just nodded. "She's scratching her ears a lot."

I sniffed Belle's ears for the unpleasant odour associated with an infection. Detecting none, I suspected she might have ear mites and told Mr. Lawlor.

"Termites! How would she get those?" he asked.

"No...EAR MITES!" I screeched. He looked at me blankly.

As I made a move towards his good ear, Mr. Lawlor stiffened and gripped the edge of his chair.

"Ear mites," I repeated slowly, lowering my voice a few decibels. "She could have picked them up from another cat."

"Oh, yes," he smiled in relief. "She does have a new friend. A gentleman caller. They share a little dish of cream on the porch every night."

"Well, I'm just going to get a sample from her ear and check it under the microscope." Delicately, I inserted a cotton-tipped swab into Belle's ear. Clutching my specimen, I left the room just as Mr. Lawlor's false teeth began squeaking again.

In the treatment area, I smeared the sample onto a slide. As I peered through the microscope, gnashing mouthparts and flailing legs revealed a parasite uglier than any alien ever imagined by Hollywood. I armed myself with ear mite medication then strolled purposefully down the hallway.

"Well," I began in a loud voice, "she does have...."

The rest of the sentence never made it to the finish line. My eyes strayed past Mr. Lawlor to the examining table, where a pair of glistening false teeth grinned hideously at me. When I was very little, my Uncle Arthur entertained my brothers and me at the dinner table with his performing false teeth. Corn on the cob, cayenne pepper, or even a good joke could summon them without warning. Far from being embarrassed, Uncle Arthur would grab them from wherever they landed and, guided by his nimble fingers, the trained teeth would sing Frank Sinatra classics. Only after several encores would they be returned to his mouth. My brothers thought this hilarious, but I had nightmares for months. Uncle Arthur's invitations to supper were understandably rare and therefore all the more memorable.

I continued to stare at the teeth that mocked me in a silent grimace. "Um...will you be taking them with you?" I nodded in their direction.

"Whath's tha'?" Mr. Lawlor mumbled through a puckered, toothless void.

"Your teeth!" I pointed. "Do you want them back?"

"Oh, yeth. I'm jutht rethting my gumth."

"Ah...would you like a container to put them in?"

"Oh, no dear. Theyw're fine."

I smiled weakly. At least the squeaking had stopped.

As I explained how to treat the ear mites, Belle jumped onto the table. Discovering the teeth, she sniffed them with enthusiasm then raised a tentative paw. In a split-second decision, I lunged for the grisly duo as she sent them hurtling over the edge with a left hook. Slowly, I reopened my fist. Later I would say that I had acted out of pure instinct. I was, after all, high school MVP shortstop on the baseball team. But as I gazed at the slimy instruments of torture from my youth, I knew that I had been tested and passed. Hallelujah. Pass the plate.

Mr. Lawlor stared in reverent silence as I handed him the teeth. Belle hopped back into her picnic basket.

"You can wait here if you like, Mr. Lawlor, while I type up the notes in Belle's medical history."

Still gripping his teeth, Mr. Lawlor could only nod.

I raced to the treatment area and scrubbed my hands with disinfectant soap. Vigorously. I inspected both sides in the bright light. There were no warts, no rash, no residual slime. Satisfied, I sat down at the computer terminal to enter my notes and the charges for Belle's visit. I was almost finished when Althea flew out of the office.

"Guess what?" she cried, unaware that Mr. Lawlor was just inside the exam room. "Bethany Marie's a hooker!"

Mr. Lawlor poked his head out the door. I noticed his teeth were back where they belonged. "Who's a hooker? One of these nice girls?" he asked.

"No one here is a hooker," I laughed. "At least I don't think so."

Lowering his voice, Mr. Lawlor whispered, "Does Dr. Doucette know?"

"NO ONE HERE IS A HOOKER!" I shouted. The repairman from Sears looked up from the washing machine with interest.

Shaking my head, I accompanied Mr. Lawlor to reception. The place was deserted so I rang through his invoice and helped him out to the car with Belle.

Back inside the hospital, a crowd had gathered around the TV in the Cat Nap Inn. A scandalized reporter claimed one Bethany Marie Carmichael had been arrested after setting fire to the elevator in her building. According to the condominium's spokesperson, a distraught woman clutching a poodle, Ms. Carmichael had been operating a home business, Erotic Aerobics for Adults; the owners were fed up with the late night traffic in their respectable building and had voted to evict her.

"I always liked her," the bespectacled little man in 7B told the reporter.

"No wonder she always has tons of money," Hilary whistled. "And such great clothes!"

Hughie's mouth was still open as he stared at the screen, even though the reporter had moved on to the weather. I couldn't help but feel a twinge of pleasure. Ms. Carmichael and I were not soulmates.

As the staff drifted back to work, Hughie moaned. "How could I not know?"

"How could you not know what?" I asked.

"Em, I went out with her!" He shook his head in disbelief.

"Oh, well." I smothered a smile. "You were just following in the footsteps of hundreds before you."

Before Hughie could respond, there was an urgent knock on

the door. Without waiting for an answer, Susan poked her head in.

"Two messages," she announced. "Dr. McBride, Mr. Lawlor wants you to call him. He said to tell you he has his teeth *and* his hearing aid in. And...," Susan drew a deep breath for what was clearly the bigger message of the two, "Dr. Doucette. A man just called. He wouldn't say who he was, just that...um...well, your voice is the outgoing message on Ms. Carmichael's answering machine."

"What?" Hughie jumped to his feet. "What else did he say?"

"Nothing. That was it. He just hung up."

"Hey, wait a minute. How did he know to call here?" I asked looking at Hughie. "You didn't leave the number."

"What *did* I say? Do you remember?"

"I remember you said something about Marcel being a lovely boy and you wanted to keep him overnight...to see how he performed."

"Good God!" Hughie ran a hand through his hair and sank back down in his chair.

"Why don't you call the number again just to make sure?" I suggested. "Maybe it's not that bad."

"I'm not calling. You call."

Closing the door, I dialed Bethany Marie's phone number. After five rings, I heard my boss' wonderfully clear voice praising Marcel and asking Bethany to call him as soon as possible.

"Well?" Hughie asked after I'd hung up.

"It's you all right."

"The police will probably want to question you," Hilary observed. She had slipped into the office to search for what was apparently the only pen in the hospital.

"Oh, Lord," Hughie sighed, drumming his fingers hard

against the desktop. "Maybe I should call the lawyer."

"What for?" I asked.

"Well, just to see if we can get someone to go and fix the answering machine. This is my reputation on the line. I mean, it could be like that for days. . . . "

"Weeks even," Hilary added helpfully.

"Communication, Hughie," I observed sweetly. "It's the key to a successful veterinarian–client bond."

Gathering my charts, I headed back to the recovery ward. Marcel had produced a nice, healthy-looking puddle of urine. I changed his litter and apprised him of the situation. "Poor baby," I crooned, rubbing his chin. "Your momma's a jailbird." He managed to look even more startled than usual.

Althea rapped vigorously on the window pane. I sighed and closed Marcel's door. "What now?"

"Ms. Carmichael's on the phone! She's calling from jail. Should I get Dr. Doucette?"

"Yes! Yes! Go!" We rushed to the office and hovered in silence as Hughie cracked his knuckles, sighed deeply, then reached for the phone.

"Hello, Bethany," he began carefully. "Yes, he's doing well... yes...I heard something about that...really?"

As they chatted, Hughie started to relax and a healthy glow returned to his pale cheeks. Laughing uproariously at something Bethany said, he leaned back in his chair and shooed us out of the room. Ten minutes later, he emerged from the office, refreshed and smiling.

"Everything's settled," he announced. "The friend who is looking after Francois will pick up Marcel tomorrow."

Humming to himself, Hughie puttered about the treatment

area.

"Well…is that it?" I asked, as the staff hovered discreetly in the background. "Did she say anything about me?"

"Did she set the fire? Is she a madam?" Althea asked breathlessly.

"And what about the answering machine?" I added.

"What? Oh, that," Hughie replied with annoying calm. "She fixed it. Just some glitch when she tried to retrieve her messages."

"Yes, but how did she find out?"

"She just said a friend told her. I didn't want to pry."

"Well, we must have a mutual client," I continued. "I mean, whoever called Bethany knows who you are."

Hughie shrugged. "Emily," he said with a stoic sigh, "I make it a policy not to interfere in the affairs of my clients."

The staff was less virtuous. For several weeks, they analyzed every voice, every nuance in conversations with clients. They were convinced that Brian Patterson had made the call until they discovered he was away on a business trip at the time.

"I still think he's creepy," Althea added darkly.

It was a mystery we never solved and one that, in time, faded from our memories, except during staff parties. But for Mr. Lawlor, there was an even greater mystery. I met him in the produce section of the grocery store a few months later. Leaning over a mound of turnips, he beckoned me closer with an arthritic finger.

"Dr. McBride," he whispered, "did you you ever find out which of the girls is a hooker?"

Chapter 9

"So, YOU CAN SEE I have a problem," Ms. Stratham-Hicks continued, with an impatient glance at her watch.

I could indeed, as her cell phone interrupted us for a third time. She snapped to attention, her lean, compact body taut with barely contained energy as she barked orders into the phone. A human terrier, I thought to myself. I half expected her to cock a leg on one of the chairs.

Gracie sat on the examining table and waited. As I stroked the soft fur, she arched her back and wiggled her tail in excitement. She was a chubby, mostly white cat with a few random patches of colour. A black smudge of fur that stretched below her nose like a mustache added a peculiar air of sophistication. We both flinched when Ms. Stratham-Hicks abruptly snapped the cell phone shut.

"Well?" she demanded, her beady terrier eyes staring at me expectantly. I opened my mouth to answer.

"Oh, for heaven's sake." She looked down at her suit. "Do you have anything I can use to get rid of all these hairs?"

I reached into my drawer. My hand closed around one of Sullivan's beloved squeaky toys. I considered hurling the toy into reception then quickly shutting the door behind Ms. Stratham-Hicks as she raced after it. Instead, I moved on to a wide roll of tape.

"Don't you have a lint brush or something?"

I shook my head.

Sighing, Ms. Stratham-Hicks grabbed the roll and, after tearing off a dozen strips, groomed with fierce intensity.

"So, Dr. McBride," she puffed in the middle of a pretzel-like contortion, "since you won't put her down, what are you going to do?"

I tore my eyes from the balled-up wads of hairy tape littering my exam table. "Well, I. . . ."

"Here's what I think." Ms. Stratham-Hicks slowly inflated to her full height of five feet and stared up at me. "You could board Gracie here until you find a home. I'll pay for a full week. That's about what euthanasia and burial would cost, right?"

How had such a wonderful cat ended up with such a horrible woman? Her son, Jason, was a terror. Now apparently he was an asthmatic terror and the cat had to go. I looked down from my lofty perch of five nine, feeling in control even as I agreed to her demands. Gracie would be better off in a new home anyway.

Her business complete, Ms. Stratham-Hicks shook my hand and left without a word to Gracie. In the parking lot I saw her reach once again for the cell phone.

I carried Gracie to the Cat Nap Inn where Susan had prepared a roomy suite with catnip toys, a fresh litter box, and a wide selection from our noon-hour buffet. Gracie inspected her new surroundings then curled up on one of two dozen cat-sized afghans crocheted by my mother for the hospital. Mom was passionate about her only handcraft. My flat was filled with crocheted gifts, the most notable being a mouse in a ball gown that covered the spare roll of toilet paper.

"We'll find you a good home," I whispered, kissing Gracie's forehead. Susan placed a heart-tugging adoption notice in the middle of the reception counter where it was bound to be noticed.

Three days later, one of our regular delivery men decided to adopt Gracie. His cat of sixteen years had recently died and Gracie looked a bit like her. Since we knew Mike well, we waived the five-day waiting period and Gracie went to her new home on Friday. On Monday she was back.

"We can't keep her," Mike explained. "There's something wrong with her."

"What do you mean?" I asked. "She's fine. She's in great health."

"She threw up on the carpet," Mike insisted.

"Oh." I smiled in relief. "All cats throw up now and then. She might have a bit of fur in her tummy. Or maybe all the changes in such a short period of time upset her. I'm sure she'll be fine."

"No, we're not keeping her!" Mike was adamant.

I was upset with Mike and his unreasonable expectations, but I suspected he wasn't telling me everything. Perhaps his wife didn't want another cat. Or maybe it was just too soon after the loss of their first cat. Whatever the reason, Gracie was back in the Cat Nap Inn. Carter and his best feline friend, Ernie, were delighted. The Inn was quiet and they missed the excitement of a full house. The pair liked to stroll through on a regular basis. Older guests often awoke to find their dishes empty. Kittens who tossed their toys too close to the mesh door of their suite never saw them again.

Back in the recovery ward, I found my boss babbling in a strained, high-pitched voice to a scruffy cat.

"Hey, Em." Hughie turned to greet me. The cat remained rigid. Its cold amber eyes stared at the back of Hughie's skull from behind the bars of the kennel.

"What are you doing?" I asked, Gracie momentarily forgotten.

"New client," Hughie explained, nodding in the cat's direction. "The owner wants him bathed and groomed without sedation. She says he hates men but turns to putty when women talk to him. Does this cat look like putty to you, Em?"

We both stared at the smoldering grey mound. His ears lay flat against his head as his tongue curled around a defiant hiss.

"Maybe he finds your falsetto offensive," I offered.

"I think he finds everything about me offensive," Hughie replied, rolling up his sleeve. Several new wounds had been patched with colourful bandages. Instead of basic beige, leopards, tigers, and panthers roamed across Hughie's forearms.

"Where'd you get the designer bandages?" I asked.

"Oh," he laughed. "Mrs. Bailey. Proceeds of all sales go to help endangered animals. This is the cat collection. I bought a bunch for the hospital."

I smiled. Margaret Bailey was one of the sweetest people I knew. Corporal William Bailey from Port Mouton, Nova Scotia, thought so, too. He met her in England while stationed there during the war. In 1945 she came to Nova Scotia as his bride despite her family's misgivings about this "rugged outpost colony." After almost fifty years in the province (and a few shopping trips to Bangor, Maine), she still spoke with a gentle British lilt. At seventy-four, Mrs. Bailey was a tireless crusader for animal welfare. She also volunteered in a literacy program and delivered home-cooked meals to disabled seniors.

Lately her little cat Tinkerbell seemed to be losing weight. She had always been a finicky eater, preferring tea and scones to cat food, but lately even fresh shrimp from the market had failed to rouse her interest. In the last few days, Tinkerbell had stopped patrolling her owner's perennial garden, although she still curled up in Margaret's lap during the British sitcoms at night. Mrs. Bailey had scheduled an appointment for this afternoon.

"I'll tell her you put the bandages to good use," I told Hughie with a grin.

That was three hours ago. Now I stared at the harsh reality of the X-ray screen in front of me which confirmed what I had felt on the physical exam. A large, shadowy image was pressing against Tinkerbell's stomach. Two smaller ones lurked in her abdomen: cancer. In just a blink of time, a few renegade cells had stolen Tinkerbell away from Mrs. Bailey. Cancer is not bound by species. Its mindless, uncontrolled growth destroys what is beautiful. In its wake, we are left with only our memories.

I clicked off the X-ray viewer and slid the films back into their file, neatly labeled and dated. Then I walked up the hall towards the exam room where Mrs. Bailey and Tinkerbell waited. Crouched in Mrs. Bailey's lap, she purred as the wizened hands caressed her fur in long, gentle strokes.

Without looking up, Mrs. Bailey said quietly, "It's cancer, isn't it, Dr. McBride."

I eased the door shut behind me. "Yes."

"Is there anything we can do?" she asked, the faintest hope still lighting her eyes as she looked to me for answers.

I paused. The doctor in me wanted to offer options, to keep that light in her eyes: surgery, chemotherapy, even radiation at the veterinary college. In the end, all I could offer was compassion.

"There are treatments that will prolong her life," I began, "but I don't think it would be the kind of life she would choose."

Mrs. Bailey continued to pet Tinkerbell. The little cat's eyes were closed. Was she remembering her days of grandeur, wild safaris in her mistress' garden? Or did she see something even more glorious? Mrs. Bailey's chest rose and fell in small, ragged breaths. A single tear fell onto Tinkerbell's fur where it glistened for a moment, then disappeared.

I turned my gaze to the wall where a painting hung. When he found out I had been accepted to vet school, my dad began work on a canvas he called *Emily's Ark*. Every species imaginable lolled about on the grass or hung out the windows of an elaborate veterinary hospital, all happily waiting to see Dr. McBride. As his own cancer progressed, he was unable to complete the work. At his request, our neighbour, herself a talented artist, added the finishing touches and dad signed his name.

"My husband believed that butterflies are souls reborn," Mrs. Bailey whispered at last. Her voice, soft and gentle like a meadow of flowers, floated towards me across a great distance. "I don't want her to suffer, Dr. McBride."

I knelt down beside her and rubbed Tinkerbell's chin. Outside, cars were beginning to clog the city streets as their owners rushed to get home for the weekend. Malls filled with shoppers as everyone searched for something to make their life better. Inside the exam room, we were wrapped in a cocoon, separated from the hustle and bustle of everyday life.

After a while, Mrs. Bailey looked up. "May I hold her while you...while you put her to sleep?"

I nodded, not trusting myself to speak.

Late on a Friday afternoon, a small calico cat died peacefully in her owner's arms. Thanking me for all I had done, Mrs. Bailey tenderly wrapped her in a blanket and left. A neighbour's son would help bury her in the garden she loved so much. In the spring, her soul would rise with the daffodils and dance among the butterflies.

Mrs. Bailey had been my last appointment until Monday morning. An entire weekend spread before me. I lingered at the hospital tidying my desk and sorting through a stack of journals. Susan and Hilary were busily washing a disgusted but compliant grey cat. Hilary had a new boyfriend and the two women were immersed in a serious analysis of his potential. From somewhere within the hospital I heard Hughie's deep laugh.

Picking up my bike from the storage room, I slipped outside. As I headed home, I saw Gracie watching me through the window of the playroom. I pedaled furiously, grateful for the wind that whipped across my face and a sun so bright I had to squint.

❖❖❖

Could we possibly find a spot for Rodney in the Cat Nap Inn?

Mrs. Picard was frantic. The clutch of robin eggs in her maple tree had just hatched and the event hadn't escaped Rodney's attention. In fact, when he wasn't asleep, Rodney had spent every spare minute spying on the robins from behind the bedroom curtains. The window was only five feet from the tree and Rodney had bided his time. With the arrival of the squawking youngsters, however, Rodney lost any measure of self-control and howled incessantly to go outside. Mrs. Picard was convinced he would head straight for the tree. Besides, she was vice-president of the Halifax Birdwatchers' Society. Its members, a select group of the bird-loving public, already frowned upon Rodney's existence. If they found out he had sampled a few of their favourite species... well, Mrs. Picard couldn't even think about that.

Fortunately for Rodney, his mother, and the robin family, we had a vacancy at the Inn. I had barely hung up the phone when a breathless Mrs. Picard arrived with Rodney in tow and a picnic basket full of his personal items. Rodney sat stiffly in his suite, scowling at his new surroundings.

"Rodney, dear," Mrs. Picard pleaded. "This is only temporary. Just till the baby robins are flying. Then you can come back home."

Ignoring his owner's pleas for forgiveness, Rodney jumped onto one of the shelves and turned his back.

"Oh, he hates me!" Mrs. Picard wailed. Dabbing her eyes with a tissue, she promised to visit every day.

Gracie eyed the pair curiously. Yesterday, Ms. Stratham-Hicks had complained bitterly about Gracie's bill. Two weeks had passed and still we hadn't found a home. When she decided to take Gracie elsewhere and have her put down, I blurted out that we would keep her at no charge until she was adopted.

I hadn't broken this news to Hughie, who only last week had delivered his standard sermon about charging for services and cutting costs. The hospital's fiscal year end was months away, but already clothing seemed to hang more loosely on his lanky frame. He was often heard muttering to himself in darkened rooms. Finding Gracie a loving home, soon, seemed like a good idea.

Gracie, however, was enjoying her stay at the Inn and the attention lavished upon her by the staff. She was also fascinated by Rodney. He was vulgar and outspoken. He complained the longest and loudest at mealtimes, demanding to be fed first. He gagged up more furballs than all the other cats combined. He snored when he slept. His bowel movements were too large to be covered.

As promised, Mrs. Picard visited her beloved Rodney every day, always remembering a treat for Gracie as well. Lately, the three of them had been lounging together in the playroom. Rodney sprawled on the window ledge chattering to the pigeons while Gracie preferred to curl up in Mrs. Picard's ample lap.

"Poor little dear," she sighed, over and over. "Poor little dear."

I had high hopes for Mrs. Picard. Gracie and Rodney seemed to get along fine and the robins would be flying soon. Gracie never went outside, a fact which would endear her to the bird lovers. When the day arrived to take Rodney home, Mrs. Picard decided she absolutely could not leave Gracie behind and left with two carriers. Like ladies-in-waiting, Susan and Althea followed behind with Rodney's picnic basket of goodies, two large bags of food, a new litter pan, and Gracie's pillow.

Spring is a busy time in a feline practice. Satisfied that Gracie now had a good home, I was swallowed whole by work. For James Herriott, a rural British vet who authored many wonderful books, spring was a time of floral fragrance, lambs, and busy farmers sowing their fields. Vivid displays of nature reborn blanketed the rolling hills of his Darrowby in the Yorkshire dales.

Spring at Ocean View Cat Hospital in Halifax was marked by cold, grey drizzle, foghorns, and abscesses. Cats who had lain dormant all winter on hot radiators now felt that ageless call of the wild. It was time to patrol the north forty and mend any broken fences. God help trespassers. In the territorial disputes that erupted, large smelly abscesses were born. So were hundreds of kittens. In the midst of war, love endures.

Names and procedures fought for space on our crowded appointment sheets. We were so busy that visiting drug reps were pressed into service, holding fluid bags or fetching nail trimmers. Kittens popped up everywhere. Hughie was ecstatic and robust once again.

He was in surgery the day a depressed, apologetic Mrs. Picard returned with Gracie.

"Oh, Dr. McBride, I'm so sorry. It just isn't working out. Look!" She pointed to a ruptured abscess on Gracie's flank. "Rodney is being hateful. He won't let Gracie eat! He guards the litter pans and attacks her every chance he gets! Oh, I feel just terrible." She crumpled into a chair. "I've tried everything!"

A month had passed since Gracie went to live with Mrs. Picard and Rodney. In truth, I had forgotten about her. Now as I examined Gracie I could see that she had lost weight. Her fur had a moth-eaten appearance where Rodney had removed a few clumps. Fortunately, the wounds weren't too serious, and she would likely just need a course of antibiotics.

"They got along so well here," Mrs. Picard shook her head.

"Well, sometimes this happens," I sighed. "I guess the Cat Nap Inn was neutral territory, but back in his own home Rodney felt threatened."

"I'm so sorry, Dr. McBride. I tried. I really did." Mrs. Picard sniffed several times and wiped her eyes. "She's a sweet little thing and I'm very fond of her. But she's terrified of Rodney. Normally, he's such a lovely animal."

"Don't worry, we'll look after her." I held Gracie close and nuzzled my face against her forehead while addressing Mrs. Picard. "This isn't your fault, you know. Sometimes things just don't work out. And you have to think of Rodney, too."

I carried Gracie back to the Inn. Ignoring her bowls of food and Carter's erratic pursuit of a housefly, she withdrew to her bed. Like any one of us, all she needed was a home and someone to love her. Yet, here she was, back again behind the green mesh door of her suite in the Cat Nap Inn.

Hilary walked in clutching an apple. "Wow. Gracie looks terrible," she observed.

"I know."

"You should call Mrs. Bailey."

I looked at Hilary in surprise. "Oh, I think it's way too soon, Hilary. She's still grieving. Besides, if she was looking for another cat, she'd give us a call."

"Maybe. Maybe not." She rubbed Gracie's ears. "People don't always know what they want."

Hilary's words ran through my thoughts all evening. When appointments were through, I picked up the phone and dialed Mrs. Bailey's number. An answering machine asked me to leave a message at the sound of the beep. I hesitated, unsure of what to say. How can you explain that opening your heart to another animal honours and reaffirms your love for the one who is gone? How do you ask someone to try? In the end, I said only that Gracie was a sweet cat who desperately needed a home. Was Mrs. Bailey interested or did she know anyone who might be?

I didn't hear back that evening. When she didn't call the following day or the next, I was sure I had intruded on her grief.

Three days later Mrs. Bailey called me. She had just returned from a visit with her daughter in PEI. Before she even said hello or we exchanged pleasantries, she said, in that soft, gentle voice, "I'll take her."

"But...don't you want to know anything about her?" I asked.

"Dr. McBride," Mrs. Bailey began, "I'm not a very religious person. And I don't believe those silly stories about the supernatural you see on TV these days. But when I came home tonight, I heard Tinkerbell's meow for the first time since she died. I really did. And I knew she was happy."

Mrs. Bailey paused. "Then I checked my answering machine…and your message was waiting for me."

I have a picture of Mrs. Bailey and Gracie on my desk. To this day, Gracie patrols Mrs. Bailey's perennial garden until four-o'clock teatime, when the two share lukewarm tea and Peak Frean biscuits. By night, Gracie curls up on Mrs. Bailey's lap, although she prefers hockey games to British sitcoms.

I don't know if Tinkerbell spoke to her mistress that night. I do know that Mrs. Bailey had the courage to follow her heart even though someday, it would surely be broken again.

Chapter 10

"OH, WE'VE BEEN to a lot of erotic places together!" Barry smiled as he patted his cat Livingston.

Hoping he meant "exotic," I replied, "That's nice."

"C'mon, buddy." Barry removed the lid from a large wicker basket. Livingston, used to the routine, jumped in and Barry raised the basket to his head.

"A trick I learned in Indonesia," he grinned. "Keeps your hands free." Barry turned to leave, the basket balanced perfectly on his head.

"Uh, Barry...the door?"

Barry ducked just in time. Maybe there weren't many doors in Indonesia. It was a pretty hot country, after all. Here in Halifax, doors were clearly a hazard to the basket-bearing public. Two older women entering the hospital didn't seem to notice the man leaving with the basket on his head.

"Did not!" the larger one spat. She was wearing a man's checkered shirt and a Blue Jays ball cap pulled down over short, grey hair.

"Did so!" her smaller companion hissed, shuffling past in a pair of pink ballet slippers.

The pair bypassed Althea at the reception counter and began wandering aimlessly through the products and displays. I ducked into the work area behind reception.

"Didn't!"

"Did!" The conversation might have continued indefinitely

had Althea not intervened.

"May I help you?" she asked.

The stocky woman looked up. Marching over to the desk, she picked up a business card and examined it.

"Mom!" she hollered. "Get over here!"

With a sudden pirouette, the wiry little woman reversed direction, and sashayed towards the reception counter. Every so often, she would raise her arms to an unseen but apparently appreciative audience, twirl, and then continue on in a mostly forward direction. Standing on her tiptoes and hanging onto the counter, she could just see over the edge. If she relaxed her grip, she disappeared altogether except for a row of pink sponge curlers on the top of her head.

"Hello!" The younger one thrust an arm across the counter. "My name is Betty Ann." As if remembering the second part of the routine, she flashed a stiff smile.

Althea shook her hand. "How do you do?"

"Don't ask!" Betty Ann rolled her eyes in the direction of her mother. Turning back to Althea, she added, "Fred needs to see the doctor."

"Fred is…your cat?" Althea guessed.

Betty Ann nodded. "He's doing a lot of crazy things. Maybe he needs a psychiatrist!"

Delighted by her own wit, Betty Ann threw her head back and cackled at the ceiling. Her mother followed suit. Then the twin cackles abruptly ceased, as if someone had pulled the plug.

"Seriously, can you help him?" she asked, narrowing her eyes.

"Well, that depends on what's wrong," Althea replied.

"You name it!" Betty Ann threw her arms wide to show the extent of Fred's illnesses.

"What's the worst thing?" Althea countered.

Betty Ann looked at her mother. They nodded in tacit agreement. "He peed on my head last night."

"That is bad," Althea agreed. "How did that happen?"

"I was sleeping. He just let loose."

"Has he done that before?"

Betty Ann shrugged. "I dunno. I'm a pretty deep sleeper."

"No, I mean, has he ever peed in places he shouldn't?"

"Don't we all?" Betty Ann winked.

Althea decided on another approach. "How old is Fred?"

"Oh, he's old. Old. Old. Old. Really old."

"How old is that, exactly?"

Betty Ann thought for a moment. "As old as the Queen. In cat years," she added.

"Prince Philip!" Betty Ann's mother gripped the edge of the counter. "Sexy!" she grinned slyly. "Good in the sack."

"So…," Althea glanced at me behind the desk. "I think Fred should see the vet. Dr. McBride can see you today at four o'clock."

I shook my head. Grabbing a piece of paper I scribbled "Dr. Doucette" in big letters but Althea ignored me.

"H'mm. Four…. We have group today, don't we, Mom? Or was that yesterday? Oh well," Betty Ann shrugged her shoulders. "Doesn't matter. C'mon. Let's go have a donut and a smoke."

"Ta-ta," Betty Ann's mother waved regally as she rose onto her toes and twirled out of the hospital.

"Looney as a toon," Betty Ann shrugged. "Oh, well. What can you do?"

Althea agreed that there weren't too many options.

"That's why we picked your place, you know," Betty Ann confided as she turned to leave. "Right next to a Tim Hortons! I'm supposed to be on a diet," she grinned, patting her considerable belly. "Ha! That's a good one!"

"Hey," she said, suddenly somber. "Don't tell Dr. Meisner."

Althea symbolically zipped her lips shut. "Mum's the word."

I never expected the pair to keep the appointment but just before four, Betty Ann's mother scurried past the reception counter and screeched to a halt under the chandelier. She had forsaken the ballet shoes for a sensible pair of red sneakers and knee highs. Mesmerized by the lights, she stared up at the chandelier.

I waited a few minutes then approached, clutching my clipboard. The little woman gave no sign that she had seen me and continued to gaze heavenward.

I cleared my throat. "Um...will Fred and Betty Ann be joining us?"

"Donuts."

"Oh." I gripped my clipboard and waited. As the minutes passed, I found myself stealing peeks at the chandelier. A client who had stopped in to buy food looked up.

"What are you looking at?" she whispered.

"I'm not sure," I whispered back. She nodded and took her food to the counter.

I began to wonder if *donuts* was some sort of secret codeword. Maybe Betty Ann and Fred weren't coming at all.

"Would you like to wait in the exam room?" I asked at last. "There's a lava lamp in there," I added hopefully.

Nodding, Betty Ann's mother followed me into the room.

I had just settled her in a chair when the exam room door burst open. A dark shadow spread like an oil slick across the floor. Squinting, I looked up. Betty Ann straddled the opening, legs braced. Under one arm she carried an unmistakable canary-yellow box, under the other a howling cat in a plastic milk crate.

"You must be the doc!" Light flooded back into the room as Betty Ann squeezed through.

"Let me help," I offered, reaching for Fred's makeshift carrier.

"Thanks, Doc. Whew! It's hot out there!" Betty Ann flopped onto a wooden chair that winced in surprise. I held my breath as the chair struggled to support as much of the woman as it could. The rest spilled out over the sides. Wiping the sweat from her brow, Betty Ann leaned forward and studied the contents of the box. After making a selection, she thrust the box towards me.

"Doc?"

"Uh...no thanks," I smiled politely.

"Go on. It'll put hair on your chest," she chided.

This was also my mother's rationale for eating porridge, Brussels sprouts, and lima beans. While it worked for my brothers, it never motivated me.

"No, thanks. Really."

Betty Ann shrugged. "Your funeral."

She popped a Timbit into her mouth. "I'm Betty Ann, by the way. That's Lillian over there."

Tired of waiting her turn at the trough, Lillian grabbed a handful of Timbits and shoved them all into her mouth. Her toothless jaws smiled at me through a gooey, unmanageable mass of custard, chocolate, and icing sugar.

Betty Ann shook her head then rummaged through the box. Selecting a plain Timbit, she broke it into small pieces for Fred who, in his haste, nearly ate her hand.

"Is everyone in this family rude?" She threw her hands into the air in exasperation. Sighing, she leaned back in her chair.

"OK. Fix him, Doc."

"Yeah, fix him," Betty Ann's mother echoed, then threw her head back and laughed maniacally.

"Too much sugar," Betty Ann whispered. "We're not allowed donuts at the home."

I nodded. Sugar and insanity were a bad combination.

Turning my attention to Fred, I began his physical exam. Although friendly and courteous, he was a veterinarian's nightmare. He was beyond old; he was an antique. He had a raging heart murmur, an enlarged thyroid gland, and breath that could wake the dead. He ate everything in his path, yet remained skinny and left gifts of urine wherever he sat. With Betty Ann's permission, I drew blood and urine samples. Tests revealed, among other things, that Fred's thyroid gland was producing too much hormone. He was hyperthyroid, a condition not uncommon in older cats.

"It's like his body is stuck in park with the engine on and the gas pedal jammed to the floor," I explained to Betty Ann. "That's why he's always eating but never gains any weight."

Betty Ann sighed. "I wish I was hyperthyroid."

"Now, we can try to control this with a drug called Tapazole." I looked from Betty Ann to her mother who was sitting demurely with her hands folded in her lap. "Do you think you could give him medication every day?"

"Piece of cake, Doc! I'm used to pills. I take a bunch every day," Betty Ann confided. "Mom takes even more."

"So...you're experienced. That's good," I bobbed my head up and down. "Sometimes it's hard to pill a cat though. You may be able to just put it in his food. With that appetite, he probably won't even notice."

"No sweat." Betty Ann scribbled in a small coil notebook. "What else, Doc?"

I started to answer just as Betty Ann passed what in polite circles is known as wind. I would describe it as more like a tornado, a raucous hell-raiser with a smell to match.

"Go on, Doc," Betty Ann urged in wide-eyed innocence.

I cleared my throat and continued.

"His teeth and gums are in pretty rough shape. Normally, I would recommend cleaning and extractions but he's a poor anesthetic risk so I'm going to prescribe antibiotics. They won't cure him but at least they'll help make him feel better."

Betty Ann leaned so far forward that her breath tickled the hairs on my face. "That's a nice necklace."

"Oh." I fingered the pendant around my neck and took a step back. "Thanks."

"Boyfriend?"

"Ex-boyfriend."

"Men!" Betty Ann snorted. "Did he break your heart?"

"Well…uh…," I stammered.

Betty Ann nodded and sat back down. "It's too painful to talk about. I understand. But," she admonished, pointing a stubby finger at me, "don't repress your anger."

"No, I certainly won't," I promised.

Fred had gathered himself into a tight little ball on the weigh scale and was snoring peacefully. I decided to forge ahead.

"So Fred here has a urinary tract infection as well," I continued. "That's why he dribbles wherever he happens to be, including your head. The antibiotics will help with that too. I'd like to see him back in a few weeks so that we can…."

This time a flurry of sound like exploding kernels of popcorn erupted from Betty Ann's mother.

"Huh?" Betty Ann asked, cupping a hand to her ear. "What did you say?"

"I'd like to see him again in a few weeks," I repeated, raising my voice. "I want to recheck his urine and do another T4 to assess his thyroid function."

In the meantime Fred woke up from his nap and, forgetting where he was, began to howl plaintively. My words were caught in the crossfire between a cat and a crone. When the popping had slowed to one every four or five seconds, I quickly wrapped up Fred's health care plan before Lillian could fire off another round.

Betty Ann studied me for a moment. A slow grin spread across her face. Overcome, she gripped her sides and bent over in a silent paroxysm of mirth. Her mother raised a tiny, veined hand to her face and giggled. In spite of myself, I started to laugh.

"Donuts!" Betty Ann gasped at last. "They go right through us!"

"With me, it's tomatoes," I confided with a grin.

"Tomatoes?" Betty Ann slapped her knees and rocked back and forth. "Doc! You crack me up!"

As the fumes began to fade, Betty Ann wiped the tears from her eyes and reached into her pocket. "Now, Doc, how much do we owe you?"

I stared as she calmly unrolled a large, colourful wad of bills. "Not *that* much."

"I have $800.00," Betty Ann announced. "Well, $794.50." She glanced at the empty donut box and shrugged. "The money is supposed to be for the psychiatrist."

"He's on vacation," Lillian chirped.

"The group took a vote and we decided to spend it on Fred instead," Betty Ann explained.

"I see," I nodded, not really seeing at all. I wondered what would happen when the psychiatrist found out he was Fred's benefactor. Opening the door, I herded my clients into reception. Althea went over the bill with Betty Ann and made an appointment for the following month while Lillian sang "Frosty, the Snowman" to Carter.

"Join in," she urged him. "You know the words."

❖❖❖

As the busy month of June sped by, I had little time to think about Fred. The herald of summer, June was one of my favourite months. Bare feet, beaches, and barbecues. Besides, my birthday was in June. A paper trail of well wishes had been trickling into the hospital from my elderly aunts who couldn't remember my home address but knew that I worked at a cat hospital. They all despised cats except Aunt Frances, who owned nine. It was generally agreed that Aunt Frances had been led astray by her second husband, who was fourteen years younger.

After an unusually quiet day, I was leaving early for my birthday party at Mom's when I heard the commotion. Peeking through the blinds in the exam room window, I saw Betty Ann, Lillian, and half a dozen people I had never met before. They were hovering around Althea like fruit flies and everyone was talking at once.

I decided to slip out the back door. Grabbing my knapsack, I headed for the storage room. Ten feet away. Five feet away.

"Dr. McBride!" My hand, only inches away from the doorknob,

dropped like an anchor. "Thank God you're still here!" Althea breathed. "Betty Ann is back. With a whole bunch of people."

"But she's not due back till next week," I whined.

"She says it's an emergency."

That was it, then. The "e" word. I was doomed. Hughie wasn't due back until five o'clock.

"All right," I sighed, taking off my coat. "Get Fred in the exam room and I'll have a look at him."

I thought sadly of the mound of presents that would go unopened and the food that would go uneaten. The aunts were very generous. As the only niece in a swarm of nephews, I was treated like an endangered species. Any flaws were clearly the result of my father's DNA and were overlooked.

I opened the door. It was like opening the hatch on an airplane at thirty thousand feet. I was nearly crushed by the rush of bodies toward me.

"Doc! Doc! Over here!"

I elbowed my way towards Betty Ann. Fred lay on the examining table, oblivious to the crowd. His eyes were closed and he was breathing rapidly. Even before I began my examination, everyone wanted to know what was wrong. They tugged on my lab coat and jostled for position as I tried listening to Fred's heart. In desperation, I looked at Betty Ann. She nodded, stuck two fingers in her mouth, and whistled fiercely.

"You guys shut up and go sit outside in those chairs. The Doc needs peace and quiet!" As I smiled my thanks, Betty Ann flashed a two-finger salute. The group filed past into the reception area. Some grasped my hand and shook it solemnly on the way out.

"Not you, Daniel." Betty Ann grabbed a stooped, gaunt man with a wool hat pulled down over his ears. He wore a pair of pants several sizes too big and held in place by a tightly cinched belt. Pinned to his shirt was a button that said "SAVE THE UNICORN."

"Go on. Tell Dr. McBride," Betty Ann prompted. Daniel hung his head, refusing to meet her gaze.

Continuing my examination, I inserted a rectal thermometer. When Fred cried softly, Daniel covered his ears with his hands and began to rock back and forth.

"Ohhh," he moaned, collapsing in a chair. "All my fault. All my fault. Fred's gonna die!"

"Why do you think he's going to die?" I prompted.

"Betty Ann said so," Daniel whispered miserably. "Because I was careless. With my stuff."

"What stuff?" I asked.

"Marijuana!" Betty Ann blurted out.

"What? Where'd you get marijuana?" I demanded.

"It's…it's mine," Daniel sniffed. "But I'm not supposed to tell anybody,"

"Hmphh!" Betty Ann snorted. "Drugs are NOT good for you. Look what's it's done to Fred!"

"I'm sorry…I'm sorry," Daniel sobbed.

Betty Ann put her arm around him. "It's all right. The Doc'll fix him. Right, Doc?"

I didn't answer. My mind was racing as I examined Fred. "Are you sure he ate some? How long ago?"

"How long ago?" I repeated when Daniel didn't answer.

"I…I don't know."

"Just before *Dr. Phil*," Betty Ann said. "We had all settled in, real comfortable, with bowls of popcorn, and then you started hollering from upstairs."

"That's right," Daniel's head bobbed up and down in agreement. "I…I left my drawer open. I had to go to the bathroom… real bad. An' when I got back, Fred was inside. It was an accident."

The door to my exam room burst open.

"Dr. Meisner!" Daniel jumped up and threw his arms around a stubby little man in shorts and a T-shirt. "It was an accident!"

"It's all right, Danny." The man hugged Daniel with one arm and shook my hand with the other. A whistle dangled from his neck. "Horace Meisner," he added, gasping for breath. "I had to park way down the street."

"Are you the psychiatrist?" I asked, remembering the misappropriated wad of bills.

"No. Dr. Ahmadi's on vacation. I'm just your run-of-the-mill family physician. The unsung hero of the medical community." He wiggled his bushy eyebrows up and down. "I'm also the only one in this bunch with a valid driver's license. How's Fred?"

I looked at Betty Ann. Betty Ann looked at Daniel. Daniel looked at the floor and wrung his hands. "He got into some of the stuff, Dr. Meisner."

"What stu…? Oh…." Dr. Meisner took a deep breath.

"You know about this?" I accused Dr. Meisner.

"Daniel left the drawer open," Betty Ann explained, without waiting for Dr. Meisner to answer. She had lowered herself to her knees and was now at eye level with Fred.

I shook my head. "I'm just going to give Fred some hydrogen peroxide to make him vomit. After that, some activated charcoal. Hopefully, it'll bind with any of the marijuana he doesn't throw up."

Dr. Meisner nodded in agreement. "Betty Ann? Daniel? Why don't you two go out with the others. I'll stay here with

Dr. McBride." Daniel gratefully rushed from the room as Dr. Meisner helped Betty Ann to her feet.

"Betty Ann's looked after Fred a long time," he said kindly.

Betty Ann snorted and scratched her head. "Got that right."

"Here," he said, removing the whistle around his neck. "Keep everyone together."

With one last glance at Fred, Betty Ann left the room, tightly gripping the whistle.

"Try to get him to sit up," I ordered Dr. Meisner as I shut the door, "and I'll start the peroxide."

Fred sputtered and gagged as I poured the obnoxious stuff down his throat but made no attempt to escape. Marijuana can have the same effect in people as in pets. Fred was probably drifting through a fog of feline fantasies.

I put my stethoscope on his chest. His tired old heart was racing.

Dr. Meisner peered anxiously at me over the rims of his glasses. They had slid down his nose and now perched on the last bump, defying gravity.

"I'm really worried about his heart," I told him. "Did you know he has a very bad heart? Along with several other serious problems?"

"Yes. Betty Ann told me she brought Fred here. She...." Dr. Meisner was interrupted by several blasts on the whistle. Lifting one of the slats in the window blind, he scanned reception. Satisfied, he turned back to me and added with a faint smile, "She said the place next to Tim Hortons."

A mournful howl resonated from the depths of Fred's bony soul. His sides heaved again and again as they gathered momentum trying to purge the horrible concoction brewing in his belly.

His stomach contents gurgled a final warning as they were forced up the long narrow esophagus. And then, like Vesuvius, Fred erupted. Everywhere. In the calm that followed, murky pools of vomit lay scattered across the landscape of my examining table. Viscous streams trickled down the cupboard doors.

"Wow!" Dr. Meisner was clearly impressed. "That worked well!"

Although exhausted, Fred seemed determined to wash his face. He still couldn't quite co-ordinate his movements so that more often than not, his tongue ineffectively licked the air as his paw passed by. I was just happy to see him make the attempt. Dying cats don't think about washing themselves.

"So… I suppose you're wondering about all this," Dr. Meisner remarked casually as he straightened his tie.

I was wondering about a lot of things. Was I out of the loop, or was it normal for a group of mental patients to sit around and smoke pot while watching *Dr. Phil*? I bit my tongue and waited for Dr. Meisner to continue.

"Dr. Ahmadi and I run a group home for mental patients who also have medical problems. They all work, at least part-time, except for Daniel and Betty Ann's mother. Daniel has leukemia," Dr. Meisner sighed as he stroked Fred. "I wish there was another way, but marijuana seems to be the only thing that helps with his nausea. I arrange for his nephew to bring it in."

In the silence that followed, I thought about my own dad's many trips to the hospital. On his final visit, I held him in my arms while he screamed in agony for more morphine. Although a palliative care patient, the only hospital bed available that day was in the urology ward where nurses had no authority to dispense a higher dose of narcotic. In the wrangle over territory and potential legal issues, my dad suffered because no one had the courage to help him.

"Aren't you worried that someone will find out?" I asked at last. "You could lose your license."

Dr. Meisner shrugged. "Worse things could happen. Besides" he grinned, "who'd believe a bunch of lunatics anyway?"

I rubbed Fred's ears. "Well, all I know for sure is that Fred nibbled on some plants and made himself sick. I'll get him settled in a kennel and call you with an update."

"Thank you. I'm divorced."

"Pardon me?"

"I love old movies," he continued with a grin. "Walks on deserted beaches and any kind of alcohol. I can do impersonations and juggle. I'm in the book under Horace Meisner, MD. My mother still can't believe I graduated and it's been twenty-six years," he winked. "I've had all the normal childhood diseases so no surprises there. I have a hamster named Matilda. I know how to cook and I mend my own socks. Anything there catch your interest?"

Laughing, I opened the door. Reception was deserted except for Althea who stood on a chair dusting the chandelier.

Dr. Meisner looked around, mouth agape. "Oh, my God! It's my worst nightmare. They've been abducted by aliens."

"Actually, Betty Ann said to tell you they were going next door for donuts," Althea explained, feather-duster in hand.

"I better go before someone's arrested. Cheerio!" Dr. Meisner waved a hasty goodbye.

We kept Fred at the hospital for several days to monitor his recovery. Thanks to the activated charcoal, loose dark stool was a common, but thankfully temporary, occurrence. Otherwise, he seemed no worse for his little indiscretion. He ate everything placed in front of him and washed his behind as necessary. For an arthritic eighteen-year-old with a bad heart, an overactive thyroid gland, and rotten teeth, he certainly enjoyed life.

On Thursday morning, Dr. Meisner arrived to take Fred home. He followed behind me chattering in excitement. The residents had worked out a medication schedule for Fred and spent hours making him a "Welcome Home" banner which they erected on the front porch. A delighted Dr. Ahmadi had leapt out of the taxi and hugged everyone, unaware it was intended for the cat.

"I've never seen them work co-operatively like this before," Dr. Meisner gushed.

"That's great. Just make sure you keep all the…houseplants… out of his reach," I cautioned, hugging Fred's tired, old body close as I said goodbye. Then I gently eased him into his new, state-of-the-art carrier. I wondered if Dr. Ahmadi had unwittingly funded this too.

"Thank you again!" Dr. Meisner sandwiched my hand between both of his and shook vigorously. Then, picking up Fred, he waved goodbye. Legs braced and head bobbing, Fred admired the view from his new carrier.

I was just about to give Albert Sponagle his pre-med before surgery when I heard the door chimes followed by the familiar squeak of Dr. Meisner's sneakers.

"Yoo-hoo! Dr. McBride!" A head appeared in the doorway.

"It's OK. Come on down. We're just getting ready to neuter Albert here."

Dr. Meisner hesitated, then eased himself down the hallway. He avoided looking at Albert altogether. "I'm not good with castrations," he shuddered.

He put a large box of donuts on the counter. "Betty Ann would kill me if I forgot to give you these. She said to tell you they'd put hair on your chest. Oh, and she sent these also."

Hilary started to snicker when Dr. Meisner pulled three fat, red tomatoes out of a bag. She was well aware of my affliction.

Dr. Meisner stared at Hilary. "You know, it's the strangest thing. When I asked Betty Ann if you especially liked tomatoes, she started to laugh too. Then Lillian started. And they didn't stop that cackling. For almost five minutes," he added in a strangled voice.

Keeping a straight face, I took the tomatoes and donuts and thanked Dr. Meisner.

"Two weeks without Ahmadi," he sighed, shaking his head. "It shows."

Chapter 11

I STOOD IN LINE with the rest of the popcorn-toting crowd, nodding politely whenever my date paused for breath. Blind dates had been unthinkable when I was in my twenties. An ad in the personals? Pathetic. But at thirty-something, I liked to believe I was more…tolerant. Besides, I really wanted to see this movie and as Hughie pointed out, only critics or serial killers went to movies alone. I stifled a yawn and reached into my bag of popcorn.

"Emily! Hi!"

Caught with a full mouth, I looked around wildly to find Benny Mombourquette standing three feet away. I sucked in my stomach muscles.

"What are you going to see?" he asked.

I chewed furiously but before I could answer, my date cheerfully provided not only the name of the movie but a synopsis of the story.

"Benny, hi," I said swallowing. "This is…." What was his name? Rod? Cod? No, that couldn't be it. "Todd!" I smiled triumphantly.

The two men shook hands.

"So. How've you been?" Benny asked. I babbled something forgettable then thought to ask Benny about his new kitten.

"Samantha? She's doing great! The other day she…." Benny paused as the blonde woman beside him cleared her throat.

"Oh, this is Jennifer, my girlfriend," he explained.

"Hello." Jennifer acknowledged me with a polite smile and

extended a smooth, polished hand free from eczema and cat scratches. Her grip had the strength of Jell-O. "You must be the vet."

"That's me," I grinned. "Benny and I knew each other way back when we were kids."

"Yes, he's told me all about you."

He had? That was good news.

"You were quite a tomboy," she smiled, bursting my bubble. "I wish I'd had brothers. Oh, well," she sighed, "being an only child has its advantages."

We all smiled awkwardly at each other until Jennifer glanced at her watch. "We really should be going, Benjamin. We'll be late." She hooked her arm in Benny's.

"Right." Benny looked from me to Todd. "Well, you two enjoy your show."

"So lovely to meet you," Jennifer added.

Todd watched her high-heeled retreat in admiration.

"Wow!" he declared, stuffing a handful of popcorn into his mouth and munching contentedly.

"Em!" Benny spun around. "I nearly forgot. Can you speak to the kids next week on Career Day?"

"Career Day? Grade Fives have Career Day?" I chuckled. The lineup suddenly came to life. Todd and I were swept along as it snaked up one cordoned-off row and down another. Benny struggled to keep up against the flow of humanity headed towards the other sixteen theatres.

"You've been locked up with litter boxes too long. They graduate from pre-school now," he grinned.

"Well…I…well…," The darkened entrance to the theatre loomed ahead as the impatient line of movie goers propelled me closer. "Ahhhh...okay, I guess," I blurted over the heads of the couple behind us.

"I'll call you!" Benny shouted as he disappeared from view.

Hughie was thrilled when Benny called the next day. "Em, this is great! I've been wanting to get a school program going! We've got to teach kids about responsible pet ownership. And," he declared, pointing at me with his index finger, "this is an excellent public relations opportunity. You can hand out business cards."

I nodded, although I wasn't sure ten-year-olds would have a lot of use for them.

"Aren't you nervous, Dr. McBride?" Althea asked when she heard the news.

"No, not really," I shrugged. I liked kids and got along fine with my nieces and nephews.

"I would be." Althea walked away, shaking her head.

Even my clients were skeptical. "My goodness, you're brave," was Mrs. Warner's comment. "My sister's boy goes to Pinegrove Elementary."

Her Siamese, Ho Lee Schitt, stared at me in cross-eyed concern as if he too couldn't believe my folly. I opened a tube of ointment and rubbed a small amount onto the tip of his tail. Ho Lee loved to suck the end of that particular appendage until it was raw. The bony tip was so inflamed it glowed with Rudolph-like intensity.

"Well," I began, as I wrapped a protective bandage around the tip to thwart his efforts, "kids love animals. I'm thinking it will go well."

Mrs. Warner sighed, "I'm sure you're right, dear." She sounded doubtful.

I had decided to take Carter with me to the school. Nicknamed the "Love Sponge" by a doting volunteer, Carter adored people and was sure to be a big hit. My eight-year-old nephew, inventor of the Gross-O-Meter, had also assured me that kids would be interested in anything gross. With his help, we rated my visual aids on a scale of one to ten for their gross-appeal. I had just finished loading the more spectacular and slimy hallmarks of my profession when a clap of thunder rattled Bill through to his carburetors. Carter meowed plaintively from his carrier in the passenger seat.

Ignoring the warnings, I slipped into the car and arrived at Pinegrove during the lunch break. Immediately a flurry of little girls surrounded the car.

"Are you Dr. McBride?" one of them asked breathlessly.

"Yes," I smiled.

"See? I told you," she turned towards her companions.

"We thought you were Jimmy Henderson's mother," a plump girl in braces explained. "He's in *big* trouble."

Six heads nodded in solemn agreement.

"Oooooh! Look at the cat!" an excited voice squealed. "He's adorable!"

Jimmy Henderson's transgression was quickly forgotten as Carter was whisked out of sight into the building. I was left alone to manage several large boxes in the rain. I trudged up to the building and somehow managed to pry open one of the heavy school doors. Wedging my foot in the crack, I squeezed inside. I had entered the world of the pre-pubescent.

The foyer was a cheerful place, alive with the colours of elementary school art. Down the hall, a seriously out-of-sync group was reciting a poem and in the distance, I could hear a piano.

My would-be helpers were nowhere in sight. Sighing, I unloaded everything on a bench and entered the office. A girl no more than ten or eleven sat behind the desk. A name tag identified her as "Jessica, Office Assistant."

"May I help you?" she asked with a bright smile.

I looked around in confusion. "Um…is the secretary here?"

"No, she's on her lunch break. Oh!" Jessica clapped a hand over her mouth. "Are you Jimmy's mother?"

I shook my head no just as the telephone rang. I had been here only ten minutes and already the name Jimmy Henderson was legendary.

"Good afternoon, Pinegrove Elementary, Jessica speaking. How may I help you?" The pint-sized office assistant expertly cradled the phone while scribbling a message. I felt like Gulliver in the land of the Lilliputians. Where were the big people?

Jessica hung up the phone and smiled expectantly at me.

"I'm Dr. McBride. I'm here for Career Day."

"Ooooh!" Jessica clapped her hands in delight. "That's *your* cat! He's cute. I wish I had a cat. I have a little brother," she sighed.

Just as I was wondering what to do, a grizzled old man, dressed from head to toe in olive green, stuck his head in the door. Ah! An adult! I smiled and waited as he blew his nose, then stuffed the hanky into a back pocket. A mob of keys jangled from his belt.

"Someone left a bunch of junk in the hallway," he sniffed.

"Oh, that's mine. I'm here for Career Day," I answered cheerfully.

He turned and headed for the foyer. I scrambled after him. "Well? Where's it going?" he grumbled over his shoulder.

"Mr. Mombourquette's room."

Without a word, my reluctant helper loaded up a dolly and

began rolling it down the hallway. With every step, great chasms of light yawned between his bowed legs. When he stopped abruptly to pry a bit of grease off the floor, I made a stab at conversation.

"My name's Emily." I waited for a reply. Except for the merciless scraping of his fingernail against the floor, there was none.

"I'm a vet here in town," I continued. "At a place just for cats." That was my trump card. Invariably, people were intrigued and had lots of questions.

"Baker," my guide grunted as he inspected his fingernail then rubbed it on his overalls. Satisfied, he and the dolly began rolling once again.

"Hey!" he hollered. "You kids quit running." Two boys, rounding the corner from another direction, skidded to a halt.

"You know the rules," Baker growled.

The boys meekly proceeded at a snail's pace while Baker and I continued down the hall, stopping in front of the service elevator. Baker pressed the button. After an eternity, the doors opened to reveal a space only slightly larger than a coffin. Baker motioned me inside then followed with the dolly. As the elevator made a painfully slow and creaky ascent to the second floor, I glued myself to a corner and studied the top of his head. A few sprigs of white clung to life on its windswept surface. Liver spots, like shadowy craters, dotted a moonscape that glowed with reflected light.

The elevator stopped, presumably on the second floor. The doors remained shut while the poor creature gathered enough strength to open them. I closed my eyes thinking that, if asked, I could identify Baker's head in a police line-up. Just when I was sure this was how I would end my days, the doors opened and we proceeded to the second door on the left.

"Is this Mr. Mombourquette's room?" I asked as Baker began

unloading the dolly. Wordlessly, he pointed to the nameplate above the door.

I knocked and was relieved when Benny appeared.

"Em. I was just coming to look for you," he said with concern.

"Uh...Baker here helped me up with everything." I turned to thank my benefactor.

"She left all this stuff in the foyer," Baker grumbled, shaking his head in disbelief.

"Oh?" Benny looked shocked but managed a sideways wink at me. "Well, I guess we can manage from here," he smiled. "Thanks, Baker."

With a dismissive wave and a grunt, Baker continued down the hall.

I followed Benny into the classroom. Carter was sprawled on a blanket in the middle of the room surrounded by his admirers. He drooled and kneaded the air in ecstasy. Assuring the girls that Carter would be fine in their absence, Benny reminded them it was time to go outside.

"Actually, Em, I have to run too. I have an emergency meeting with the principal and one of my parents," he explained.

"Oh? You're leaving?" I asked casually.

"Sorry. This just came up. The staff room's down the hall if you need anything," he added. "I'll see you in the gym at 1:15. Good luck. You'll be fine."

It occurred to me that my parents had said exactly the same thing when they dropped me off at summer camp. That was the time Angie-somebody cut a hole in my new sweater and I came home with the measles.

I set up my display, put Carter back in his kennel, and then left for the gym. The guest speakers for Career Day would be introduced by the principal during general assembly at 1:15. We would then return to our assigned classrooms where the Grade Five, Six and Seven classes would visit in turn.

A stout, middle-aged man in a business suit looked up as I wedged myself into my assigned seat next to him at the head table.

"Jeremy Townsend, lawyer. Defender of the Oppressed and Injured," he grinned, extending a business card. "Do you have a will?"

As 150 students began filing into the gym, I began to wish I had. The younger ones looked harmless enough but some of the older ones had pierced body parts and unusual clothing. I wondered which one was Jimmy Henderson. I hoped that his deed had been so foul that he was sent home for the day. Benny caught my eye and waved reassuringly.

The children hushed as a cherubic little man stepped up to the podium. He was dressed in a checkered polyester suit, the kind you buy from a thrift store for Hallowe'en. Squinting benignly at the students, he rummaged through his pockets for a pair of glasses.

"Ah…that's better," he sighed, polishing the glasses then anchoring them behind his ears. "Now I can see everyone. Good afternoon, boys and girls. Welcome to Career Day." There was scattered applause, mainly from the teachers.

"Today, boys and girls, we are fortunate to have seven professionals from our community who will speak to you about their career choices."

As Dr. Watkins paid each of us a glowing tribute, cold sweat began to trickle down my arms. My fellow professionals seemed calm and relaxed. Had none of these people heard about Jimmy

Henderson? Or run into Baker? I tried to focus on the basketball hoop at the end of the gym.

"And now," I heard Dr. Watkins say, "our guests will proceed to their assigned classrooms."

As the noise level rose in the gym, Dr. Watkins raised an arthritic finger. "Remember, there will be no profanity or chewing of gum."

Jeremy kicked me under the table. "Jesus Christ!" he winked, swallowing his gum.

With that, we, The Magnificent Seven, arose as one and filed out of the gym. Career Day was about to begin.

My first group of Grade Sixes was delightful. They were followed by Mrs. Jamieson's sullen Grade Seven class. Mrs. Jamieson disliked cats and so did the majority of her students, it seemed. When I opened Carter's door, hoping to pique their interest, she recoiled in horror.

"I'm sure he's a lovely animal," she announced, "but we have to think about disease."

I explained that Carter had been de-fleaed, de-wormed and de-testicled, but Mrs. Jamieson had already shut the door. Her class quickly lost interest.

The second Grade Six class was an exuberant group and included Arthur, who headed directly for a back seat where he proceeded to sew his fingers together with a needle and thread. By the time Benny's group arrived, I felt only compassion for the school teachers in my life.

Fortunately, Benny's students were a happy bunch: polite, curious, and well-prepared. They peppered me with questions. I was particularly impressed with a frail-looking child whose feet just scraped the floor. He had a mouth full of hardware and an endearing lisp. His worn corduroy pants only reached mid-calf, revealing a pair of white socks and loafers. Far from being ridiculed, his classmates liked and respected him. As the students gathered around Carter, I whispered to Benny, "Who's the cute little guy with all the questions?"

"Oh, that's Jimmy," Benny whispered back.

"Jimmy? Jimmy Henderson?"

Benny looked surprised. "Yeah. Do you know him?"

I hesitated. "I know the name."

There was a loud knock at the door. I grabbed Benny's sleeve. "Wait!" I hissed. "What did he do?"

"What did who do? Oh, you mean Jimmy?" Benny paused, his hand on the doorknob. "How do you know about that?"

I shrugged my shoulders. "I have my sources."

The knocking grew more insistent.

"He hacked into the principal's personal PC and made some, shall I say, creative changes," Benny whispered, opening the door. "It was his mom I met with at lunch."

"Oh...." Relief flooded over me. The face of crime in elementary school was changing. Jimmy Henderson was not a knife-wielding, dope-pushing delinquent. I relaxed for the first time since arriving at Pinegrove Elementary.

"Found it outside," I heard a familiar voice mutter. Baker reached past Benny to hand me a large cardboard box.

"Oh, thanks, Baker, but this isn't mi...," I gasped as the box began to jiggle. A large black beak pierced the cardboard, narrowly missing my hand.

Baker began undoing the flaps of the box.

"No, wait a minute, Baker! I don't think...."

Too late. A large bedraggled crow catapulted to the floor

where it proceeded to twirl around in circles. Several students rushed forward to help but Benny sent them back.

"Dr. McBride is trained to handle these kinds of things," he said in a calm voice. "Let's give her some space."

My lips parted in an anemic smile. My professional training about birds was limited to a two-hour seminar in my third year of vet school. I loved birds and thought the world was a far better place with them in it. I enjoyed their cheery morning conversations outside my window, admired their graceful flight, and marvelled at the intelligence of crows, especially. But up close and personal, I had an irrational fear they'd get tangled in my hair and poke at me with their beaks. My mother said this was because, against her direct orders, I watched Alfred Hitchcock's *The Birds* at a sleepover when I was twelve.

I had enough presence of mind to grab a jacket and began creeping forward. My audience was spellbound. The unfolding drama was more than they could have hoped for. I hovered over the bird, fearful that he would try to fly and crash horribly, but after a series of somersaults, he suddenly lay still.

"Oh, no!" the kids cried. "Is he dead?"

Several of the girls burst into tears.

Without a word, I grabbed the bird, Benny grabbed the box, and Jimmy Henderson grabbed a roll of masking tape.

"Wow! This is the best Career Day ever!" someone exclaimed. There were murmurs of agreement.

I brushed the hair out of my eyes and turned to Benny. "I'll take him back to the hospital right away. He's having seizures."

Benny nodded. "Sure. I can bring Carter and the rest of your stuff after school."

Baker materialized with a thick pair of gloves. "You might

need 'em. In the car," he hinted darkly.

I looked at the box. If this bird got loose while I was driving, I would need friends in the police department and a good lawyer.

"Lots of tape, Jimmy," I ordered.

I said goodbye to the class and was rewarded with an enthusiastic round of applause.

From Pinegrove Elementary to Ocean View Cat Hospital, there are eleven sets of lights. I know because every one of them turned red as we approached. I gripped the steering wheel and stared straight ahead, refusing to make eye contact with the box. Every so often the crow regained consciousness and tried desperately to escape his cardboard prison. I whipped in and out of lanes, honking my horn and gesturing rudely if required.

We roared down a back street and then careened into the hospital parking lot just as the crow's head popped out. He looked around and after sizing up the situation, began pecking a hole large enough for the rest of his body. I flung open the door and grabbed the box. A quick-thinking Tim Hortons patron, coffee in one hand and donut in the other, stuffed the latter into his mouth and held the hospital door open for me.

I nearly bowled Hilary over as I rounded the corner.

"You're back early," she called after me.

With no time to spare, I rushed past her into the isolation ward. The dozing occupants looked up with interest at the new arrival. I thrust box and all into the kennel then left to find Hughie.

He was in the office studying an ECG strip. "You have a what?"

"A crow," I repeated.

Hughie's lower jaw dropped open, exposing several jelly beans. "Weren't you supposed to be talking to little kids about being a vet?"

"Well, yes. And they're not so little, by the way. But then Baker brought in this crow."

"Who's Baker?"

"A funny little man. The janitor, I guess. He brought in this old box with holes in it. And then there was the whole thing with Jimmy Henderson." I rolled my eyes. "Anyway, it wasn't mine. Then he started opening the box. I told him not to. But he did. And it was a crow!" The words flew out of my mouth in a torrent. "We tried to catch him and he went crazy. . . ."

I could tell by the look on Hughie's face that he wasn't following any of this. "Anyway, he's having seizures."

"Who? Baker?"

"No!" I cried, throwing my hands into the air. "The crow!"

Hughie jumped up. "Where is he?"

"Isolation," I answered, trailing behind my boss.

A curious crowd of cats was gathered on the window ledge outside isolation, chattering in excitement. They were used to spiders and the occasional mouse; a crow was big game. The bird had freed himself and from his perch on top of the box eyeballed the furry onlookers suspiciously. Hughie consulted the emergency manual then drew up some Valium.

"Em," he ordered, "why don't you give D'Entremont at Shore Road Vets a call? He's into birds."

Grateful for the reprieve, I fled to the office. Herb D'Entremont was a pleasant and fortunately long-winded man, not one to say in two minutes what could be stretched into ten. By the time I returned, all was quiet. The crow was resting on a mound of towels and shredded cardboard. Hughie sat in the chair, idly picking bits of black feathers out of his hair. Susan was scrubbing a wound on her arm.

"So, Em, what did D'Entremont have to say?" Hughie asked, examining the rip in his new lab coat.

"Valium to control the seizures. Activated charcoal and fluids if necessary. He thinks the bird was likely poisoned."

"Yeah, that's what I figured. Anything else?"

"He owes you five bucks from the Saint Mary's–Dalhousie game. He has an old X-ray machine for sale. He's thinking about stocking a new cat litter and wants to know what you think. He and the missus are going to Scotland in a few weeks. Oh, and he's having prostate trouble too, so he hopes that doesn't flare up in Scotland."

Hughie grinned. "That's Herb. Honest to a fault. Well, we'll have the results from the blood sample tomorrow. In the meantime, call the school and let them know. If there's some wacko out there putting poison out, other animals or maybe even kids might get into it."

Benny arrived later that afternoon with Carter. A column of worker ants carrying my boxes trailed behind him. Several of the students smiled and waved.

"Is the crow okay?" one little boy asked.

"Well, so far, so good. Come have a look," I offered.

The students gathered at the window to watch Mr. Russell Crowe, as he had been dubbed, snoozing contentedly. The cat in the neighbouring kennel knew something was amiss but was hazy on the facts following an injection of morphine.

As the children chatted among themselves, Benny turned to me. "Do you remember when Forty Watt put that dead rat on your desk? You started to cry. Everyone thought it was so funny."

Forty Watt. His name was Robert but he wasn't too bright so people called him Forty. He used to scour the golf course for lost balls and sell them. After the rat incident, I read about golfers being struck by lightning and hoped that Forty would become another golf course statistic.

"Yeah," I answered, watching the kids. I had felt so sad and helpless as I stared at the lifeless rat. His little body was cold, his fur splattered with mud. His eyes saw nothing and nobody cared.

"I took the rat home after school and buried him," Benny said quietly.

I looked up but Benny had already begun herding his flock together. "Okay, guys," Benny clapped his hands, "we've been here long enough. Dr. McBride has work to do. Let's go."

In the morning, Russell Crowe's demanding squawks echoed throughout the hospital. He had devoured one can of cat food and several of Susan's breakfast hash browns. His water bowl was flipped upside down and wet strips of towel were flung far and wide. There had been no more seizures but the lab results were inconclusive. If Russell had been poisoned, we would never know what it was.

I was with Hughie a few days later when he released Russell at a nearby provincial park. We removed the top of the cage and waited. The bird just sat there for a moment, blinking in the bright sun, studying us and his surroundings. Then gathering himself, he lifted his great black body into the air with powerful sweeps of his wings. I watched him soar as he banked and turned, gliding on an updraft. The crows down below in the trees cawed noisily. Maybe they were cheering him on, or maybe they were telling him to get out of their airspace. But somewhere in those trees was a friend.

Chapter 12

"Come in," Hughie croaked feebly when I knocked on the office door. He sat in the middle of the floor in a rumpled heap, his tie undone and his hair poking up like a tornado had sucked him up and spit him out.

"What are you doing?" I asked, glancing around the paper-strewn landscape.

Hughie squinted at me through bloodshot eyes. "Resumes."

A month had passed since Althea tearfully explained she had been accepted to a fashion design school out west. Hughie had hugged her and wished her well. We threw a big party and joked that someday McCloskey-Birnbaum would rival Hilfiger and be splashed across all the clothing we wore. Employment ads were placed, and then Hughie promptly avoided all the resumes that flooded the hospital.

"She can't be replaced," he moaned. Now, on the eve of Althea's departure, he was desperate.

I picked up a resume and began skimming through. The unsigned cover letter had eight spelling mistakes and wild, carefree sentences. This applicant freely admitted she had been a hostess at McDonald's where she "*severed* people and cleaned up afterwards." A serial killer with a conscience.

Dropping the resume back onto the floor, I picked up another. A note from Althea stapled to the first page warned Hughie that this potential employee had green hair and wore a studded dog collar. It was going to be a long night. I poured my boss a fresh cup of coffee and rounded up some jelly beans.

"Emily, you're a godsend."

"I know." I slung my knapsack over my shoulder.

"You're not…leaving?"

"I'll be back in the morning."

"I may be dead by then!" he called desperately to my retreating back.

When I arrived the following morning, there was no sign of Hughie. If he had died overnight someone had removed the body, but not before arranging the resumes into three neat stacks: YES, NO and MAYBE. NO was by far the largest with MAYBE a distant second. There were five resumes in the YES pile. Curious, I began leafing through the five survivors of the late night cull.

Absorbed in the resumes, I didn't notice the eerie silence that had enveloped the hospital, as if we were shrouded in fog. No phones rang. No cats cried. The amiable chatter of people at work was absent. Carter fled past the office door, followed by Ernie. I felt the hairs rise on the back of my neck.

"He must be looking for Dr. McBride!" I heard someone cry.

"Claude!" a voice demanded. "Come back here!"

I froze. I could hear slow, deliberate thuds on the ceramic tile. The stale coffee in my cup trembled with each step. And then… nothing. In slow motion, I turned my head. Claude stood in the doorway, motionless, his eyes malevolent slits. A long pink leash trailed behind him.

"Claude! There you are!" Anne grabbed his leash. "Good morning, Dr. McBride!" she added, catching sight of me pressed against the back wall. "We're here for our manicure."

"Oh?"

"Yes, I'm afraid Claude's nails got a little long while I was in

Florida."

"Really? Are you sure?"

"My friend Bernie looked after him while I was away. But between you and me," Anne lowered her voice, "I don't think she took him out for his regular walks." A pair of gaudy birds swung from Anne's earlobes as she shook her head. "His nails always grow more quickly when he doesn't get out for his walks."

I couldn't imagine that Claude wore his nails down one little bit during these daily strolls. He was not the kind of cat to expend energy needlessly.

"Anyway, your dear, sweet receptionist said you were fully booked but if we came in first thing this morning, you could do his nails before your regular appointments. We wouldn't want him to be uncomfortable, would we?"

"No, we certainly wouldn't," I agreed.

Anne tugged on Claude's leash and rattled a bag of kitty treats. "Come along, Claude."

With a withering glance, Claude turned his back on me and proceeded into the exam room where Susan and Hilary were waiting with the usual arsenal.

"Girls," Anne said with a smug smile, "you can put all that away. You won't need 'em."

As Claude flexed his nails, I wondered if Anne had forgotten to wear a sunhat when she was in Florida.

I kept a cautious eye on Claude while his mother rummaged through a cavernous tote bag, the kind designed with tourists in mind.

"Here we are!" Anne produced a flimsy plastic bag from the drycleaners for our inspection. "Danger," it read. "May cause suffocation if worn over the head."

I looked at Anne in concern.

"Watch and learn, girls," Anne winked. "Here Claudie. Here baby," she cooed, waving the bag in front of him like a bullfighter.

Claude waddled over and allowed Anne to drape the plastic bag over him like a see-through negligee. Standing still, he closed his eyes. She then began caressing his body with the thin film, back and forth, back and forth. Claude arched his shoulders and kneaded the floor. Finally, he toppled over onto his side and stretched luxuriously. Gobs of happiness drool appeared at the corners of his mouth. I was shocked to hear a loud rumble. Claude was purring.

I had heard about this kind of phenomenon before but never actually witnessed it. Some cats can have an extreme reaction to tactile stimulation, both positive and negative. Fortunately, in Claude's case, it was the former.

"Quick, girls," Anne whispered, "get the trimmers!" Claude appeared to be in a trance. So was I.

"Dr. McBride!" Anne nudged me.

"Right!"

I got down on my knees and tentatively touched a paw while Anne swished the bag over his body. After several cautious pokes with not so much as a blink, I grabbed a foot in earnest and began trimming. With every effortless snip, my little pile of nails grew. So did my confidence. I was merciless. Claude's nails had never been shorter. I was just finishing foot number three when disaster struck. The seventy-two-year-old Anne suddenly developed a muscle spasm in her back and dropped the ball, or in this case, the plastic bag.

I looked up. "Anne, are you. . . ."

I never got a chance to finish. Claude's eyes flew open and my hand was the first thing he saw. Slimy yellow fangs disappeared into my thumb joint. I howled. He howled. Anne held onto her back and howled.

"Oh, Claude, Claude!" Anne cried when she saw my hand. "Dr. McBride, I'm so sorry!"

I gripped my throbbing hand and scowled at Claude. He scowled right back.

In a few short minutes my hand looked like a cranberry muffin, swollen and covered in red blotches. An untreated bite wound can cause serious infection. Luckily for me, Hughie had made a favourable impression on Dr. Lisa Greer, who practiced family medicine in an office upstairs. A queue of waiting patients turned their heads irritably as I was ushered past into her examining room.

"So how's Dr. Doucette these days?" she asked casually as she disinfected my hand.

"Oh, he's good. Busy. You know."

Dr. Greer nodded her head sympathetically.

"I think maybe he's a bit lonely since the divorce," I couldn't help adding.

"H'mm," Dr. Greer wrapped my hand in a sterile bandage. "I may give him a call. My cat's been throwing up furballs."

My tetanus shot was up to date so she prescribed a course of antibiotics. But in spite of the pretty pink pills I took three times daily, my right arm swelled to the elbow and throbbed constantly. My digestive system, never one to be finicky, balked at antibiotics. I was home for almost a week, most of which time I spent on the toilet or eating yogurt. Melody, Mickey, and Lionel enjoyed having me at home and took full advantage of my left arm which could still open cans and doors.

In my absence, a beautiful bouquet from Anne and Claude arrived at the hospital, followed by an assortment of homemade sweets. Susan salvaged the flowers as well as a jar of pickles for me but the cookies were never heard from again. Mom made a chicken dinner for two and had Benny Mombourquette deliver it. She claimed she just happened to run into him out mountain-biking. Hughie called often to see if the swelling was down in my arm. I noticed an increasingly high-pitched quality to his voice.

By the time I returned to work, a paper skyscraper of my own had risen from the desk. At the very top was a note that said Anne had adopted a stray kitten. When I heard her urgent voice on the phone a few weeks later, I was sure Claude had eaten the kitten and was now suffering from indigestion. Instead, Anne informed me that the kitten wasn't feeling well.

She arrived for the appointment with her Irish cat-sitting friend, Bernice, in tow. I had met the fifty-plus Bernie, as she was known to her friends, at Claude's birthday party last winter. The fact that the cat of the hour was locked in a bedroom didn't stop his guests from having a good time. After several glasses of sherry, the flamboyant Bernie, accompanied by her feather boa, led us in a rousing rendition of "The Rocky Road to Dublin" followed by "Old Black Rum." She was silent now, her kind face wrinkled in concern as I began examining the tiny kitten.

Isabella was everything Claude was not: delicate, pretty and friendly. She seemed quiet, however. Anne said she had been vomiting and hadn't eaten since yesterday. I wondered if perhaps Claude was terrorizing her. She was very small for her age. Anne insisted that the two were getting along just fine and produced a picture of Isabella nestled in the vast warm expanse of Claude's tummy.

"I know you've only seen his bad side," Anne sniffed, wiping her eyes. "But he can be very sweet."

So was the apple that poisoned Snow White, I thought bleakly. Cradling Isabella in my arms, I explained that I first wanted to test her for feline leukemia and feline immunodeficiency virus. These AIDS-like viruses cause severe illnesses and death in persistently infected cats. Before proceeding with treatment, we needed to rule out this possibility.

While Isabella squawked in helpless protest, we wrapped her in a pink blanket and drew 0.2 mL of blood from her baby veins. I waited while Susan ran the test. She worked silently and efficiently, oblivious to the mindless chatter of the radio station. When an abandoned animal was adopted by someone prepared to offer a loving home, it was heartbreaking to get a positive test result. If the cat was sick at the time, like Isabella, the prognosis was very poor, and we usually recommended euthanasia.

I heard Susan exhale. "It's negative, Dr. McBride."

I breathed a sigh of relief. We were over our first big hurdle. Since Isabella was dehydrated from vomiting, I gave her some fluids and an injection to reduce the nausea. I didn't know yet what was wrong but hoped that with supportive care, she would improve over the next twenty-four hours. When I returned to the exam room, I found Hughie chatting with Anne and Bernie.

"Good news," I smiled.

"Isn't that grand!" Bernie cried, throwing her arms first around me, then Anne, then Hughie in turn.

"That's a big relief," Hughie agreed with a smile. "Well, it was nice chatting. I must get back to work. Thank Claude for those delicious cookies, Anne. And Bernie, you'll have to tell me more about your Uncle Seamus. Maybe he can give me some investment advice."

"Who's Uncle Seamus?" I asked after Hughie had gone.

"He's away in the head," Bernie explained.

"He has fits," Anne translated.

"Afterwards he can see into the future," Bernie whispered reverently.

"Oh," I nodded politely. I wondered if he was anything like my uncle Arthur with the performing false teeth.

"Oh, that dear, wee man," Bernie sighed.

"It must be very hard on him and his family," I agreed. "Does he take medication?"

Puzzled, Bernie looked at me. "Oh no, dear. I mean your Dr. Doucette. I'd just love to sit him down at a table with a good meal. Fatten him up a bit. He works so hard. He must be knackered."

"Yes, he does work hard," I admitted. Poor wee man indeed! He'd single-handedly eaten most of the cookies in my gift basket. When I cornered him, he had promised to bring me some of his mother's famous Cape Breton oatcakes. I was still waiting.

As if reading my thoughts, Anne declared she was making a big batch of fudge tomorrow. "Do you think Isabella will be able to go home by then?" she asked.

"I hope so, Anne," I replied. "We'll see how she does."

But in the morning, Isabella was no better. She had eaten nothing overnight although she had somehow managed a scrawny deposit in her litter box. A fecal flotation showed no evidence of parasites. Similarly, her urinalysis was normal. With Anne's permission, we drew more blood for a serum chemistry profile. Other than the expected changes due to vomiting, everything looked fine. I had no idea what was wrong with this kitten. My original euphoria over a negative test result was fading.

As the afternoon progressed, she became weaker and more withdrawn. Huddled in the corner of her kennel, she refused to eat. Hilary prepared a nutritious paste and together she and Susan began force-feeding little bits at a time. No sooner had they finished than Isabella started to retch. Within minutes her stomach contents lay undigested on the floor of the kennel. While Susan disinfected the space, Hilary cuddled the exhausted kitten in a flannelette blanket. As I watched, she moistened a gauze pad with warm water and gently washed the little face.

"Should we try again?" Susan asked when she emerged from isolation.

"No," I sighed, gazing past her into the ward. "Let's take a pair of X-rays. Maybe she swallowed something she shouldn't have." I was also worried about an intussusception in which a part of the bowel folds back on itself. Either condition would require surgery and right now, Isabella was a poor surgery risk.

While Susan set up for X-rays, I spoke with the internal medicine specialist at the Atlantic Veterinary College in PEI. Most of his suggestions I had already tried. Slowly, I hung up the phone and looked at Hughie. He had been listening thoughtfully to our conversation. Leaning forward in his chair he rested his forearms on his legs and clasped his hands together.

"I don't know, Em," he shook his head. "You could try an exploratory but she's pretty weak."

"Yeah," I agreed. "I don't think that's an option."

Susan poked her head in the door. "X-rays are up."

Hughie joined me in the treatment area as we pored over the films. Other than a lot of gas in the intestines, they looked normal. I looked at my watch. Evening appointments were starting in a few minutes.

"Try her with a little more food in an hour or so," I told Susan. "Let me know if there's any change."

Evening clinic was busy. In between appointments, I checked on Isabella. Anne was sprawled on the floor, her head and shoulders out of sight inside Isabella's kennel. I adjusted the flow rate on the IV and gave Isabella her evening injections. We had stopped oral medications because she just couldn't keep anything in her stomach. The only sound in the room was the mechanical click of the IV pump as it delivered the life-sustaining fluids and nutrients through a vein in Isabella's front leg. Bending over, I laid my hand on Anne's shoulder.

She reached up and patted my hand reassuringly. It was a hand that had traveled great distances and experienced much. One day my own hand would be gnarled and arthritic, the skin hanging loosely over tired old veins. I hoped it would feel as warm as Anne's felt upon mine.

After a restless night, the morning came early. I stumbled to the kitchen table with a cup of coffee and watched the sun rise. Gaining strength, it began to dissolve the morning fog. The fragrant scent of my neighbour's yard wafted in through the kitchen window. Clarence was a devout gardener who spent his spare time hatching elaborate schemes to keep the neighbourhood cats out of his garden. Most failed but he remained cheerfully optimistic.

The ringing phone shattered the early morning calm.

"Hi, Dr. McBride. I know it's early but you asked me to call." Hilary was apologetic.

"How is she?"

"Well, no worse, but...," Hilary hesitated. "Anne just called. She's bringing Claude in. He's sick too."

"Oh no," I sighed. First Isabella and now Claude. "Okay. Thanks, Hilary."

I dumped my coffee in the sink and headed for the shower.

When I arrived, Hughie was examining Claude on the stainless steel table in the treatment area. Anne was convinced Claude had caught something from Isabella. He refused to eat, an unheard-of event in the household.

"Where's Bernie today, Anne?" Hughie asked pleasantly as he lifted the snarling but otherwise inert Claude onto the treatment table.

"She's working," Anne replied, her eyes upon Claude.

Hughie pulled back an ear flap and peered down each ear canal with his otoscope. "A little waxy. Claude, when was the last time you washed your ears?"

Switching off the light, he asked Anne, "What does she do?"

"She's a receptionist. Doctor's offices mostly. She works for a temp agency," Anne explained without a trace of her usual exuberance.

"Oh?" Hughie lifted Claude's lip, exposing the lethal weapons within. Claude rattled off a series of spine-chilling death threats followed by a long, sustained scream. Here it comes, I thought. Hughie had been lulled into a false sense of security. A lesser vet might have crumbled under the barrage but Hughie seized the opportunity to get a good look in Claude's mouth.

"M'mm...no ulcers. A lot of tartar. Looks like a broken molar back there...Oops!" Hughie jumped backwards as Claude clamped down on the dental probe.

"Does she like cats?" Hughie continued, palpating Claude's belly

"Oh, she loves cats!" Anne smiled at last. "She has four, you know. Took in a pregnant stray last year."

Hughie listened to Claude's chest then slung the stethoscope around his neck. I gasped as he reached for the digital thermometer and inserted it somewhere I never would have considered unless Claude was comatose. Holding it in place, he whistled cheerfully through his teeth.

"Would you have her phone number?" he asked Anne.

Anne looked surprised. "Well, yes. Of course. She's one of my best friends."

Hughie passed Anne his little black datebook. "Can you jot it down?"

Anne picked it up gingerly. "Anywhere in particular?"

"Alphabetically," my boss replied.

"Bernie's very attractive for her age," Anne commented, just as the thermometer beeped. Claude hissed in response.

"Mm'm? What's that?" Hughie was preoccupied with Claude's behind. Removing the thermometer, he squinted at the digital read-out. "Normal."

"What do you think, Dr. Doucette?" Anne asked.

Hughie took a deep breath. "Well, I can't seem to find anything unusual on his physical exam."

"Just like Isabella," Anne said, reaching for my hand.

"Well, let's not jump to conclusions," Hughie tried to reassure her. "He's not dehydrated and he's well equipped to handle a day or two without eating. There's no fever and his vital signs are good. He certainly is quiet, though...for Claude, I mean."

Anne nodded in worried agreement.

"I think it would be best to keep him at home today, Anne, and see how he does," Hughie continued. "I'm sure he'd much rather be home than here. But if he gets worse, we'll admit him and do a work-up. Is that okay with you? "

"Okay." Anne's voice seemed small in the large treatment area with its stainless steel table, high ceilings, and rows of hospital-white cupboards.

"I'll help you out with him," Hughie offered.

As they turned to leave, I noticed Anne's sweater lying over the back of the chair. "Anne!" I called, holding out the sweater.

"Oh, thank you, dear. Isabella just loves this sweater. Maybe...," Anne looked thoughtful. "Could you put it in the kennel with her? For company?"

"Sure. But after it's been in isolation, you probably shouldn't take it home," I explained.

"It's just a sweater, dear," she whispered. "I can buy one anywhere."

By early afternoon I had finished my surgeries and just had time to swallow a peanut butter sandwich whole and wash it down with a Coke before Arnie Rossiter arrived. Arnie was an amiable, outgoing tabby who couldn't keep his nose out of other cats' business. As a result, he was a regular at Ocean View. Abscesses, colds, and ear mites were routine events for Arnie.

"Dr. McBride!" Hilary knocked on the door. Without waiting for an invitation, she popped her head inside. "I'm sorry to interrupt but could I see you for a minute?"

Excusing myself, I followed Hilary to the treatment area.

"What is it?"

Hilary pointed towards isolation.

Fearing the worst, I peered through the window. Isabella stood at the door of her kennel looking out through the bars.

"She just ate a plate of food," Hilary grinned. "And look at this!" she added, proudly holding out a litter tray. She might have been showing off the crown jewels. Instead, I gazed down upon a single piece of stool pock-marked with tapeworm segments.

"She threw up a bunch too. See?" Hilary lifted up a piece of paper towel.

I had never seen so many parasites in one place unless you counted The Liquor Dome on a Friday night in downtown Halifax. Given the severity of the infestation, I would have expected to see eggs when I examined her fecal flotation under the microscope. Cats develop tapeworm when they ingest an infected flea while grooming. It usually takes at least a month for the tapeworm egg to develop into a mature intestinal parasite capable of shedding segments in the stool. In this case, Isabella had somehow become infected before she was even old enough to groom herself. I had only given the tapeworm medication last night as an afterthought along with a cornucopia of other drugs.

Isabella spied us in the window, and began climbing the crossbars of her kennel door, crying for attention.

Grinning, I turned to Hilary. "I'll call Anne as soon as I finish with the Rossiters."

Hilary nodded and returned to the ward. Although the waiting room was full, I lingered outside the isolation window for a few moments longer, savouring the sight of a happy, active kitten. Giving Isabella the right medication had been a lucky guess, a matter of covering all the bases. I smiled as the kitten crawled up Hilary's shoulder and began playing with her hair.

Reluctantly, I turned away from the window and grabbed an antibiotic for Arnie from the cupboard. When I was finally able to call Anne, her joy over Isabella was tempered by the fact that Claude seemed worse. He ignored a plate of Ritz crackers and Cheez Whiz that had been left unattended and refused to leave the basement. She found him sleeping in a box of rags in a dark corner.

"I'll bring him in first thing tomorrow," she sighed. "By the way, Dr. McBride, do you know if Dr. Doucette called my friend Bernie? I just hate to pry," she added.

"Yes, he did. I believe they're getting together after work tonight."

"Oh, that's wonderful!"

"He was so grateful to meet Bernie," I added. "He's been looking for someone for quite awhile. He put an ad in the paper over a month ago."

There was a pause. "He put an ad in the paper? I wouldn't think a man like him would need to do that." Anne sounded surprised.

"He usually does when he's looking for someone new. He had a bad experience on the Internet." I smiled, remembering my own experience with Hughie and computers.

"Did lots of people respond?" Anne asked curiously.

"Quite a few," I babbled. "Mostly women, but there were a few men. One was a professor at the university. I guess he was just looking for a change."

"Well…," Anne hesitated. "I've always thought Dr. Doucette was very open-minded. Anything goes these days, I guess." Thanking me again, she promised to bring in a chocolate cake along with Claude.

Isabella continued to improve. By mid-morning, she had polished off her third meal of the day and was touring the hospital in Hilary's lab coat pocket. Hughie had improved as well. I found him in the office with an orange juice instead of the usual black coffee. He looked rested and smiled benignly when Susan told him Mrs. Jefferson was refusing to pay her bill. Normally that would send him into an apoplectic fit.

"Come in!" Hughie waved his arm expansively. I noticed the mountain range of paper, an office landmark for so long, was gone.

"So, how did the interview go?" I asked.

"The woman is a national treasure," Hughie glowed.

"When does she start?"

"Monday. You know, I think I may go home for the weekend. Relax a bit. Play some golf." Hughie leaned back in his chair and flashed a beatific smile. "'All things cometh to he who waits.'"

"I don't think God was referring to he who procrastinates, Hughie." I reminded him about my Cape Breton oatcakes. "And I've *been* waiting."

"All in good time, Dr. McBride. All in good time," he replied with a non-committal shrug.

Meanwhile, Anne arrived with the morose Claude. He allowed Hilary to lift him into an isolation kennel then promptly turned his back on all of us. Anne held Isabella in her arms as she stood in front of Claude's kennel.

"There's your big brother," she cooed. "Claude...Claudie...."

Claude gave no indication that he had heard or was even interested in anything Anne had to say. Tired of being held, Isabella struggled in Anne's arms. Now that she was feeling better, she was anxious to explore her surroundings and complained when Anne tried to restrain her. I saw Claude's ears twitch.

"Anne, maybe you should put her back. I think Claude's getting upset."

Isabella climbed up the front of Anne's chest and perched on her shoulder. Unsure what to do next, she started to meow.

Claude's big orange head turned in slow motion. I watched in disbelief as he hauled his great self up and lumbered over to the front of the kennel. Seeing me, he snarled hatefully, then turned his attention to Isabella.

Anne peeled Isabella off her shoulder and dangled her in front of Claude. Instead of the lunge and scream I expected, Claude sniffed the little face.

"Do you want to visit your brother?" Anne asked Isabella as she opened the kennel door.

"Oh, Anne, no," I began. "That's not a good...."

I was too late. The sacrificial lamb looked around innocently as the great jaws descended from above. I grabbed the leather gloves to snatch Isabella away just as Claude's personal paddle brush began washing her forehead. Once cleaned to his satisfaction, he moved on to the delicacies within her ears. He washed her back in long gentle strokes while Isabella closed her eyes in ecstasy. When Anne placed a dish of food in the kennel, Claude allowed Isabella to eat her fill before lowering his gigantic head into the bowl. Who would have thought Claude was the motherly type?

We ran some bloodwork on Claude just to be safe but his results were normal. It appeared that the big, tough guy had been pining for Isabella. I decided to send them both home on a trial basis but felt fairly confident that everything would be OK when Claude tried to shred me en route.

In reception, Anne hugged and thanked everyone, including the unsuspecting delivery boy. Nudging Hughie in the ribs, she winked, "How was your date with my friend Bernie? We're the same age, you know," she winked.

All heads turned in Hughie's direction. He sputtered as

orange juice dribbled down his chin onto the green scrubs.

"What date? It wasn't a date!" Hughie called after her, tiny sparkles of juice glistening on his chin. Giggling, Anne waved good-bye and disappeared through the doors. Hughie smiled self-consciously at the sea of staring faces.

"It wasn't a date," he explained. "It was to interview for a new receptionist." Then he fled out back to the treatment area.

In the corner of the room, Frank Delamare turned to his wife of forty-one years and shook his head. "Slept her way to the top, eh?"

"Em!" Hughie grabbed my arm when I came through the doors. "She thinks we had a date! Bernie's old enough to be my mother!" Hughie was horrified. "You've got to set her straight!"

I looked at my boss sympathetically, then patted his arm.

"All in good time, Hughie, all in good time."

Chapter 13

WHEN THE PHONE RANG, an avalanche of bodies rushed to answer. School had just closed for the summer. In the brief lull that always followed, the staff rather joylessly painted, cleaned, and oiled. A phone call in the desert of appointments was fertile with far more exciting possibilities. I could hear the rich Irish rhythms in Bernie's voice as she reached the phone first and then the patter of her clogs down the hall.

"Dr. Deeeeee, Dr. Deeeeee." A few seconds later her freckled face appeared in the doorway. "There's a lovely gentleman on the phone. He wants to know if you'll do a house call to Tatamagouche."

She peered at Dr. Doucette over the rims of her bifocals. "Do we do house calls that far away? For fourteen cats?"

"Oh, that'd be Herbert Grant." Hughie beamed from underneath the desk, screwdriver in hand. "He used to live here in town. See if this Sunday is good for him."

As Bernie clattered back into reception, Hughie asked, "Em, how would you like to visit Catopia?"

"In your Jeep?" I made a face. Tatamagouche was a hundred and sixty kilometres away on Nova Scotia's north shore.

"Herb's right on the ocean," Hughie continued, hauling himself out from underneath the desk. "We can spend the day, go for a swim. And he's a gourmet cook."

I was convinced. Nevertheless, it was my car we loaded on Sunday morning. Bill might be a geriatric with exhaust problems, but the windows worked, the roof didn't leak, and the trunk was not a compost bin. Hughie sighed as we pulled away, leaving the Jeep behind in the deserted parking lot.

"The Jeep would have been more fun."

Bill rolled out of Halifax on a gorgeous summer day. Although Nova Scotia has several large urban areas, the province is mostly rural. We drove past flowing tracts of emerald green farmland dotted with grazing cows. Just past Truro, in the centre of the province, we left the divided highway and eventually picked up a quiet two- lane road.

"It's hot," Hughie complained. "If we had the Jeep we could have taken the roof off."

"Roll your window down."

Five minutes later, I heard snoring in the passenger seat. His Jeep forgotten, Hughie had succumbed to the country air. Sunshine pooled on him like golden taffy.

Following Herbert's directions, I turned right onto a skinny, threadbare road. Trees embraced overhead as Bill wound his way through the dappled light underneath. Gradually, the hardwood forest gave way to rocky pastures. The road alternately dipped and rose like a rollercoaster but followed a straight course. Bill chugged up the third hill, unaware that a rather dim-witted Holstein lurked in the hollow just beyond.

I slammed on the brakes. Hughie pitched forward against the seatbelt then jerked back, biting his tongue.

"Ow!" he cried, glaring at me. "What the...?"

I pointed to the large black and white cow staring calmly at the car through a dust cloud. She considered us for a moment then resumed chewing her cud.

Hughie leaned over and tooted on the horn. The creature

flattened her ears and rolled her eyes but refused to budge. I turned on the four-way flashers and waited.

"This is why I work with cats," Hughie sighed. Opening the door, he eased his lanky frame outside.

"Shoo!" he ordered, waving a hand. The cow looked at him and idly flicked her tail.

"Shoo!" Hughie hollered and flapped his arms. "Move it, Bessie."

I poked my head out the window. "Why don't you give her a little slap on the rump to get her going? We could be here all day."

Hughie gave me a look then circled behind the cow who watched his approach with suspicion. When he got within striking distance, her eyes rolled back in her head and a right hind leg shot out menacingly. Hughie hopped back into the car.

"Well, that was a good idea, Em."

"We've got to do something," I pointed out. "She'll end up in a fast food restaurant."

"Maybe we can find out who owns her," Hughie suggested. "There's a house up there on the hill."

Squeezing past the cow, we drove a half kilometre down the road to the rutted, boulder-strewn driveway of E. Hobbs. Mr. Hobbs didn't get a lot of visitors, nor, judging by the lean on his mailbox, a lot of mail. I hesitated.

"The Jeep could make it."

With a withering glance at the passenger seat, I slowly eased Bill up the rugged incline. Chickens scattered as we detoured past an abandoned car and a rusted box spring. The grey farmhouse stood alone at the top of the hill. Its spine sagged in the middle, exhausted from holding up the house for so many years. No flowers or shrubs softened the landscape.

Hughie opened the car door. Immediately, a large German shepherd materialized.

"Em! Em!" Hughie hissed. "Any muffins left?"

As I rummaged through the remains of a McDonald's breakfast, a gaunt man wearing an undershirt appeared behind the ripped screen door. A fragile arc of cigarette ash dangled from the side of his mouth. E. Hobbs didn't look any more prosperous than his house.

"Oh…hello!" Hughie's smile faded as Hobbs continued to stare. The dog bristled and curled his lips in an unfriendly sneer.

"There's a cow in the middle of the road just down there," Hughie turned and pointed. A frenzied outburst of ill-tempered barks pinned him against the car. "My friend and I are worried she might get hurt."

Squinting in the sun, Hobbs shifted his scowl to the road and then back to us. Deciding we were neither salesmen nor religious zealots, he took one last puff of his cigarette and squashed the remains on the porch. A sharp whistle silenced the dog in mid-bark. Disappointed, the animal slunk along the side of the house, muttering half-heartedly to himself. At the corner, he gave a final woof and disappeared.

With one eye on the back of the house, Hughie brushed the dust off his clothes and approached Hobbs.

"So…do you know who owns that cow?"

Hobbs gathered some phlegm from the back of his throat and spit over the rail. Removing a package of cigarettes from the pocket of his trousers, he selected one and popped it into the space recently vacated by the previous cigarette. He lit it with a practiced hand and inhaled deeply. After a moment, he tipped his head back and exhaled in a slow, satisfying release. Folding his arms across his chest, he stared at Hughie.

"Yup."

"Does he live around here?"

Hobbs curled his shoulders in a disinterested shrug.

"Do you know his name?" Hughie persisted.

A hovering mosquito landed on Hobbs' neck and was quickly dispatched. He scraped away the carcass with a fingernail and wiped the remains across his pants.

"Tom Keddy."

"Well, do you think we can call him?"

Hobbs took a thoughtful drag on his cigarette. "Nope."

"Oh." Hughie was silent for a moment. "Why not?"

"Don't got a phone."

"You mean you don't got a phone or he don't…doesn't?" Hughie corrected himself.

While Hughie waited for Hobbs to think the question through, I noticed a coyote trotting through the field. Apparently, E. Hobbs did too. Hughie, facing the opposite direction, did not.

"Gawd damn!" The farmer roared to life, snatching a shotgun from inside the porch. Hughie threw his hands into the air as Hobbs hurtled past. But the coyote, cunning from centuries of persecution, had already melted into the landscape.

"Aw, shit!" Hobbs kicked the ground in disgust.

Hughie thanked Hobbs for his help and hopped back into the car. Rocks flew in Bill's wake as we tumbled down the driveway, the shepherd in hot pursuit.

Fifteen minutes later we were sipping tea in Herbert Grant's garden that overlooked the shallow, warm waters of the Northumberland Strait. Strains of classical music wafted through the French doors, which opened onto a flagstone patio.

Colourful annuals filled every kind of container imaginable, while beds of black-eyed Susans bobbed like synchronized swimmers in the gentle breeze. In the centre of the garden, three cherubs peed lazily into a fountain.

Cats spilled out from the house into the sun-soaked yard. A retired history professor and cat devotee, Herbert rescued animals that other people had thrown away. In Catopia, they lounged on antiques and designer cat trees, drank distilled water from crystal bowls, and played with organically grown catnip. All were named after historical figures.

For the next two hours we examined, de-wormed, vaccinated, and trimmed the nails of fourteen cats. As it turned out, Pierre Trudeau was pregnant and Churchill's flea allergy was acting up. Otherwise, the cats were in good health, due in no small part to superior nutrition and Herbert's watchful eye. We had just settled down to lunch when the phone rang.

Excusing himself, Herbert padded out to the kitchen in his yellow flip-flops. I took a sip of wine and leaned back in my chair. Hughie grinned at me across a white linen tablecloth laden with delicacies. Selecting a tea biscuit from the basket, he slathered it with butter as we waited for our host to return.

"Oh dear! Oh, my goodness!" Herbert reappeared in the archway, his face ashen.

I sat up straight in my chair. "What's wrong?"

"There's a cow in the road a few kilometres back. She's foaming at the mouth. Acting strangely. People are saying it's rabies!"

"A cow?" Hughie asked, glancing at me.

Herbert wrung his hands. "I've got to get the cats in!"

Most of the cats had been overcome by the aroma of tuna rolls and were already inside. While I helped Herbert with the rest, Hughie made a call to the Department of Agriculture. Although there had been a recent report of rabies in the area, it hadn't involved a domesticated animal. If this was rabies, the cow's brain would need to be sent to Ottawa for confirmation. A recorded message advised him to call back during regular hours.

He then tried the local RCMP detachment. Marjorie, the dispatcher and Constable MacDonald's wife, explained that her husband was currently investigating a break-and-enter at the sausage factory. Someone had left the cash but taken several boxes of schnitzel. She promised to send him along as soon as humanly possible.

Hughie grabbed his tea biscuit off the table. "Let's go, Em."

We jumped into my car and sped towards the hapless cow, not quite sure what we would do when we got there. We had a few leftover feline vaccines, an ice pack, a stethoscope, and a pair of nail trimmers. Somewhere in the back seat was half a muffin.

Bill skidded to a stop on the crest of a hill where an agitated knot of farmers and their trucks had gathered. Beyond them, the dazed cow sputtered and gagged. She looked wretched, her earlier confidence gone. A small man with delicate features broke free from the group.

"Are you the vets?" When Hughie nodded, the little man grabbed his hand and pumped.

"Tom Keddy," he announced. "That's my cow, Mabel." The other farmers eyed Hughie's Hawaiian shirt suspiciously.

"What should we do?" Tom asked, his eyes wide.

"Shoot her!" someone said.

Tom gasped. "But...but...she's a pet! You just can't...shoot her!"

"Look, buddy." A large man with bulging arms and a grimy

ball cap faced Tom. "You got yerself a coupl'a goats up there. A fat, lazy pig that shoulda gone to market last summer. A bunch o' chickens. They all prob'ly sleep on the bed at night! Christ, we got families, livestock to protect."

Others nodded in agreement and the crowd grew louder.

"We don't know this is rabies," Hughie said.

"We don't know it ain't!" A man in the back clutched his rifle and stared at Hughie.

I tugged on Hughie's sleeve. "This feels like a cow-lynching!" I whispered.

"Em, I don't think this is rabies. Besides," Hughie added in a low voice, "she was fine this morning."

Looking around for the first time, I noticed the fallen apples littering the roadside. The hard green globes were the size of golf balls, unsuitable for human consumption but a delicacy for a creature with four stomachs. Hughie picked one up and rolled it thoughtfully in his hand. Then he turned to me.

"I bet she's got one stuck in her throat!"

I saw the gleam in his eye and shook my head. "No!"

"You hold her mouth open," he continued, "and I'll look inside."

"Are you insane?"

"Okay, I'll hold her mouth open and you look inside." He strode toward the cow.

Reluctant to be left behind, I followed. Consumed by her own misery, Mabel was oblivious to our approach.

"Does anyone have some thick gloves?" Hughie addressed the crowd who had fallen silent.

One of the farmers rummaged in the back of his truck. With a furtive glance at Mabel, he handed a mud and hay-encrusted pair of gloves to Hughie then shrunk back into the circle of safety. The crowd watched with morbid curiosity as Hughie pried open the cow's jaws and peered inside. Tom Keddy hopped from foot to foot alternately moaning about his misfortune and trying to soothe his cow.

As Hughie tried to hang on and look inside the cow's mouth, Mabel twisted and tossed her great head. "I can't...see...anything!" he grunted in frustration.

"Hey Hobbs!" someone called as a familiar figure emerged from the crowd. "Catch yer coyote yet?"

A few farmers snickered but most were quiet as Hobbs took the gloves from Hughie's outstretched hand. Anchoring his feet in a broad stance, he unlocked Mabel's jaws with plier-like arms. A cigarette dangled from the corner of his mouth. Looking at Hughie, he nodded.

Hughie rolled up his shirt sleeve and stretched his arm down the cow's throat until it disappeared altogether. They stood cheek to cheek. Mabel's great tongue thrashed about with no sense of purpose, drenching my boss in slimy gobs of saliva. He grimaced as he probed blindly.

"Oh!" His eyes opened wide. "There it is. If I can just.... SHIT!" The mesmerized crowd which had drawn closer for a better view jumped back.

"Oh, no!" Tom Keddy wailed. "Is she OK? What is it?"

"There's something stuck there all right." Hughie wiped his face with the drool-free arm. "But it's so slippery. My hands are too big."

"Yuh ken crush it in'er throat," Hobbes announced.

"We could," Hughie admitted. "But I think a smaller pair of hands could get it out without that kind of trauma."

Sixteen heads turned towards me. I shivered as a cloud passed over the sun.

"What about Tom Keddy?" I hissed. "It's his cow and he's got little arms."

"You can do this, Em." Hughie's calm voice propelled me closer to Mabel's mouth.

I glanced at Hobbs. Only a glowing stub remained in the corner of his mouth. Closing my eyes, I eased my arm down the viscous road to hell and thought of Dr. Helmut VonVaggelin. As a fourth-year veterinary student, I spent two months on his large animal rotation. All I could remember from those two months was his pragmatic message delivered in a crisp, German accent:

"Never…nein, nein, nein…put you hand in de mouth of de animal unless you are sure she does not have de rabies! Ya?"

Ya! Right on, Helmut!

Yet, here I was, my hand roaming an unknown cow's esophagus. As I wondered how many needles I would need if Mabel was rabid, my fingers locked onto the offending apple. A music teacher had once praised my long, thin fingers, claiming they were born for arpeggios and bar chords, and now, as it turned out, retrieving apples from cows. Victorious, I held it up to the crowd like a football player who had just scored the winning touchdown.

"Oh, thank God!" Tom Keddy broke out of the pack. Sputtering with emotion, he threw his arms first around Mabel and then me. I searched for Hobbs in the crowd but he had disappeared. As I shook hands with everyone, I thought I saw his lanky frame flicker through the trees. But maybe it was only a shadow, like the coyote he pursued.

In the meantime, Constable MacDonald had arrived followed

by Harvey McClintock, editor, publisher, and photographer for the monthly *Tatamagouche Times.* My complimentary August issue featured side by side photos of Mabel and me on the front page. "Cat Vet Saves Cow" was the heart-stopping headline.

Mom had been very helpful when Harvey called for some background information. My childhood was described in some detail along with a few other facts: "She's always been a cow-lover," Dr. McBride's mother stated proudly, adding that her daughter was not married.

We left Tatamagouche that day as the sun was setting. Along the horizon, the sky was swathed in a kaleidoscope of colour where an angel had spilled her paints. I glanced at my boss, who lay sound asleep thanks to a broad sampling of Herbert's homemade liqueurs. I had just turned off the radio, preferring the music that played before my eyes, when a ghostly shape ran across the road: Hobbs' coyote. As I slowed down, he turned to watch my approach but then slipped silently into the woods when I stopped. From somewhere nearby, a white-throated sparrow sang to the first star.

Chapter 14

DIARRHEA. The word strikes a chord of unrest in every veterinary hospital. It can appear without warning, anywhere, anytime. At Ocean View, we had developed our own vocabulary to describe its rich diversity: the Soft Serve, a tubular mound that rose skyward in diminishing circles and culminated in a curlicue, the H-Bomb, diffuse and horrific, and last but definitely not least, The Platter (self-explanatory). On a day that began innocently enough, I spent my shift immersed in excrement.

"Good morning!" Bernie sang out as she handed me a specimen jar. "Stool sample. Joshua Simmons. His mom said it was fresh."

I shook the container. The contents rattled forcefully against the plastic walls. Joshua was nineteen years old and his stool sample looked even older. Under the label heading "description," Bernie had written "petrified." Oh well, at least it wasn't diarrhea.

"Lovely. Thank you, Bernie." I slipped in behind the counter to check the schedule.

In reception Janice Fleiger shifted uncomfortably in the wooden chair. With a dramatic sigh, she glanced at her watch.

"Where's Hughie?" I whispered.

"I don't know. Do you think I should call?" Bernie's eyes were round with worry. Dr. Doucette was never late.

The hospital doors suddenly flew open as the cannons of Tchaikovsky's 1812 Overture fired from the speakers overhead. The blast of fresh air tickled the feather toys and sent wayward cat hairs scurrying for quiet corners. Face flushed and tie askew, my rumpled boss tore through reception carrying an orange garbage bag under one arm. Sullivan's head poked through one end while his tail thumped enthusiastically against the other. Hughie nodded but didn't break stride as he disappeared into the bowels of the hospital.

"Oh no…not again!" I whispered to Bernie.

Mrs. Fleiger rose expectantly then clutched her throat. A spasm of pain crossed her face. "What's that smell?" She looked at the door through which Hughie just disappeared.

Bernie grabbed Sylvester's medical chart. "Why don't we get the two of you settled in the exam room, luv?"

Mrs. Fleiger picked up the cat carrier with one hand and held a scarf to her nose with the other. Trailing behind, Bernie grabbed the bottle of Cherry Orchard concentrate and sprayed the air.

I followed Hughie to the treatment area where a crowd had gathered. The unmistakable odour was much stronger here. Its epicentre was immersed in the stainless steel tub. Long gooey strands of feces clung to his wavy coat like garlands on a Christmas tree. Poor Sullivan. His smooth-coated counterparts were just as motivated to roll in poop but the effects were not as profound.

"I think he ate some too!" Hughie fumed as he rolled up his shirt sleeves. To a cat, voiding is a necessary evil. Do it quickly, hide the evidence and vacate the area. Dogs on the other hand view body waste, anyone's body waste, as an opportunity. Living in a wooded area with wildlife provided lots of opportunity. Hughie poured a generous amount of shampoo over Sullivan and began to scrub.

"Mrs. Fleiger is here," I announced.

"Oh?" Hughie looked at me as the rest of the staff quickly dispersed. "Em, could you finish bathing him?"

Sullivan gazed at me with mournful eyes. He loved to swim but warm water and soap was a different situation entirely. "Hughie, this is the third time this month."

"Yes, but Em, Mrs. Fleiger is a good client. Odd," he added thoughtfully, "but good. She doesn't like to be kept waiting. I'd do it for you."

"I don't have a dog."

"Ah, Emily," Hughie sighed with exaggerated patience. "You have to look at the bigger picture. It's the principle of the thing. The dog is merely a metaphor." He waited but when I didn't respond he raised the stakes.

"Friday afternoon off?"

"Deal!" I took the gloves and smiled at Sullivan. Shedding his soiled lab coat for a fresh one, Hughie grabbed a stethoscope and bolted down the hall to the exam room.

"Cherry-flavoured dog shit, Dr. Doucette," a high, shrill voice complained. "And me with environmental sensitivities!"

I finished rinsing Sullivan, then rubbed him down with a thick beach towel. He may have hated the bath but he loved to be blown dry. Perched on a stool, he closed his eyes while the hot air rippled through his fur. As his thick, long coat began to dry he looked more like a cloud than a Jack Russell terrier.

"Dr. McBride?" Hilary peeked around the corner. "Harold's splint needs to be changed."

"Why? Is it loose?" I asked above the loud hum of the dryer.

"No." Hilary wrinkled her nose, a gesture that could mean only one thing.

I tuned off the dryer and lowered the freshly-minted Sullivan onto the floor. He danced in excitement as I reached into the cat food bag for his special après-bath treat. Holding the kibble in his mouth, he raced back to the office where it could be enjoyed away from the evil tub. I joined Hilary in the surgical ward. Harold was fast asleep in his litter box along with several coiled mounds of stool. The white bandage covering his splint was smeared in feces.

"Harold, Harold," I moaned. Cats were supposed to have more sense.

Harold opened one eye then resumed his snooze.

"Dr. McBride?" Bernie tapped on the window. "The lab just called. They lost the culture results for your patient in isolation with the bloody diarrhea."

I sighed.

"And here's the chart for your next patient."

I glanced at the chart and noticed with relief it was a routine check-up for a healthy kitten with normal bowel movements. Inside the exam room, Mr. and Mrs. Noble and their three-year-old daughter, Helena, were waiting with Princess. We chatted amiably for a few minutes while Helena kept opening the door and peering down the hallway. When I began to examine the kitten, she stopped fidgeting and grabbed her father's pant leg.

"Daddy, what is she doing?"

"Well, Dr. McBride is going to examine Princess and give her a vaccination to make her strong. Just like your doctor does," Mr. Noble explained.

"But where's the kitty doctor?" Helena persisted.

Puzzled, Mr. Noble looked at his daughter. "Dr. McBride is the kitty doctor, sweetheart."

"No! I mean the real kitty doctor!" Helena pointed accusingly at me. "She's not a kitty!" The parents exchanged worried glances as a storm gathered on Helena's face.

"Honey," Mrs. Noble made one last valiant effort, "Mommy didn't explain very well. Dr. McBride is the lady doctor who looks after kitties. Isn't that exciting?"

I smiled my biggest, widest smile. Kids, after all, liked me. Helena looked up at my face and burst into tears. Clearly, I was no substitute for a well-educated Siamese in a lab coat.

"She's been sick," her mother whispered apologetically.

Helena sobbed throughout the entire visit. The intestinal bug that had infiltrated her daycare, causing cramps and diarrhea, reared its ugly head. Mrs. Noble excused herself and ushered Helena to the washroom while I finished my examination of Princess. Helena was still whimpering by the end of the appointment but managed, at her father's urging, to disengage a shriveled thumb from her mouth and wave good-bye.

Outside, the glorious day had deteriorated. Sunlight pouring in through the windows faltered, rallied, then disappeared for good behind a horde of black clouds. Inside wasn't much better. Susan stomped by, muttering something about a mixed-up supply order. In the office, Hughie glared at the phone in his hand then pressed the speed redial.

"Still busy!" he seethed as I grabbed a pen. "Why do they tell me to call then yack on the phone with someone else for half an hour! I've got a surgery to do."

"Yoo hoo! Dr. McBrrrrride!" Bernie trilled. "There you are, dear. Will you be able to see a drop-in? They've just come in from the country so they don't have an appointment."

"What's wrong with their cat?" I narrowed my eyes.

"Diarrhea?"

"Ooooh, no dear. I think they just want a rabies vaccination." Bernie removed her bifocals. "They read about you in the *Tatamagouche Times*!" she added with a touch of pride.

"Fans?" Hughie looked up.

"Oh. Well, okay!" I replied, flattered. My public needed me. "I just need to change Harold's splint first. That shouldn't take too long."

Predictably, I was wrong. Harold was resistant to change. I had to sedate him first before removing the old bandage and reapplying a new one over the splint. Almost half an hour had passed by the time I was ready for my appointment. Reaching for the clipboard, I glanced at the chart. "Mr. and Mrs. Tid," it read. "From Tidsville." Their cat was none other than Titus Tid III. I shook my head. Feeling a bit giddy, I opened the door and introduced myself to the Tid trio.

"Hi. I'm Dr. McBride. Sorry to keep you waiting."

"Ethel Tid." A tall woman with tightly permed hair nodded towards her husband in the corner. "That's Tobias. One in the carrier's Titus." Apparently, Mrs. Tid spoke for all the Tids.

"How's the big, handsome boy?" I cooed.

"Just fine, thank you," Mr. Tid beamed. Mrs. Tid glared at him.

"Titus don't like the vitnery much," she continued, folding her arms across her chest. Mr. Tid's head bobbed in vigorous, but silent, agreement.

"Okay, then." I rubbed my hands together. "Let's have a look." I opened the kennel door. "C'mon, Titus," I urged, "time to come out and be a brave boy."

The Tidsville Terror had no intention of either coming out

or being a brave boy. I exhausted my bag of tricks and still Titus remained in his carrier, teeth glistening. His front paw was raised like a viper ready to strike.

"Whew!" I tucked a damp curl behind my ear and looked up at the Tids. "I'm just going to get one of the technicians to help me. I'll be right back."

As I eased the door shut, I heard Mr. Tid whisper, "I guess she's better with cows."

I collected a thick towel, gloves, and reinforcement, then headed back to the disillusioned Tids. Hilary, seasoned veteran of cat rebellion, suggested we remove the top half of the carrier.

"Good idea!" I smiled at Hilary. "Why didn't I think of that?"

Why indeed? The Tids exchanged knowing glances as Hilary and I removed the twelve plastic screws holding the two molded halves of the carrier together. Once exposed, Titus lost his bravado and allowed me to examine him.

The Tids watched in silence as I weighed Titus then probed his mouth, throat, and ears. I listened to his heart. I checked the condition of his skin, palpated his internal organs, and took his temperature. Surely, I must be gaining their confidence. Titus was putty in my hands. Before injecting the rabies vaccine into his left hind leg, I warned the Tids it might sting a little. Titus never even whimpered.

Instead, he began to drool, small amounts at first, then viscous rivers that dangled from his chin. Smacking his lips, he leapt onto the floor where he paced frantically. When he started to pant, I realized Titus was in trouble. I had seen an anaphylactic vaccine reaction only once before. The body's immune system overreacts, causing severe agitation, sometimes accompanied by vomiting and diarrhea. As blood pressure falls and heart rate rises, the patient goes into shock. Death can occur in just a few minutes.

Grabbing the emergency kit, I explained this to the horrified Tids. Titus had stopped pacing and started crying. His mournful howl brought them both to their feet. As I drew up some epinephrine to reverse the reaction, Titus began to retch. His sides heaved in and out like an accordion, faster and faster until finally a torpedo tube of matted fur shot out of his mouth. This was followed by an assortment of grasshopper parts.

Leaving the mess for someone else to clean up, Titus jumped into a chair and began washing his face. The unused syringe lay slack in my hand. While Titus' performance was certainly a show-stopper, it was not an anaphylactic vaccine reaction.

I took a deep breath. "Well. That was a bit of excitement, wasn't it?"

The Tids were silent.

I reached for a tube of fur ball remedy from the shelf. It worked by coating any fur a cat ingested while grooming, thus allowing it to pass smoothly through the digestive system. Most cats loved the taste.

"It won't help with the grasshoppers, though," I smiled in a feeble attempt at humour.

Wordlessly, Mrs. Tid took the tube from my hand. Picking up the carrier, she turned to her husband. "Come along, Tobias."

Mr. Tid leapt to his feet.

"Let me know if Titus develops any problems," I called out as Mrs. Tid departed, husband and cat in tow.

Of course, Titus Tid the Third from Tidsville developed problems. Just before closing, an agitated Mrs. Tid called to say Titus had rabies. He was foaming at the mouth and running all over the house like a crazy thing. Mr. Tid wrenched his knee chasing after him and was now confined to the sofa. He couldn't even go to the bathroom by himself, and she, Mrs. Tid, certainly wasn't able to carry him.

Bernie assured Mrs. Tid that Titus could not get rabies from his vaccination but recommended that I re-examine him. Mrs. Tid grew even more agitated at the mention of my name.

Bernie held her hand over the mouthpiece. "Mrs. Tid wants you to do a house call."

"What? I'm not driving to Tidsville!"

"No, no, dear. They're just a wee bit down the road. At Mrs. Tid's cousin's. And Mrs. Tid doesn't drive after dark."

As it turned out, a wee bit down the road was near the grain elevators. Properties were cheaper here because of the rats, the graveyard, and the noisy proximity to the dockyards. Prostitution was a seasonal problem.

Armed only with an angler's fishnet, I picked my way along the path leading to the house. Broken concrete pavers alternately rose and fell, sometimes disappearing altogether. The only light came from the flickering blue glow of a TV in the living room. At the steps, I paused and tested my weight against the frail boards. When I looked up, a tall figure was silhouetted in the doorway.

Startled, I grabbed the railing for support. "Oh, hello," I gasped, recognizing Mrs. Tid's sparse frame. I navigated the last few steps and slipped inside. Mrs. Tid closed the door behind me and pointed to a closet at the end of a long, narrow hall.

"He's in there."

The route was dimly lit by a single bulb overhead. I hesitated, then clutching my fishnet, began inching forward. Mrs. Tid remained by the door in case a quick escape was necessary.

Decades earlier, someone had painted the walls an institutional mustard. I passed a row of faded rectangles, the ghosts of pictures past, then came upon a large iron grate in the floor. Hot air blasted from the furnace below. I would have loved to linger there. My grandmother's home had been heated in the same way. In cold weather, I used to stand on the grate as forced hot air blew up my pant legs, enveloping me in its warmth. But in my grandmother's house, no child had ever been swallowed alive by the furnace. There was always apple pie and ice cream, and a series of fox terriers named Skippy. I had no reason to believe anyone in the Tid household was concerned about my well-being or maintained the grate. I hesitated, then leapt over the grate and continued down the hall as the closet loomed ever closer. The light flickered but remained lit.

At the door of the closet, I paused to listen. If Titus was having some kind of fit, he was having a quiet one. Crouching on my hands and knees, I opened the door a crack and peered inside.

Fortunately, the closet possessed electricity. I flicked on the switch and cautiously opened the door a crack. Titus was nowhere to be seen until I lifted up an old tarp. A pair of green orbs stared balefully at me.

"Titus," I said softly. "There you are. Good boy."

Titus lunged. Raising the fishnet for protection, I leapt backwards against the door which came to a sudden stop against Ethel Tid who had apparently slipped down the hall for a better view. When the dust had cleared, Titus was in the net and Mrs. Tid had an awe-inspiring welt on her forehead.

Although Titus complained bitterly about a second examination in one day, I could find nothing wrong with him. I did notice a lump of stool clinging to the long fur on his backside.

While Mrs. Tid held him down, I cut it off with a pair of scissors.

"Where'd that come from?" Mr. Tid had wandered in to the hallway to watch the proceedings.

Mrs. Tid shook her head in disbelief. "Where does it look like it come from?" she spat.

Mr. Tid wisely hobbled back to the living room.

Mrs. Tid turned her attention to me. "Says this stuff can cause diarrhea." She held up an empty tube.

"Yes, that's true," I replied. "You should only give a small amount every second day. The main ingredient is mineral oil."

"I bin cleanin' up shit all night."

"Oh."

In the silence which followed, at least Titus seemed happy. Once freed of his Klingon, a word we borrowed from Star Trek to describe a particularly tenacious piece of poo, he relaxed and wrapped himself around Mrs. Tid's legs in the pursuit of food. I hadn't known what to expect on this house call and was rather pleased with myself for Titus' instant recovery.

Mrs. Tid escorted me to the door. A cold ocean fog shrouded the city and seeped through my clothes. Hugging my body to keep warm, I stepped into the night and began the perilous journey back to my car.

From the step, a lone figure with an ice pack pressed to her forehead called to me, her words echoing down the street.

"An' you needn't think I'm payin' for this visit neither!"

Chapter 15

I AM, BY NATURE, a worrier. A firm believer in Murphy's Law. I chew the dry skin around my fingernails and have more than my fair share of grey hairs. When my mother warned me that Uncle Mortimer worried himself into a heart attack, I hung "Desiderata" in the office, a daily reminder in gilt-edged parchment to "go placidly amid the noise and haste." In the late sixties and early seventies, "Desiderata" was standard issue in university dorms as students tried on new beliefs and values. Today, its simple message of nurturing inner peace was often lost among my stack of files to be updated, patients to be seen, and a constantly ringing phone.

I glanced through my next patient's medical records. Misty Love: her name always evoked images of an exotic dancer, not a cat, although with one green eye and one blue she could certainly be considered exotic. Her owner, Mark, was a graduate student in biology. To make ends meet, he worked part-time as a teaching assistant and on weekends he cleaned the biology building. Thanks to his close ties with the janitorial staff and a shared enthusiasm for poker, Mark was able to rescue Misty from the university's research colony.

Mark and his wife, Julie, shared their tiny attic apartment with several species including a parrot named Yves who, in the wee hours of the morning, liked to imitate an air-raid siren. This was followed in quick succession by a bomb whistling through the air and an impressive explosion. As the cats scurried for cover, Yves would laugh maniacally and call himself a naughty bird. One night, Misty managed to pluck several tail feathers from this avian psychopath and earned a nip at the base of her glorious, feather-duster tail. Although treated with antibiotics, the small wound was slow to heal. Misty seemed to be eating less and sleeping more, but Mark attributed this to tension in the apartment. Yves was the kind of bird to hold a grudge.

Now the small, delicate creature stretched out on the exam table was struggling for air. There was panic in her eyes as she looked from Mark to me, her sides heaving.

"How long has she been like this?" I asked, listening to her chest and lungs.

"It just started a few hours ago. She was really quiet yesterday but I didn't want to bother you on a Sunday." A long strand of shoulder-length hair escaped Mark's ponytail, brushing his face as he leaned forward to rub Misty's chin.

I palpated her belly. "Has she eaten anything today?"

"No. Nothing since yesterday."

Unlike most of my clients who wanted to know what was wrong with their pet as soon as I entered the room, Mark was quiet. His watchful eyes never left the little white cat on the table. As I continued my examination, I became reasonably certain she hadn't swallowed anything that was blocking her airway. Her temperature was normal and her heart, although pumping rapidly, sounded fine.

I straightened up. "We need to do some X-rays right away, Mark. I'd also like to take some blood for a feline leukemia test."

"Do you think she's infected?" he asked.

It was a simple question but the answer was complex. It would influence how we treated Misty and ultimately determine the outcome. Feline leukemia is an AIDS-type virus that affects the immune system, making infected cats susceptible to many other health problems. Some cats are able to fight off the virus on their own; others become persistently infected. For them, there is no cure.

"I hope not," I answered. I scooped Misty into my arms. "Do you want to wait or should I call you with the results?"

"I'll wait," he replied without hesitation.

In the treatment area, we drew 0.2 ml of blood for the test. Even the mild stress of this procedure forced Misty into open-mouth breathing. Unlike their extroverted canine counterparts, cats rarely pant. While Susan ran the test, Hilary and I set up for X-rays. Getting good resolution was difficult. We had to time exposures in between her shallow rapid breaths. Finally, after three attempts, we had acceptable X-rays. Hilary rinsed the films under the tap and slipped them onto the viewer.

"Oh," she said.

I joined Hilary in the darkened room. We stood beside each other in silence as I studied the portrait of shadows that was Misty. Radiology has always held an air of finality for me. Invisible beams of energy slice through skin, soft tissue, and bone. Their silent passage reveals the innermost secrets of the body's core, a black and white view not softened by the gentle muting of colour. Misty's spine glowed white, her ribs fanning out like the prongs on a rake. Her intestines were empty and appeared as darkened coils within her abdomen. But in her chest, a large greyish mass was squeezing out her lungs for space. No wonder she was having trouble breathing. As I studied the X-rays and the extent of the mass, Susan poked her head into radiology.

"It's positive," she said quietly.

She waited. Water dripped from the X-ray films onto the collecting tray below. I removed the first pair of X-rays and slipped a second pair in their place. Taken at a different angle, they nonetheless showed the same invasive growth.

"Okay." I flicked the switch on the viewer and the grim pictures disappeared. "Let's get a fluid sample."

While Susan held Misty, Hilary shaved a small patch of fur on her chest then prepped the area. With a fine-gauge needle, I withdrew some fluid and prepared a slide. Under the microscope, it was filled with completely abnormal blood cells, confirming the diagnosis.

Back in the exam room, Mark sat beside an untouched cup of coffee. He looked up as I entered.

"It's not good news, Mark." I lowered my voice as if this could somehow soften the impact. "She has a large tumour occupying more than fifty percent of her chest cavity. That's why it's so hard for her to breathe."

Mark sighed and studied his hands.

"It's what we call a mediastinal lymphoma," I continued. "Her thymus gland is cancerous." The thymus gland plays a vital role in the body's immune system. As a graduate biology student, Mark would be well aware of the implications.

"She's positive for feline leukemia too," I added gently. "I suspect the virus probably triggered the cancer. We should test Tyrone to make sure he's not infected. It can be spread from cat to cat in body fluids. I'm sure they probably share a food bowl from time to time or wash each other."

Mark leaned forward in his chair. Elbows resting on his knees and hands clasped against his forehead, he gave no indication he had heard me. The tail on my cat clock clicked back and forth like a metronome, marking each second.

"Are those yours?" he asked suddenly. "On the wall?"

I glanced over my shoulder at the mosaic of my pets, past and present. In the centre, my first pet, Bootsie, lay sprawled illegally in Mom's flower garden. During her twenty-one year reign, Boots ruled the neighbourhood with an iron paw. Fools were not suffered kindly. Yet with me, she endured the humiliation of leash walks, doll clothes, and tea parties. She was driven to these soirees in Barbie and Ken's convertible, which Dad had refitted with the bottom of a large Moir's Mix chocolate box. As I pulled the non-motorized car by a string, Bootsie would gaze serenely from her perch like a queen while we toured the downstairs. Perhaps it was the anticipation of the cat treats at the tea party that encouraged her participation, but she became the confidante and best friend of a lonely, quiet child. When she was finally euthanized, I felt like I had lost a part of myself.

But Misty was only two years old. How much living had she done in a research lab? When had she felt the wind tickle her whiskers with stories? When had she discovered the joy in a windswept leaf? When had she sent a dog three times her size scurrying home to mama?

Mark gripped Misty's harness in both hands. "Is there anything we can do?"

I slipped into the chair beside Mark. "I can make her more comfortable for a few days…to give you and Julie some time to say good-bye."

"No, I mean any long-term treatment?"

"Well," I hesitated. In a study I had read recently, two cats and a dog survived six months before relapse. Most clients chose euthanasia as the humane choice. Chemotherapy drugs were expensive and by their very nature, toxic. There were no guarantees that treatment would be effective.

Mark twisted the wedding band on his finger as I explained the procedure and possible outcomes. For the first time, I noticed his frayed flannel shirt and the worn knees of his corduroy pants.

"Julie's pregnant," he said. "We just found out."

"Oh...congratulations."

Mark allowed himself a brief smile. How well I remembered my own student days of Kraft Dinner and leaking basement apartments. I couldn't imagine trying to support a child while I was still in school.

"Look...let me check into the costs," I added as an idea began to take shape in my mind. "In the meantime, we'll look after Misty and I'll call you this afternoon."

In a country where we take free medical care for granted, it is sometimes difficult to understand the costs associated with medical care for our pets. To become a veterinarian requires a minimum seven years of university. Many support staff, including technicians, receptionists, groomers, kennel attendants, and practice managers, depend on the veterinarian for their livelihood. Overhead expenses, medical supplies, and equipment costs are enormous. Besides being a general practitioner, the vet must also be skilled in radiology, internal medicine, oncology, psychology, anesthesiology, and surgery, to name a few.

Still, veterinarians often give services away, absorbing the costs associated with caring for sick or abandoned animals. Although Hughie preached about charging for services, he was the worst offender, especially with seniors.

My plan was simple. As a specialty practice, Hughie felt we should be on the leading edge of new technologies and therapies.

The key was to spark his interest, show him the obstacles in the way, then sit back and watch as he jumped over them. For good measure, I had a spare ticket to the NBA exhibition game in Halifax next month.

I slipped unseen into the office. Selecting the review article I had recently read on cancer treatments, I laid it on Hughie's desk and filled a bowl full of jelly beans.

After a busy morning, Hughie finally retreated to the office with an egg salad sandwich and shut the door. I paced and fidgeted in the treatment area until I couldn't stand it anymore. Dragging myself into the office, I collapsed in a chair. Hughie was asleep in the other. I sighed loudly and rattled some papers.

When that had no effect, I knocked the stapler off the desk. It landed with a satisfying metal *thunk*. Hughie's eyes flew open.

"Oh, sorry. Were you asleep?"

"No, Em," he rolled his eyes. "I always read with my eyes shut and my mouth open."

"What were you reading?" I asked innocently.

Hughie wiped the corner of his mouth where a tiny drop of drool glistened. "Actually," he began, rummaging through the disarray on his desk, "a review article of cancer protocols."

"Really? Did you hear about Misty Love?"

"I know she's in the hospital." Hughie peered at me over the rims of his reading glasses. "What's wrong with her?"

"Cancer. Thymus gland. We're probably going to euthanize her tomorrow. Mark just wanted his wife to see her."

"Where's his wife?" Hughie asked.

"In the hospital." This was not a complete lie. Julie worked part-time in the hospital gift shop.

"Is she all right?"

"Pregnant," I sighed.

"Oh...." Hughie took a bite of his sandwich and changed the subject. Female things were best left to females. "How big is the tumour?"

"More than half of her chest."

Hughie whistled under his breath. "You know, Em, what an odd coincidence. I was just reading about the treatment of mediastinal lymphoma."

"I mentioned chemotherapy to Mark."

"And?" Hughie sat upright, his eyes bright.

"Well, they're both students," I sighed again. "They don't have the money."

Hughie nodded. "Chemo can be expensive."

I stared sadly at the floor, waiting for Hughie to say more. When he didn't, I forged ahead.

"I think Mark's worried about putting Misty through more pain for only four to six months, maybe less."

"But maybe more, Em! I know four to six months may not seem like much but if it's good quality time...."

"I know."

"And lots of pets do great. There's such a stigma attached to chemo. But anytime we treat a disease with drugs, that's chemotherapy. Would you not treat your cat for worms? Would you not give heart medication? Thyroid medication? Antibiotics?" Hughie's eyes glowed with conviction. "It's all chemotherapy."

"I know."

"If Melody was miserable, dying, and you could give her four to six months, good months, would you?"

"Yes, but...."

"Em! We have to look at the big picture. We need to face

disease, not run from it! Cancer doesn't have to mean the end of the road." Hughie tore a bite off his sandwich and began chewing with enthusiasm.

This was my boss at his best – a zealous visionary. It was time to reel him in.

"So…can I order the drugs?"

Hughie swallowed and gagged. Sullivan scrambled to clean up the little bits of egg that flew onto the floor.

"I'd like to help, Em. I really would. But I can't just do all this for…for…*free*!" he sputtered, throwing his hands into the air. "It'll probably cost over a thousand if you count veterinary services!"

"I know, but…."

"No. I'm sorry." Hughie checked his watch. "Oops. I've got to get going." He wiped his mouth with a paper napkin and left the room.

I kicked off my shoes and savagely bit into an apple. Only the mauled core was left when Hughie poked his head back into the office a few minutes later.

"When were you going to offer the NBA ticket?"

I threw the remains of my apple at him. "How did you know?"

"Because I'm God-like, Em. Omnipotent. All-knowing." Hughie grinned, then his expression became serious. "See if Mark can make payments on the wholesale cost of the drugs. We'll provide the veterinary services at no charge."

I looked at my boss. Hughie bore the perpetually windblown look of a busy man: the tousled hair, the five o'clock shadow at one o'clock, the bulging pocketful of memos. Balancing a business with a big heart was not always easy.

"Thanks," I said quietly.

Susan's abrupt "Dr. D!" yanked him away then. Within minutes, the noon hour lull gave way to the busy hum of people at work. A centrifuge rumbled, water ran as surgical instruments were scrubbed, doors opened and closed. From deep within the Cat Nap Inn, a lonesome boarder stretched his vocal cords. And tomorrow, a small-for-her-age white research cat would get a second chance.

The drugs arrived in the morning: cyclophosamide, vincristine, and cytosine arabinoside. The fourth drug used in the protocol, prednisone, was a steroid we normally stocked in our own pharmacy. The bottles looked harmless but I hoped the lethal combination would destroy the advancing tumour.

"Where's Hughie?" I asked, as we sedated Misty for the first of six weekly treatments.

"He called this morning to say he wouldn't be in," Susan answered, deftly inserting a catheter into Misty's vein. The drug would be delivered through the catheter into Misty's bloodstream. With the patient sedated, there was no chance that the needle could slip out of the vein, allowing its poisonous cargo to destroy the surrounding tissue.

We were silent for a moment. The procedure demanded concentration and precision.

"Good," I breathed, capping the empty syringe and placing it in the hazardous waste disposal.

"So, is he sick?" I asked, thinking of the busy day ahead. My own schedule was daunting. I had precious little time to see Hughie's patients as well.

"I don't know. He didn't say." Susan removed the catheter from Misty's leg and applied light pressure with her thumb and forefinger to prevent bleeding. As if reading my thoughts, she added, "We rescheduled most of his appointments."

Placing the stethoscope on Misty's chest, I rechecked her heart rhythm. "Sounds good." Grabbing a pen, I began updating her chart.

"Uh, oh. Dr. McBride!" Susan called out in alarm. I turned to see Misty's sides heave and her neck arch as she lay on the table.

"Get her upright," I ordered. "She's probably going to vomit." While nausea and vomiting are not uncommon with cancer drugs, Misty was still unconscious. I didn't want any fluid to drain back into her lungs and cause pneumonia.

Misty's tiny body struggled against the nausea until finally a river of bile erupted from her mouth. We washed her face and white bib, now stained yellow. Limp and exhausted, she lay in her kennel for the rest of the day, refusing even a tiny lick of food. Mark and Julie spent the entire evening with her. Julie sat in a chair, her hand caressing Misty's head through the open kennel door. Just before closing, Mark stepped out of the recovery ward and taking me aside, confessed that they were considering euthanasia.

"She's so sick," he said quietly. "If you could see what she's normally like and then to see her like this. . . ." Mark shook his head. "I appreciate everything you and Dr. Doucette have done for her. And for us. But maybe I'm just being selfish. Maybe it's her time."

"I'll do whatever you think is best, Mark. It's your decision."

"She's been through so much." Mark thought for a moment. "What would you do?"

I'm often asked this question when clients are faced with difficult decisions. I wish I had a crystal ball. The decision to end a life can only be made if the purpose is to end incurable pain and suffering. The difficulty is knowing, with a certainty that frees us, when that time has arrived.

In the recovery ward, Misty lay still, her eyes closed against the reality of a stainless steel kennel, the nausea, the bewilderment of disease. Mark gazed through the window, unable to penetrate that emotional space into which sick cats retreat. Shoulders hunched and hands thrust deep inside his pockets, he struggled in silence. Finally he turned back to me, a decision made.

"I can't give up until I know she has," he said softly.

We agreed that if her condition worsened over the next forty-eight hours, I would euthanize her.

I stayed late that night. I wanted to keep an eye on my patient, and I had a bloodthirsty backlog of paperwork. Long after the staff had gone, I heard a key turn in the lock and then the patter of toenails. Sullivan poked his head into the office. Seeing a familiar face, he plastered his ears against his head while his little behind wiggled a doggy dance of joy. Hughie joined us a few minutes later.

"You're here late, Em. How's Misty?"

"Well…we'll see. She was in rough shape after her first treatment. Where have you been all day? It was crazy here! You've got a ton of messages!"

Hughie nodded as he pored over several files then checked the message board. Satisfied there was nothing urgent, he began searching the library shelves. Tired of waiting, Sullivan barked at the box of dog biscuits on the desk. I reached inside to give him one.

"Oh, Em." Hughie turned around quickly. "He can't have any hard food."

"How come?" I looked at Sully whose eyes were bright with

anticipation. Drool began to form in the corners of his mouth at the unexpected delay.

"He just had a biopsy done. I found a lump in his mouth when I was brushing his teeth a few days ago. I'm really sorry about the short notice," Hughie apologized. "Bridgeview called this morning to say they could squeeze him in."

Instantly, I regretted my annoyance over Hughie's absence today. "You should have told me! Is he okay? Did you get the results?"

"Yeah." Hughie whistled for Sully who leapt from the floor into his arms. Cradling the little terrier under one arm, he picked up his briefcase with the other and stood in the doorway. The light from the hall silhouetted his tall frame and cast a shadow across his face.

"It's a fibrosarcoma."

The words dropped like an anchor.

"Oh, my God!" I breathed.

A fibrosarcoma is an aggressive tumour with long tendrils that invade the surrounding healthy tissue. Sullivan's only chance would be surgical removal of part of his jaw. The procedure and the months following surgery would be painful. The success rate was low. Yet to do nothing would sentence him to six months at most.

Blissfully unaware of his fate, Sully stared at the box of biscuits, his little tail stump quivering in excitement. It was hard to believe anything was wrong.

"What are you going to do?" I asked at last.

Hughie hesitated. "I don't know. The surgery itself is risky and it'll be putting him through hell for whatever little bit of time he might have left. If I do nothing, he'll be dead in four to six months. Jesus."

Before I could say anything else, Hughie left. I heard the lock turn in the door and then silence. Staring at the chart in front of me, I wished I could erase this day between yesterday and tomorrow. I missed having a dog of my own and loved to doggy-sit when Hughie was away or tied up at work. Sullivan was an irrepressible little fellow. He made people smile with his rolling gait, perky ears, and appetite for life. Althea had once told me that Hughie's only request in his divorce settlement had been to keep Sullivan, the three cats, and the Jeep.

I picked up Sully's little doggy T-shirt that lay draped over a chair. "LIFE'S SHORT, BITE HARD" it declared in bold, red letters. It was a catchy phrase that embodied the beliefs of a modern society, a sentiment that sold fancy cars, soft drinks, and extreme sports. But for Misty and Sullivan, it was so much more.

When I got home that night, I called Hughie, but there was no answer. Picking up my well-worn copy of The *Wind in the Willows* by Kenneth Grahame, I read for a little while. One rainy summer between Grade Eight and Grade Nine, I had discovered Toad, Ratty and Mole while rooting through my oldest brother's room. This gentle tale of love and friendship was my safe place in the storm of adolescence. Even now it could whisk me away to a time before anybody I loved died or left.

I was tired but, when I turned out the light, my mind was unwilling to let go of the day. Melody, Lionel, and Mickey were draped over me. It was a cool night and I was grateful for their warmth.

When I arrived at work the following morning, I was expecting the worst. Instead, Misty had devoured a plate of food. Thirty hours after her first treatment, she was demanding to be let out of her kennel. Forty-eight hours after treatment, she was clinically normal. Chest X-rays revealed a ninety-five percent reduction in the size of the tumour. It was that simple.

Meanwhile, at the Atlantic Veterinary College, Sullivan underwent surgery to remove most of his lower right jaw. Hughie stayed in Charlottetown a few days to be with him. The surgery went well but Sully was very depressed and in a great deal of pain afterward. According to the harried fourth-year student on ward duty that night, Sullivan was "adorable but very needy." When Hughie offered to keep Sully at the motel the second night, the hospital manager readily agreed.

The Sullivan who returned to Ocean View Cat Hospital was a very different creature from the one who left. He slept his days away in a wicker basket surrounded by untouched toys. Water poured out the side of his mouth when he tried to drink. He showed no interest in food and had to be hand-fed. Hughie blamed himself for making a selfish decision and ruining what little time Sully had left.

The return of the Jack Russell spirit was gradual, marked by the occasional theft of cat food or the frenzied outburst of a squeaky toy in the office. And there were unexpected benefits. Without the stabilizing influence of a lower right jaw, Sullivan's bark was now accompanied by a menacing sneer. His status among the neighbourhood dogs rose considerably.

The day he arrived at work in an orange garbage bag, we celebrated.

Linked by time and disease, both Sullivan and Misty defied the odds. Maybe they were blessed with extraordinary immune systems. Or maybe they were just lucky. But they are the survivors and they give us courage. It is not the courage to cheat death, because death is inevitable, but the courage to face life.

"You are a child of the universe, no less than the trees and the stars; you have a right to be here. And whether or not it is clear to you, no doubt the universe is unfolding as it should."

Chapter 16

"So, Doc...do you love animals?"

Stethoscope to my ears as I listened to Reggie's heart, I smiled in response.

"Ever been arrested for it?" Jack "just call me J.C." Cruickshank bent over at the waist and shook in silent appreciation of his own wit. While I continued to examine his cat, Mr. Cruickshank pulled a hanky out of his pocket and wiped away the tears.

"Ah," he sighed, "I've been waitin' to use that one."

"It's a zinger," I agreed.

I finished clipping Reggie's toenails. The little cat jumped onto the floor and lovingly rubbed figure eights through Mr. Cruickshank's bowed legs.

"So Doc, how's my boy?" he asked, bending down to pat Reggie.

"Well, Mr. Cruickshank...J.C.," I added hastily as a pair of bushy eyebrows was raised to their full height. "Reggie's in great shape. And he's not cryptorchid."

"But Doc! He's gotta be," J.C. protested. "Cecil said he was. Just like P.C."

Ah, Cecil. Halifax's own cat guru. Cecil had become a legend among the cat-loving patrons of his neighbourhood pub thanks to his own cat's unusual anatomy. Talk which normally centred on women, beer, sports, and combinations thereof, now included cats. If Cecil didn't know the answer, he would call his good friend Emily. While he supplemented my advice with his own recommendations, Ocean View had seen a significant influx of new clients, for which we were grateful.

"Well," I grinned, "even the great ones can make mistakes."

J.C. remained unconvinced. "Doc, I bin in the navy for twenty years. Seen a lot of things." He thrust Reggie's hind end in my face. "An' there's somethin' I don't see here."

"There's a good reason for that," I replied, brushing Reggie's tail out of my face.

J.C. leaned forward. "Has he got some strange disease?"

"*He* is a *she*."

"What? No way, Doc. I mean, he does guy things."

"Oh?" I peered at J.C. over the top of my glasses. "Like what?"

"Well, he…he…you know," J.C. stammered.

I drew my eyebrows together in a thoughtful frown as J.C. fidgeted. A rose-coloured flush spread upwards from his neck and boiled over into scarlet on his cheeks. In vain, he searched for the politically correct word.

"He humps things!" J.C. spluttered at last.

"Humps things?" I asked. "M'mm. What kind of things?"

"Jeez, Doc. Does it matter?" J.C. wiped his forehead.

"Oh, yes!" I nodded, trying to keep a straight face. "It could be very significant." J.C. looked miserable. His sexual bravado didn't extend much beyond off-colour jokes.

"Well…," he squirmed. "I guess blankets."

"Patterned or solid?" I asked.

"What?"

"The blankets. Does Reggie prefer solid colours or patterns?"

J.C. cleared his throat. "Solids. He likes the yellow one on the wife's bed."

"I see. Anything else?"

J.C. hesitated. "The wife's new bowling bag. There was hell to pay over that one," he added.

Even though I had only been teasing, it suddenly occurred to me that Reggie might be jealous of J.C.'s wife. J.C. seemed to think this was hilarious and immediately volunteered to "get rid of the old girl" for Reggie's sake.

"She could also have a urinary tract infection," I explained. "We can check her urine when she's in for her spay. Or she may just have growing pains. Reggie's not sexually mature yet. She may just be a little confused, like your typical teenager."

"I was never confused, Doc," J.C. winked.

"Uh huh." I clicked my pen with a flourish.

Whistling, J.C. stuffed Reggie through the narrow door of the homemade carrier that Mrs. Cruickshank had picked up at a flea market. With a shingled roof and painted flower boxes under the screen windows, it looked more like a portable dollhouse. Reggie's worried face loomed large behind the lace curtains Mrs. Cruickshank had added.

"Let's go, sweetheart." J.C. opened the door leading into reception. "See ya, Doc." Reggie wailed mournfully as she rose and fell with his rolling gait.

"Hello, girls," I heard him call out to the staff. "You love animals?"

Shaking my head, I closed the exam room door.

On Friday of that week, Hughie and I enjoyed our usual lunch at Cecil's. As always, the food was simple but delicious. Cecil had prepared an apple crisp especially for me and beamed when I confessed it was better than my mother's. I took a sip of my Coke and leaned back in the booth.

"Hughie, do you love animals?"

Hughie opened his mouth to answer, then blanched and shrunk in his seat. A beautiful, long-legged brunette had just entered the pub. Her emerald eyes flickered over each table. Hughie studied his empty plate as her heels clicked mercilessly against the hardwood floor, coming to rest at our booth. After a moment of silence, he looked up.

"Michele," he said with a tight smile.

"Douce. Thought I'd find you here." The gorgeous face turned to me. "You must be Emily."

I reached for her outstretched hand.

"I'm the ex," she said, adding, "you may have heard of me?"

"Yes. Of course."

"May I sit down?"

Catching my eye, Hughie shook his head back and forth.

"Sure." I shuffled over to make room for Michele. Hughie glared at me.

"So…how are you enjoying Ocean View?" Michele asked, slipping in beside me. She smoothed her skirt, then crossed her legs and looked at me expectantly.

"Oh, very much. I really love working with just cats."

Michele's polite smile made me think she had seen one too many litter boxes.

"So…you're an accountant?" I struggled to keep up the conversation, receiving no help from my sullen boss.

"Yes. Actually, that's why I'm here." Michele turned to Hughie. "Did you fill out those forms I gave you for the year end?"

"Ah…they're not quite done." Hughie glanced at his watch.

"Why not? I gave them to you last month."

"Well, it's been really busy. Em can tell you."

Michele glanced at me.

"Not that busy." I shook my head, enjoying Michele's faint smile of approval.

Her manicured nails tapped against the table as she stared at Hughie. "As you know," she began in the slow measured voice of a parent to a child, "the government does not like to be kept waiting. You could be fined."

"I'll finish them today."

"So, I can pick them up on Monday?"

Hughie squirmed. "How about Tuesday?"

Michele opened her appointment book and made a notation. Hughie leaned forward to read her neat script but jumped back when she snapped the book shut. With an efficient click, the briefcase opened and closed, swallowing the appointment book whole.

Michele stood up. "Nice to meet you, Emily. I'll probably see you again soon." Turning to Hughie, she nodded curtly. "Douce."

"Michele."

Every male head in the pub except one turned as Michele's snug cream-coloured suit and shapely legs left the building. Hughie loosened his tie and slumped against the chair.

I grinned at my boss. "Douce? Is that a pet name? A term of endearment?"

Hughie ignored me. "God, I could use a beer!"

When Michele arrived the following Tuesday, neither the required paperwork nor Hughie could be found. Unsightly red blotches erupted on Michele's face.

"Please tell him," she said sweetly, "to courier them to my office by Friday." The smile never left her face as she leaned over the counter and whispered to Bernie, "Or I'll cut off his balls." Straightening up, she smoothed her suit then picked up her briefcase and left.

A flabbergasted Bernie fanned herself with a brochure on flea control. "Oh, the dear, wee man!" she gasped.

When I left at six that night, the dear, wee man was hunched over a mound of papers. Pen in hand, he alternately sighed and muttered to himself. I had to admire Michele's ability to get the job done.

August 31 dawned a brisk, no-nonsense kind of day that marked the end of two things: Ocean View Cat Hospital's fiscal year and Reggie Cruickshank's ovaries and uterus. The sultry summer heat had been replaced overnight by a blast of arctic air. Michele had commandeered the office, fortifying her stronghold with a sign on the door that said "No Cats." Held hostage by overflowing boxes, laptop computers, a printer, and an adding machine, Hughie sat tucked away in a corner looking miserable as Michele fired questions at him. Sometimes, he smiled in relief and rattled off the answer, but for the most part he mumbled and studied his fingernails.

Mrs. Cruickshank dropped off Reggie at the hospital promptly at nine. Resplendent in her curlers and satin bowling jacket, she explained that J.C. was up to his eyeballs with a flooded toilet in 5C.

"Speaking of which," she said, tapping a nicotine-stained finger on the admission form, "Reggie's litter box smells awful strong, honey. You gonna fix that?"

"Hopefully," I smiled. "I told J.C. that we should check Reggie's urine when she was in for her spay. She might have a bladder infection."

"Sweet Jesus!" Mrs. Cruickshank exclaimed. "I get them! Have to pee every five minutes!" Poking the retired Herb Hennigar in the ribs as he waited in line to buy cat food, she winked "Hard on the sex life too!"

Speechless, poor Herb could only bob his head in agreement.

Grimacing with the memories of her last bladder infection, Mrs. Cruickshank gnawed on a large wad of gum. "Where do you want me to sign, dearie?"

I finished my morning appointments and then pre-medicated Reggie. Her urinalysis, bloodwork, and ECG were all normal so we were proceeding with her spay. Reggie lay on her back. A sterile surgical drape covered all but her shaved belly, now stained golden with disinfectant. Within minutes after beginning the surgery, I had located her ovaries and uterus. Using an instrument which closely resembled my mother's number four crochet hook, I eased them through the opening of the incision. I paused to look more closely.

"Hilary, check these out."

In response to my muffled excitement, Hilary leaned forward. Reggie's uterus was unremarkable but the ovaries at the end of each uterine horn were smooth and darkish-blue. Normal ovaries are a light tan and a bit lumpy from the development of egg follicles.

"They look like testicles."

"They do, don't they?" I explored Reggie's abdomen a bit more but could find nothing unusual.

"Strange," I remarked to Hilary. "They're in the right place for ovaries. I'll send them off to the path lab just to make sure."

I removed the mysterious organs and placed them in a vial of formaldehyde. Along with a medical history, they would be sent to a pathology lab in Guelph, Ontario, and we would have the results in a few days. Then I finished suturing Reggie's abdomen.

As we waited for her to wake up, Hilary began to tidy surgery, humming as she worked. Unused gauze was reshelved. Alcohol and prep solutions were returned to the drawer. The surgical instruments were gathered for cleaning and sterilization in the autoclave.

"Whoa!"

Hilary stopped humming and looked at me in alarm. "What's wrong?"

"It's Reggie's....Can you ask Hughie to come in for a second?"

"Sure." Hilary slipped out of surgery and in less than a minute, reappeared with Hughie. He looked haggard and worn.

"Thank you," he breathed. "What's up?"

"Have a look at her genitals."

Puzzled, Hughie gently probed Reggie's vulva while she was still asleep.

"What the...?" He looked at me in surprise then pulled a pair of reading glasses out of his pocket. Whistling under his breath, he took a closer look at the tiny penis nestled inside Reggie's vagina. "Wow! You read about stuff like this but you never actually see it."

I dangled the floating ovaries in front of him.

"Those look like testicles."

"That's what I thought. They were attached at each end of the uterine horn, right where ovaries should be."

"Has the cat been acting normally?"

I explained that Reggie's urine had a strong odour and that she humped things, according to J.C.

"This is Jack Cruickshank's cat?" Hughie peered at me over his reading glasses.

I nodded.

Hughie began to laugh. He pushed the door open and exited surgery, still laughing. His good humour echoed throughout the treatment area and down the hall until it was abruptly silenced at the entrance to the office.

Reggie's post-op recovery was uneventful. J.C. sounded out of breath when I called him later to discuss Reggie's surgery. "Gimme some good news, Doc."

"Reggie's doing great," I began, "but…there is this one thing."

I began explaining Reggie's peculiar anatomy in detail. The air whistled in and out of J.C.'s nose as he listened intently, trying to digest the information. In the space of a week, Reggie had gone from being cryptorchid, to female, to both male and female. It was a lot to absorb.

In the background, a woman's voice hollered, "What about that smell?"

"What about that smell?" J.C. repeated.

"Well, her urinalysis was normal. My guess would be the testosterone from the testicles was causing the strong odour, just like a tomcat."

"But, you say the testicles…no, I mean them other things, the ovaries…," J.C. sighed. "No, I guess…testicles. You say they were inside Reggie's belly?"

"I think they're testicles. We'll know for sure when we get the lab report back. But yes, they were inside her belly."

"Balls are supposed to be on the outside, right, Doc?" This, at least, was familiar territory.

"That's right. I don't think she would have ever come into heat. And any sperm wouldn't likely survive either. It would have been just too hot for them tucked up inside her abdomen."

There was a minute of silence as J.C. digested this information.

"So Doc," he asked at last. "Are you saying Reggie is a *he* and a *she*? At the same time?"

I hesitated. "Well, yes, I guess that's true. But you don't have to worry. All this happened before she was even born. She's coping quite well."

"Coping?" J.C. began to chuckle. This gave way to belly-wrenching guffaws that left him gasping for air. I held the phone a safe distance from my ear as J.C. cackled and wheezed due, in no small part, to a pack-a-day habit and the enlisted man's pre-occupation with sex.

"Doc?" he finally managed in a choked voice. "Seems to me that cat's got it made. Everything he needs in one place! That's way better'n cryptorchid." Fresh howls erupted, leaving J.C. speechless. He was still howling when he hung up the phone.

"How did it go?" Hughie asked, spying me in the hallway.

"Better than expected. What about you?"

"Better than expected. Michele's not so bad after five cups of coffee and new batteries for her adding machine. Hey," Hughie warned as I continued down the hallway, "Remember she'll be back in the morning for the completed inventory count."

I grimaced. The drug inventory was my responsibility. Hughie had not yet computerized the practice, although he dabbled on his new home computer. His confidence was growing and next year, he promised, the annual all-you-can-count inventory buffet would be just a bad memory. In the meantime, every pill, every can, every piece of gauze had to be counted by hand.

By 10:30 that night, I realized why no one else had chosen the drug inventory. I had been lured by the injectable drugs and tubes of ointment which were easily counted. It was the silent shelf of pills that tested my character. There were antibiotics, anti-depressants, and anti-convulsants. There were steroids, dewormers, pain medications, muscle relaxants, appetite stimulants, heart pills, thyroid pills. All came in bottles of fifty to a thousand pills. All had to be counted before midnight.

I resorted to the professional version of an old birthday party stand-by. Instead of a jar of jelly beans, I studied bottles of pills. I shook them for good measure, then recorded a number unlikely to be challenged like 378 or 691. I never rounded off. By 11:30, I was home snug in bed.

The next morning, a silver BMW pulled into a parking spot right in front of the hospital.

"She's here!" Hilary hissed, returning from Tim's with an armload of treats.

The staff scattered. Stuck on the phone, I could only watch as Michele strode purposefully through the doors, oblivious to the cheerful welcome of the door chimes, and up to the reception counter.

I flashed her a nervous smile while I explained the results of Squiggy's bloodwork to Hilda McCarthy. Unfortunately, Hilda was a nurse and required little explanation. She thanked me and hung up. I considered talking to the dial tone but thought better of it.

"Good morning, Emily." Michele pointed to a large cat food box swathed in duct tape. "Is that for me?"

I nodded. Inside was Ocean View's paper trail for the last twelve months: receipts, cash register tapes, deposit books, accounting journals, bank statements, and cheque stubs. On top lay the completed consumable inventory list.

Michele looked at the box and clicked her tongue. Most of her clients probably just handed over a disk at year end. Reaching inside, she picked up the inventory list and began flipping through.

"Who did the drug count?" she demanded.

"That would be me," I smiled.

"Good." Michele tossed the list into the box. "Because last year the kennel girl did it and I know she just guessed."

I shook my head in disbelief. "Unbelievable."

Hughie peeked around the corner. "Need any help with that box?"

"No. I'm fine." Michele effortlessly lifted the heavy box and headed toward the doors. "I'll be in touch, Douce," she called over her shoulder. It sounded more like a warning than a pleasantry.

The closer Michele got to the door, the further Hughie emerged from the shadows.

"Mitchy, baby!" boomed a familiar voice as the door chimed once again. "Here, let me carry that for you, doll face." J.C. grabbed the box Michele had been carrying.

"Thanks, sweetie," Michele beamed. "What are you doing here?"

"Comin' to visit my cat, Reggie. He had surgery yesterday." J.C. waved at me. "That's his Doc! Hi, Doc."

I smiled and wiggled my fingers in greeting.

"That's my ex," Michele pointed to Hughie, who looked like he'd been hit in the head with a frying pan.

"You two know each other?" he asked, leaning against the wall for support.

"Oh my goodness, yes!" J.C. glowed with enthusiasm. "Mitchy here's our best bowler!"

"Mitchy?" Hughie tried the nickname on for size. "Bowler?" he added in a strangled voice.

"It's for charity!" Michele snapped.

"She has her own ball, too," J.C. added proudly. "With a big silver M."

Standing beside me, I could feel Hughie start to twitch. The corners of his mouth curled upwards ever so slightly as a stifled snort escaped through his nose.

"Sorry," he grinned. "Allergies."

Ignoring him, Michele turned back to J.C. "So, what did your cat need surgery for?" she asked, changing the subject.

"Oh, my!" J.C. winked at me. Balancing the box under one arm, he opened the door for Michele with the other. "I'll tell you the story at practice tonight."

"Don't forget your bowling shoes," Hughie called out to Michele.

A few days later, the pathologist's report confirmed that Reggie had indeed possessed testicles. Dr. Maurice Beaulieu, a serious man as befitting his profession, had signed his name with an unusual flourish. In a rare flirtation with humour, he added that if Reggie was human, he would likely be a cross-dresser.

I decided not to share that with J.C.

Chapter 17

"Dr. McBrr-rride! Dr. McBrr-rride!"

Bernie sprinted the fifty-metre dash from reception to storage in record-breaking time.

"There you are!" she gasped, looking up. I was perched on top of a stepladder in the storage room. An elusive bag of food was just out of my reach.

"A dear, wee puss has just been hit by a car!"

I hopped off the ladder and followed Bernie into the exam room. An attractive woman in her early thirties stood off to one side. Her suit was stained with dark splotches of what appeared to be blood and little bits of fur.

"Oh dear God," she cried when she saw me. "Please help him."

A small orange tabby lay on the table, oblivious to the flurry of activity around him. His long fur was matted with blood, dirt, and bits of leaves. Judging by his thin frame and freckled eyes, he was probably an old-timer.

"Airway's clear," Hilary announced as she bent over him with a laryngoscope.

"What happened?" I asked.

"I didn't see him," the woman sobbed. "He must have been behind the car when I backed up."

I listened to the cat's chest and then checked the colour of his gums. They were pale, indicating he was in shock.

"He's not getting enough oxygen. Susan, set up the oxygen hood," I ordered. Our oxygen hood was a customized Javex bottle. The lower third had been cut away to make room for a cat's head. Oxygen flowed from the tank through a line in the top of the bottle. This arrangement was economical and effective. We could examine the patient while saturating him with oxygen.

When Susan was ready, Hilary and I pulled the blanket under the cat taut, stretcher-like, and carried him into surgery. Susan attached the pulse oximeter to one of the cat's toe pads. The proximity of the blood supply here would allow us to read his blood oxygen levels.

"How old is your cat, Miss...?" I asked. The woman had followed us, her tear-streaked face framed by loose wisps of hair that had escaped a ponytail.

"Sandra. Sandra Smith. I don't know," she sobbed. "He's not my cat."

I heard a crash in the treatment area and then a desperate voice. "Caramel? Caramel?"

Caramel Liebowitz! I knew this cat looked familiar.

"A friend just called me!" Dr. Liebowitz cried. "Is Caramel going to be OK?"

I glanced up. Myles Liebowitz was a gelatinous blob of a man. His careful comb-over now flopped sadly to the side where it dangled like the ear of a basset hound. After his wife died, the former physicist with the National Research Council had moved to Halifax and bought a second-hand bookstore. Caramel came with the shop.

Dr. Liebowitz blinked at me through a sensible pair of black-rimmed glasses held together at the nose junction by a strip of white athletic tape. Using both hands, he carefully removed the glasses and used his wrist to wipe away the sorrow in each eye. He looked at me, his face naked. Then slowly, methodically, he slipped the glasses back over his ears and took a deep breath.

The woman who had been quietly standing in the corner offered him a tissue. "Do you know what happened?" he asked, causing her a fresh outburst of tears.

I turned back to my patient. As pure oxygen flowed into his lungs, Caramel's heart pumped the oxygenated blood throughout his body. His gums returned to a healthier shade of pink. Now that his blood oxygen levels had improved, I could take the time to examine him more closely.

The flesh on his left leg was torn and bleeding in several places. I could feel a lump in his pelvis where the dislocated head of his thigh bone, or femur, had been yanked out of position. On the same side, Caramel's knee was also dislocated. Miraculously, his bladder and other internal organs seemed intact, but we would need to watch his stool and urine output to be sure. Sometimes, nerve damage resulting from trauma was irreparable and not always immediately apparent.

"Dammit!" Susan muttered under her breath as she and Hilary struggled to insert an IV line. "His veins are so tiny."

"That's from the shock," I explained as I drew up the first of a series of drugs.

Working against the clock, Susan and Hilary stubbornly kept trying to raise a vein. Twice they were in but the needle punctured the other side of the narrow vein. On the third attempt, they were successful. The life-sustaining fluids would help raise Caramel's dangerously low blood pressure. Susan let out a deep sigh as we taped the catheter in place. With the fluids now flowing freely, I injected pain-killers and antibiotics to prevent a secondary infection caused by shock.

For the moment, Caramel was stable. While Hilary monitored

his vital signs, I stepped outside to talk to Dr. Liebowitz. Still in her blood-stained clothes, Sandra sat beside him. She looked up at my approach, and in an unconscious gesture, reached for Dr. Liebowitz's hand.

"Caramel is OK for the moment," I began.

"Oh, thank God," she sighed.

Dr. Liebowitz closed his eyes and exhaled. "There, you see," he said turning towards her, "Dr. McBride is an excellent veterinarian."

"He's not out of the woods yet," I cautioned. "I'd like to take some X-rays and keep him on an IV drip for at least twenty-four hours. Then we'll reassess."

"Of course," Dr. Liebowitz nodded. "Whatever you think is best."

"Dr. Liebowitz, I'm going to pay for this," the woman announced. Reaching into her purse she pulled out a credit card. "This is all my fault."

"Nonsense, my dear." Dr. Liebowitz shook his head. "This is no one's fault. Yours is a very kind and generous offer," he added, "but Caramel is my cat and I am responsible for his well being. Put your card away."

"But…," she protested, weakly, I thought.

"No buts," Dr. Liebowitz replied.

If Caramel pulled through, he would need extensive surgery to repair the hip and knee. The medical costs would be high. Although worrying about the hospital's finances was Hughie's albatross, it was a comfort that both parties wanted to pay the bill.

Without warning, Dr. Liebowitz's arms shot forward and grabbed me in an enthusiastic embrace. "Thank you! Thank you, Dr. McBride!" he cried, as I disappeared into a soft cushion of flesh.

"You're welcome," I mumbled from somewhere in the vicinity of his armpit. "I'll call you in the morning with an update."

Smiling, Dr. Liebowitz unlocked his grip. Now that Caramel was at least stable, Sandra suggested she pay for lunch at a small family restaurant just down the street.

"It's the least I can do," she said.

In the morning, Dr. Liebowitz met me at Caramel's kennel with two cups of coffee. "I couldn't wait!" he announced with an apologetic grin. "Isn't it a glorious day, Dr. McBride!"

"Yes, it is. Thank you," I smiled taking a cup from his outstretched hand. He didn't look quite so much like his second-hand books today. A pair of gold-rimmed multifocals had replaced the battle-weary goggles. His pants were neatly pressed and he wore a matching tweed jacket.

"I hear Caramel did very well last night!" he beamed.

"Yes, his bowels and bladder are working fine. That's great news. And he had a big breakfast."

Dr. Liebowitz and Caramel chirped at each other.

"The X-rays confirm a dislocated hip and knee," I continued, "so if Caramel continues to do well today, we'll be able to do the surgery in a couple of days."

"Wonderful! Wonderful!" Dr. Liebowitz murmured as he fussed over Caramel, rearranging the little cat's pillow and adding a few more toys to an already impressive collection. At fourteen, Caramel probably did more sun-worshipping than toy-chasing, but it was a comfort to be surrounded by familiar things. Anyone who has ever had to stay in a hospital can attest to that.

"Oh, Dr. McBride. I almost forgot." Dr. Liebowitz scribbled a phone number on a piece of paper. "I bought a cell phone. Sandra thought it would be a good idea. She says I need to modernize," he explained with a shy smile. "We're going for a stroll in the park this afternoon but this way, you can reach me wherever I am."

He handed me the slip of paper and, turning back to Caramel, began to hum. I didn't know exactly how old Dr. Liebowitz was but I suspected he might qualify for Seniors' Tuesday at Shopper's Drug Mart. Still, it was nice to see him blush at the mention of Sandra's name.

In the hallway, I overtook Hughie as he alternately limped and moaned his way to the office.

"Here," he said, thrusting a tube of Preparation H into my hand. "I don't know why you couldn't get it yourself." He sighed dramatically.

"Thanks."

I turned the tube over in my hand. It looked innocuous enough, but the five-centimetre-long applicator suggested otherwise. I noticed it was still canary yellow, presumably to make it easier to find should someone accidentally manage to misplace it. "Prep H" had been a staple in our home when I was growing up. Once when we ran out and my father was apparently in dire need, I was coerced into picking some up at the nearby pharmacy. To my horror, Tony Marino, the heartthrob of my Grade Ten homeroom, was working cash.

Fifteen years or so later and scarred for life, I still couldn't bring myself to pick up a tube unless it was anonymous in a cart full of groceries. Recently, though, I had read an article in the Canadian Veterinary Journal that elevated the status of Preparation H. Not only did it "shrink swollen hemorrhoidal tissue" but it had amazing, scientifically-proven wound healing properties in cats. I thought the ointment might be useful in Caramel's case.

"So what's wrong with your foot?" I asked, following Hughie down the hall.

"Sprained my ankle last night."

"Oh. Basketball?"

Hughie hesitated. "Ping-pong."

"What? How do you sprain an ankle playing ping-pong?"

"Yeah, well, that's not the worst of it." Hughie lowered his voice. "The pharmacist saw me hobble in and grab three tubes of Preparation H. Not the old crank but the really pretty one. She said if they were that bad I should really see a doctor."

I started to laugh.

"It's not funny. She thinks I have hemorrhoids," Hughie hissed.

"I don't imagine she's going to spend her whole day thinking about you and your hemorrhoids. Tell her it was for a cat the next time you see her," I suggested.

Hughie rolled his eyes. "Oh, who'd believe that!" he grumbled.

To quash the rumours that were undoubtedly circulating, I took Hilary into the recovery ward that night to change Caramel's dressings. He was such a cooperative patient, I had been doing it without any help. After we removed the old bandages, I added a dollop of the ointment in question to each of his wounds. Already, granulation of healthy new tissue had begun. While I wondered what had motivated the researchers to scientifically study the use of Prep H in cats, I was grateful they had.

Tomorrow's surgery would be lengthy, but we would take all the precautions necessary for a senior citizen. I made a note for the technician on duty to remove his food by 10:00 P.M., then joined Bernie, who was already in her coat waiting for me. We planned to have a bite to eat and then I was headed home for an early evening. Hughie, always in demand, was speaking to the Ladies' Auxiliary of the local fire station after work. Earlier in the day I had caught him practicing his speech and murmuring thank you's to an empty, but apparently appreciative, office.

"Have a good night, Em," he called out. "Don't forget your... ointment."

"Break a leg, Hughie."

I rose early the next morning and went for a run, feeling guilty about last night's pizza. Morning newspapers lay untouched as the neighbourhood's mostly solid citizens still lay in bed. I jogged down quiet, tree-lined streets through filtered sunlight. The lab-dachshund mix three doors down barked encouragingly until silenced by a sharp "Simon! Shut the f--- up!" After a quick shower, I left for work, refreshed and ready to tackle Caramel's surgery.

"Oh, good morning, Dr. McBride!" As Dr. Liebowitz rose from the rocking chair, I noticed his groomed head. Sometime in the last twenty-four hours it had met with a professional. The comb-over was gone and a mustache was taking shape over his upper lip.

"I hope you don't mind us staying for the surgery," he continued. "It's just that...well...." As Dr. Liebowitz struggled for words, Sandra leaned over and grasped his hand.

"I understand. I'm glad you're here," I answered truthfully. Dr. Liebowitz nodded and began lowering himself back into the chair.

"Myles!" Sandra's urgent warning stopped Dr. Liebowitz in mid-descent. Carter had reclaimed his favourite chair and refused to budge even as the light overhead was eclipsed.

"Oh, my goodness. That was close." Dr. Liebowitz turned and

patted Carter.

With the good doctor at a loss for somewhere to sit, I suggested he and Sandra join me in the treatment room while I examined Caramel. The little cat was bright and alert although concerned that everyone else but him was eating breakfast. His bloodwork and an earlier ECG were fine so I gave him an intramuscular pre-med of pain-killer and sedative. As I waited for the latter to take effect, Dr. Liebowitz cleared his throat.

"Dr. McBride, will you join us in a circle of prayer?"

I hesitated. No one had ever asked me to pray before I performed surgery on their cat.

"Um…of course," I replied with a self-conscious glance at Susan, who would be assisting me during the operation. Caramel lay on a blanket on the treatment table. Holding hands, we formed a circle around him.

As a child I was required to attend Sunday school. Every September, Mom took me shopping for a new Sunday hat and gloves, suitable for worship. I found organized religion pretty boring unless I was sitting next to Peter Newton, who smuggled in Archie and Veronica comics. But in Grade Six, I met Mr. Bent. He is the only Sunday school teacher I remember, not for what he taught but for what he didn't teach. There was no memorizing of catechism in Mr. Bent's class. Instead, we learned about truth, compassion, and respect from a man who loved life and loved his God.

In a voice reminiscent of Mr. Bent, Dr. Liebowitz began to recite Albert Schweitzer's "Prayer for the Animals." As his words washed over me, I closed my eyes.

Hear our humble prayer, Oh God
For our friends the animals
Especially for animals who are suffering;
For any that are hunted or lost or deserted
Or frightened or hungry;
For all that must be put to sleep.

We entreat for them all
Thy mercy and thy pity
And for those who deal with them
We ask a heart of compassion
And gentle hands and kindly words.
Make us be true friends to the animals
And so to share the blessings of the merciful.
Amen.

I looked up. The room was strangely quiet, as if we had been put on hold. Hilary stood still, clutching a basket of laundry. Carter had followed us into the treatment area and was perched on a stool, watching. The fridge in the surgery ward suddenly shuddered as the compressor kicked in, breaking the spell.

"God speed," whispered Dr. Liebowitz.

Gathering Caramel in my arms, I carried him into surgery. Because he was a senior cat, we used the gas induction box to anesthetize him. Once he was asleep, I inserted the breathing tube, then gowned and gloved. Susan prepped his leg and placed a sterile surgical drape over the area. The IV line was running at one drip per second. Caramel's breathing was deep and regular.

"OK, little buddy. Here we go."

I felt at home in the peaceful isolation of surgery. Humming softly, I made an incision in Caramel's upper thigh and removed the head of the femur which protruded into the pelvis. Following prolonged cage rest and physical therapy, Caramel would do fine without it. Then I began to repair the knee, a much more delicate procedure. The ligaments holding the knee in place had been badly damaged. I stabilized the joint with permanent sutures, which would act as artificial ligaments. Pleased with my work, I began to close. Caramel had been under anesthetic for just over two hours.

"Uh...Dr. McBride?" Susan checked her log book in which she had been recording Caramel's vital signs throughout the surgery.

"Mm'm?"

"Caramel's blood oxygen saturation is down a bit."

"What's the reading?"

"Ninety-eight percent."

"Check the pulse oximeter cable attached to his tongue. It probably slipped."

Susan wiggled the cable. "It's fine," she said after a moment. Then she began reporting the rapid changes out loud. "Ninety-seven percent...ninety-six percent...uh-oh."

The pulse oximeter alarm, which had been preset at ninety-five percent, began beeping.

"Talk to me, Hilary."

"His respiration rate's falling! So is his heart rate!"

I stopped suturing and looked over at Caramel's ECG tracing. In place of a regular rhythm, the screen began filling with erratic spikes and dips. Hilary had correctly turned off the anesthetic so only oxygen was flowing through the line. But Caramel wasn't breathing.

"Start bagging him!" I ordered.

Hilary pinched the end of the rebreathing bag, allowing it to fill before pushing the oxygen into Caramel's lungs. Imitating a cat's normal respiration rate, she repeated the procedure every few seconds.

I studied the ECG screen.

"Shit! His heart's stopped!" Immediately I began chest compressions. In cats, the heart can be felt on the forward part of the rib cage. Compressions are done by squeezing the chest with the thumb and fingers. As Hilary forced oxygen into Caramel's lungs, I was trying to pump oxygenated blood to the rest of his body.

"C'mon! C'mon, Caramel!" I pleaded. "Not now, buddy!" My fingers sought the tiniest spark of life, but Caramel's heart was still.

Hilary glanced at me over her face mask.

"Keep going!" I urged.

My hand engulfed the tiny chest. Compress. Release. Compress. Release. Perspiration on my forehead began to trickle into my eyes. I held the stethoscope to Caramel's chest and stared at the ECG monitor.

Nothing.

"Hilary, get me the...." I stopped my compressions. Closing my eyes, I waited for what seemed like an eternity. Had I imagined the single pulse? No! There it was again! An almost imperceptible shiver against my touch. A fleeting blip on the ECG screen. Once more. Slowly at first and then with conviction. Caramel's heart resumed beating. I felt the message of life tapped out like Morse code between my fingers.

"Stop bagging him for a minute."

We waited. Caramel's blood was well oxygenated so it was

almost thirty seconds before he took his first breath. Then his chest began to rise and fall in the calm, predictable pattern of normal respiration.

"Thank God," I murmured, exhaling.

I finished suturing quickly. As Caramel began to wake up, we removed his breathing tube and carried him into the intensive care ward. Hilary had prepared a kennel with warm blankets and a heated Magic Bag. We monitored him closely for the rest of the day, but there were no further complications. In the evening, Caramel ate a small meal that Dr. Liebowitz lovingly hand-fed him.

I pulled up a chair and sat down beside him to discuss Caramel's prognosis and homecare. Dr. Liebowitz listened attentively as he dipped his index finger into the cat food and held it out for an appreciative Caramel. Many post-op cats won't look at a bowl of food but will willingly lick a human finger spotless. Some will eat if they are petted. I think in their vulnerable, weakened condition, they choose to relinquish their independence for the comfort of a human hand. This trust that they extend to a completely different species is at once an enigma and a precious gift.

"We almost lost him today," I acknowledged quietly.

Dr. Liebowitz continued to feed Caramel, smiling when the little cat reprimanded him for being too slow. "I know."

I was surprised. None of the staff would disclose that information before I had a chance to talk with the owner.

"Around 11:30," he added.

"Yes," I nodded. "His heart stopped. How did you know?"

Dr. Liebowitz shrugged. "I don't know. Just a feeling. It was just before a gentleman came in looking for an illustrated copy of The *Wind in the Willows* for his granddaughter."

"*Wind in the Willows*?" I repeated.

"Have you read it?" Dr. Liebowitz asked. "Lovely book. Just lovely."

I nodded slowly. "Many times."

"After he left, I waited for the phone to ring," he continued. "When it didn't, I knew Caramel was going to be okay." Dr. Liebowitz patted my shoulder in a fatherly gesture.

I stayed a few moments longer before other, more mundane work pulled me away. As I trimmed nails, discussed flea control, and vaccinated reluctant patients, my thoughts drifted back to the mysterious little butterscotch cat with the white bib in kennel number seven.

In the morning, I removed Caramel's IV line and Dr. Liebowitz bought a sailboat. He had sailed as a boy, but his wife had grown up on the prairies and did not share her husband's enthusiasm for water adventures of any kind other than a good soak in the tub. I kept the little cat at the hospital for almost a week to restrict his activity and monitor his progress. In between visits to the hospital, Myles and Sandra explored the small islands and sheltered coves dotting Nova Scotia's south shore. Next summer, they were planning a trip to the Caribbean with Caramel.

After his near-death experience, Caramel never looked back. But I did. I replayed those two hours over and over in my mind. I don't know why Caramel's heart stopped. I don't know why it started beating again. And I find myself wondering what elements in the cosmos joined forces at 11:30 on a Thursday morning in August to save him.

Caramel continued to do well at home. Dr. Liebowitz called regularly with updates and was ecstatic when Caramel caught his first post-accident mouse. I ran into him and Sandra one

Friday night when Bernie dragged me out to a trendy new club downtown. The happy couple was celebrating Myles' birthday with some of Sandra's friends. As the lights flashed and the music bounced off the walls, an exuberant Myles shouted over his iridescent cocktail that I should visit someday.

It was almost a year before that came to pass. In the meantime, Dr. Liebowitz sold his bookstore and bought a small home in an older section of town. He was painstakingly restoring its charm and had already transformed the backyard into a rambling country garden. Clever landscaping hid the tall cedar fence that would protect the aging Caramel from marauding cars and canines.

Dr. Liebowitz poured me a glass of wine and we relaxed in the sunroom overlooking the backyard. Caramel lay sprawled across his lap in the rocking chair.

"Where's Sandra?" I asked.

Dr. Liebowitz cleared his throat. He had lost thirty pounds thanks to a vigilant Weight Watchers' group and daily exercise.

"Well," he began with a rueful smile, "last time I heard she was in Florida."

"Oh." I took a sip of wine and studied the floor. The hardwood was worn smooth and mellow. As I racked my brain for something intelligent to say, a warm pink glow washed over the rich grain. The sun, after battling clouds all day, had finally escaped their clutches and begun a glorious descent to the horizon.

Dr. Liebowitz looked out the window as he patted Caramel. "You know," he said quietly, "my sister called me a crazy old fool. Maybe I was...but I wouldn't have traded these last ten months for anything."

Chapter 18

"Good morning. Ocean View Cat Hospital. How may I help you?"

Bernie's voice rose and fell in the rich rhythms of her native country. Dressed in a crisp white lab jacket with a smiling cat pin fastened to the lapel, she glowed with a cheery professionalism. Clients felt confidence in her gentle wisdom and matronly figure, although she was trying to lose some of the latter.

"I see. Yes. Just one moment please." Bernie pressed the hold button and then stared vacantly at the receiver in her hand.

"Bernie?" I asked, after a moment.

In a most un-Bernie-like manner, she leapt out of her chair sending it on a hair-raising skid to the far wall. "Oh, my goodness!" she gasped, fanning her flushed face. "Oh, my goodness! Where's Dr. Doucette?"

Without waiting for an answer, Bernie kicked off her clogs and raced to the treatment area. Her legs, wrapped in Sears Best support hose, swished in protest.

"What's wrong?" I called out, racing after her.

"Dr. D.!" she hollered. "Wait!"

Three faces looked up from the treatment table, including Patches Fleming, whose astonishment gave way to incontinence. Still holding onto Patches, Hilary tried unsuccessfully to dodge the yellow stream that poured over the treatment table and spattered onto her shoes.

Hughie looked up. "Might as well get a urine sample." He

held onto Patches while Hilary reached inside the cupboard for the urinalysis test strips.

"Oh dear! Oh, I'm so sorry! Pardon me!" Bernie smoothed her hair and adjusted her skirt. Straightening up, she took a deep breath.

"Dr. Doucette," she announced at last, "Kim Basinger is on the phone!"

"Tell her I'm with a patient," Hughie reached for Patches' eye ointment. Gently he ran a strip in each eye, then massaged the lids.

"The Kim Basinger? Are you sure?" Hilary asked, grabbing a roll of paper towel.

Bernie nodded enthusiastically. The staff looked at Hughie with new respect.

"Aren't you going to talk to her?" Tanya was incredulous.

"I talked to her three times yesterday. And every time I told her the same thing. Bring the cat in. I can't make a diagnosis over the phone. What am I? Some kind of psychic healer?" Hughie grumbled.

"Ah…Dr. D., that was Kim Bessonette," someone said.

"Well, who's this?" Hughie asked with a puzzled frown.

"Kim Basinger! The actress!" Bernie was beside herself. She loved going to the movies and often spent lunch breaks poring over glossy entertainment magazines.

"Surely now you've heard of her!" Bernie cried. "She wants to talk to you about the circus protest."

In addition to her busy acting career, Ms. Basinger was a strong opponent of exotic animal acts in circuses. On a national talk show, she showed secret footage taken by an organization called PETA (People for the Ethical Treatment of Animals) that depicted an elephant being beaten and abused as it was "broken" for circus life. In fact, stories of beatings at the hands of caretakers and trainers are well-documented.

"Why didn't you say so?" Hughie passed me the disgruntled Patches. "What line?"

"Line two!" Bernie led the swarm of staff that pursued Hughie to the office.

Everyone crammed into the small space, chattering in muffled excitement. Hughie loosened his tie and lowered himself into the chair. Leaning back, he stretched both legs out on the desk. We held our breath as he reached for the phone and released the hold button.

"Good morning, Ms. Basinger!" he boomed in his most professional voice. "Dr. Doucette here...oh, certainly."

We leaned forward as Hughie held his hand over the receiver.

"Secretary," he whispered.

While we waited for Ms. Basinger to finish in make-up, speculations ran wild.

"Maybe she's coming to the protest," Hilary suggested.

"Oh, do you think?" Bernie asked, her hands clasped reverently in front of her.

"She goes all over the place for movies," Susan shrugged. "Why not?"

Bernie looked thoughtful. "I wonder what she'll be wearing. She has a gorgeous...."

"Yes, hello!" Hughie bolted upright and motioned for us to be quiet. "Oh...it's a beautiful day here too.... Well, thank you," he beamed. "A lot of people contributed....I couldn't agree more.... This Saturday....Well, we appreciate your support. Call me if you have any cat questions," he added.

Sighing, Hughie hung up the phone and flopped against the back of the chair. Clasping his hands together behind his neck, he began to rock back and forth as he smiled at the ceiling.

"Be Jaysus!" Bernie's freckles were ready to pop off her face. "What did she say?"

Ignoring Bernie, Hughie stared at his feet where both shoelaces had come undone. "Will you look at that. Brand new laces."

He bent down to tie them.

"Dr. Doucette!" Tanya groaned.

"What?"

"Kim Basinger!"

"Is she coming?" Susan asked impatiently.

"No," Hughie shook his head.

"Fiddlesticks!" Bernie grumpily folded her arms against her chest.

"Actually," he said, turning serious, "she heard about VOICE and called to say 'Congratulations and keep up the good work.'"

My boss had founded VOICE (Veterinarians Opposed to Inhumane Circus Environments) a few years earlier. After intense lobbying efforts, he had recently convinced the Nova Scotia Veterinary Medical Association to pass a bylaw against the use of exotic animal acts. This was the first veterinary body in Canada to oppose the physical and psychological cruelty circus animals are forced to endure.

As the staff bundled out of the office, Hughie took Patches from my outstretched arms. "Kim Basinger!" He shook his head in disbelief. "I'll have to tell Abby!"

Abigail MacIsaac was one of our favourite clients. A tireless campaigner for animal welfare, she had recruited Hughie in the fight to end circus animal suffering. Far from being a group of radicals, her organization included housewives, retired seniors, and secretaries – ordinary people who believed that cruelty is not entertainment.

Not surprisingly, Abby's home was a haven for all kinds of animal refugees, including eight cats. Bob, her diabetic, hadn't been doing well and was scheduled to see me this morning. With calm restored to the office, I picked up the phone to make a call when Hughie's head reappeared in the doorway.

"Kim BASINGER, Em!" he sighed, shaking his head. Halfway down the hall, he was still repeating her name in awe.

Bob arrived that morning with Abby in tow. She was thrilled to hear Hughie's news but concerned about Bob. He was a grossly overweight charmer who could hear a tin of cat food open in another country. His diabetes was almost certainly linked to his weight. Although Abby tried to keep him on a strict diet, he was an opportunist in a house full of opportunities. Until yesterday, he had been passionate in his pursuit of food, but he had eaten nothing in the last twenty-four hours and had vomited several times. Wisely, Abby had withheld his insulin.

"How's my big, handsome Bobby Boy today?" I crooned.

Bob blinked at me from the chair where he had established himself but refused to be sociable. I rummaged in the drawer for a healthy treat and held it out in my hand. Bob promptly turned his back and faced the wall.

"This is what he's been doing at home." Abby's brow was creased in a worried frown. "He's not the least bit interested in food."

"He might be feeling a little nauseous," I replied. "Let me feel your tummy there, Bob."

Bob grunted as I raised the upper part of his body with one

hand and tried to palpate his abdomen with the other. All I could feel were rolls of fat. I listened to his chest, examined his mouth and throat, and checked his body for evidence of physical injury. Bob ignored both me and the usually eye-opening insertion of the rectal thermometer.

"Well," I crossed my arms and stared at my patient. "I can't find anything wrong on his physical exam, although I couldn't feel his abdomen very well."

"Bob," Abby scolded, "what did I tell you about those extra helpings?" Bob refused to meet her gaze.

"Let's do some X-rays to make sure there's nothing stuck in there," I suggested. "We probably won't need to sedate him. He's a pretty easy-going guy."

"You go right ahead, Dr. McBride. Whatever you think."

Bob squeaked as I struggled to lift him from the chair, remembering to bend my legs and keep my back straight. In the treatment area, Susan held him while I set up for X-rays. I hoisted the heavy lead apron over my shoulders, attached the throat shield, and donned the lead gloves. Snapping the protective goggles over my head, I waddled out to Susan.

"Ready," I announced. Bob screamed in horror and scrambled out of Susan's arms.

"Bob! Bob! It's me, buddy."

Unconvinced, Bob stared back at me from underneath the X-ray machine where he had managed to squeeze all but one leg. Cats, even very large ones, have an amazing ability to cram themselves into the smallest of spaces and look comfortable.

"He's never going to sit still for an X-ray now, Dr. McBride," Susan said helpfully.

"See that leg sticking out?" I drew up a syringe of intramuscular anesthetic and explained to Bob that it was for his own good.

Wedged firmly in place, Bob was helpless to prevent the injection. He snoozed his way through two pairs of X-rays and woke up in the recovery ward next to his teddy bear. Meanwhile, I showed Abby his X-rays.

"See all those mottled areas of white?" I asked, pointing to his intestines.

"Oh, God!" Abby clapped a hand over her mouth. "Tumours?"

"No, no! He's full of stool. I mean full with a capital *F*! I don't think I've ever seen so much in one place. When was the last time he had a bowel movement?"

"I'm not sure." Abby shook her head. "We have so many cats. You just assume what goes in comes out. Oh dear."

"Well, Bob's a big guy," I continued. "It's probably hard for him to balance on his tippy toes and assume the position. So, if one little plug comes along…poof! The whole system backs up."

Abby's blue eyes blinked in slow motion. "Can you help him?"

"Well, we'll start him on stool softeners right away and begin some warm water enemas. Hopefully, we can get rid of what's in there now. But some of these guys develop megacolon," I cautioned.

"Megacolon?"

"Over time, the bowel gets stretched and becomes lazy," I explained. "It doesn't push stool along the way it used to. He may do just fine, though. We'll have to keep a close eye on him."

Abby nodded. She was used to caring for animals that other people had discarded. Back in the exam room, she picked up a bulging briefcase twice Bob's size.

"I'm making a presentation to City Hall this afternoon," she explained.

Four municipalities in the province had already banned circuses with exotic animal acts. Abby, Hughie, and other dedicated animal welfare groups were determined that Halifax Regional Municipality should do the same. Cruelty issues aside, public safety was a major concern. Frustration and psychological distress cause animals to react in unpredictable ways. There were many documented cases of rampaging elephants and tiger attacks in North America. Recently an uncontrollable elephant had bolted from the ring and, in a telling act, trampled her trainer's car. In a bloodbath that required over three hundred rounds of ammunition, she was eventually killed. As one caller to a radio talk show had asked, what if six children had been astride her back?

I wished Abby luck but doubted city council would pass such a bylaw. Incidences such as these were considered rare. Most circuses were brought into the province under the guise of fund-raising for charities. It seemed a cruel irony that money for the less fortunate members of our society should be raised by oppressing other sentient beings.

After Abby left I returned to Bob, who was awake, suspicious, and preparing for the worst. I have never met a cat who enjoyed enemas or appeared grateful for the relief which usually followed. Two or more people were required, depending upon the cat's mood and the number of days that had passed without a bowel movement. The magic potion was delivered through a plastic catheter attached to a large syringe.

We gave Bob eleven enemas without so much as a rumble or even a whiff of gas. Number twelve caused a shift in the earth's mass. Tidal waves of warm water, fur, and excrement flooded Bob's kennel. Since he was too large to do his own dirty work,

Hilary and Susan had the unenviable task of washing his backside while Bob howled indignantly. When Abby arrived to take him home, he scrambled into his carrier with far more enthusiasm than he had shown coming to the hospital.

Not surprisingly, city council had tabled the proposed by-law for further study. Always optimistic, Abby shrugged her shoulders and smiled.

"Oh, well," she declared. "Better than rejecting it outright."

With Abby on one end of the over-sized carrier and me on the other, we waddled to the door. Bob was mute. He was probably worried that if he complained, we would remember he was inside the carrier and haul him out for another round of enemas.

Outside, a wizened old man shuffled past with two wizened old dogs. All were traveling at the same arthritic pace. There was no clear leader. If someone in the trio stopped to investigate a good smell or pick up a penny, the others waited patiently until their companion was ready to continue.

"There's that funny little man," Abby whispered. "He was looking at the poster in your window about the circus protest when I brought Bob in today."

"Oh, you mean Mr. Magoo. He's harmless."

Mr. Magoo wasn't his real name although I suppose it could have been. No one knew. He only talked to his dogs. The staff had dubbed him Mr. Magoo after the cartoon character, a mumbling, little old man with round thick glasses and checkered pants. We were on his route. Twice a day, he and his companions shuffled through the parking lot with a bag of breadcrumbs for the pigeons.

Abby fastened a seatbelt around Bob's carrier then hopped into her car. "See you Saturday at the protest!" she waved.

I was just heading into an appointment when Abby and her husband rushed through the doors less than four hours later. Their cat Snowflake had been hit by a car. Last winter, Abby had discovered the terrified young stray huddled inside a dumpster at work. With the help of co-workers, she crawled inside and rescued the starving cat. While Snowflake grew sleek and glossy under Abby's loving care, she always maintained a wild streak. Now she lay limp and broken, her free spirit crushed by a ton of steel.

"We were eating supper and…and we heard the screech of car tires," Todd explained in a broken voice. "We ran outside. Snowflake was just lying in the middle of the road. The car was gone." He looked away, unable to continue.

Tears coursed down Abby's cheeks and glistened on Snowflake's ravaged body. Even as I reached for my stethoscope, I knew there was nothing I could do. Snowflake took one last gasp and died in Abby's arms.

Abby hugged the small, white bundle and wept for the short life that had endured so much. "I shouldn't have let her outside," she sobbed, her voice ragged with grief. "But she cried and cried to go out, right from the first. She was miserable in the house."

"This isn't your fault," I whispered. My fingers caressed Snowflake's small, delicate face. "You gave her the freedom she needed…that's love, Abby, not neglect."

I felt tears rise unbidden to my own eyes. Sometimes, it was so hard to bear the grief of others, to feel helpless in the face of their loss and angry at those members of society who condone widespread abuse and slaughter of animals. I grieve for what we become when we chase wolves to exhaustion and shoot them from our Ski-Doos or poison them by the thousands, when we explode bombs inside whales, when we leave a small, white cat alone on the road to die.

Abby rocked back and forth, clutching Snowflake to her chest. Finally, she kissed her forehead one last time and rose from the chair. Together, she and Todd wrapped Snowflake in a blanket. I watched from the doorway as Todd helped Abby into the car then placed Snowflake in her outstretched arms.

But time doesn't wait for hearts to heal. In its forward march, we eat, we sleep, we go to work. The days leading up to the circus protest rolled by in a blur of meetings and phone calls. Four different animal welfare groups were coordinating their efforts at this silent protest. Circus performances were scheduled for 11:00, 2:00, and 5:00 so most protestors would spend the day. Our goal was to educate. We held banners and passed out information, believing that once people were aware of the cruelty behind the sparkles and glitz, they would no longer support exotic animal acts. In fact, circuses which do not exploit animals such as the Montreal-based Cirque du Soleil are hugely successful.

The day of the protest was bathed in grey drizzle with gusting winds. We were not allowed on the circus grounds so we stretched our small numbers along the sidewalk, trying to make fifty people look like two-hundred-and-fifty. A few cars zipping past tooted their horns in support. A man we didn't know brought us coffee and donuts. But mostly, the mood of the crowd matched the day.

Abby slipped in beside me.

"Abby. Hi!" I said, surprised. "I didn't think you'd be here today."

Before she could answer, a large woman hauling four kids marched over. The kids studied Abby's poster of an elephant in chains with the caption: "If you love animals, don't go to the circus!"

"Mommy, what does that say?" one of them asked, tugging on her coat.

"Nuthin'!" she snorted. "These people are a bunch of crackpots. They don't want you to have any fun!" She yanked the nearest child towards the circus entrance and the rest followed. Even as he was being propelled forward, one of the children turned back, curious, dissatisfied with his mother's explanation. Abby waved to him. Tentatively, he waved back.

As she continued to hold her sign straight and true against the wind, Abby turned towards me.

"Someday," she said.

Our protest made the regional TV evening news. Within twenty four hours, coverage of the circus debate had reached as far away as Prince George in northern British Columbia. Spokespersons interviewed for the Nova Scotia Department of Natural Resources and the provincial SPCA claimed strict regulations governing the treatment of circus animals were already in place.

A disgusted Hughie, representing VOICE, claimed the regulations were pitifully inadequate and never enforced anyway.

"Tigers spend up to fifty weeks a year in tiny transport cages," he declared. "That's where they *live* in between performances. Regulations that require their cages to be fifteen centimetres longer are ludicrous!"

The reporter then asked why VOICE and other animal welfare groups wanted to deny children the opportunity to learn about real tigers and elephants. Hughie squinted at the microphone. Rain pasted dark columns of hair against his forehead and drizzled into his eyes.

"And what do children learn when they see a tiger dragged by his tail?" he asked the reporter. "Or muzzled bears in pink tutus and leg chains forced to dance on their hind legs?"

Behind Hughie, and perhaps more powerful than any words, four elephants who would normally roam eighty kilometres a day with their herd, swayed back and forth in their leg chains while circus-goers thronged at the gates, anxious to be entertained.

By the end of the day, tired and cold, we returned to our regular lives. We were making some progress but we knew to measure success in baby steps. Juggling a cup of hot chocolate and my protest sign, I unlocked the hospital doors to check on my patients. The rain had stopped and a few bold pinpricks of light appeared in the black canopy.

Three arthritic figures rounded the corner of the building and shuffled past me.

"No one should live in a cage," Mr. Magoo muttered.

Really, it's as simple as that.

Chapter 19

"I TALK TO ANIMALS."

Eunice Dalrymple straddled the entrance to the exam room with a shopping bag in one hand and cat carrier in the other.

"Mrs. Dalrymple? Hi. I'm Dr. McBride. Come in."

Mrs. Dalrymple eased herself through the opening and, still clutching her cargo, paused to study my credentials on the wall. Satisfied, she lowered herself into a chair, carrier on one side, groceries on the other. She was a large woman dressed in sensible clothing that had not been fashionable in any decade but nonetheless served its purpose. The exception was a brown fedora garnished with silk flowers, a purple ribbon, and the feathers of several local birds. It was neither fashionable nor functional but suggested a certain flair for the unusual.

"This is Darryl with a *Y*," Mrs. Dalrymple announced, pointing her head in the direction of the carrier. She opened the door and a grey and white extrovert with sage green eyes strolled out.

"Hi Darryl," I cooed. Tail held high, he strolled over and rubbed against my legs.

"My goodness," I laughed. "You're not the least bit shy, are you?"

"Shy?" Mrs. Dalrymple rolled her eyes. "You should have heard what he said to that pretty little tortoiseshell out there. I'm still embarrassed. He can be so vulgar sometimes!"

Darryl with a *Y* jumped up on the examining table and posed demurely at its edge, staring at his mistress. "Of course," she added, blowing him kisses, "he was a street cat, the darling."

Darryl's eyes opened and closed in a slow, seductive blink.

All of my clients talked to their cats, many understood body language and vocalizations but, prior to Mrs. Dalrymple, none claimed the ability to communicate telepathically.

"So...why is Darryl here today?" I asked with a wary smile.

Mrs. Dalrymple folded her arms across her chest and sighed.

"I have to move into an apartment and Darryl is upset about the move. I've tried to explain things to him," she shrugged, "but it's like talking to a brick wall."

Lowering my clipboard, I studied my client. "Well, you know, cats are like people," I began. "Most of us don't like change either. I bet once he gets in the new place surrounded with all his familiar things, he'll do just fine."

"You don't understand, Dr. McBride. He's not worried about himself. He's worried about his friends. He has tea with Edna every morning." Mrs. Dalrymple lowered her voice and whispered, "Nobody else can stand her. And he loves to ramble in the garden. How can I take him away from all that?"

Mrs. Dalrymple patted Darryl as he perched on the edge of the table.

"Tell you what," I said at last. "I notice he's due for a vaccination so I'll give him a thorough examination today and vaccinate him. That way, we'll keep him healthy for when he visits his old friends or they come to visit him."

I put the stethoscope to my ears and reached for the amiable Darryl. He seemed healthy but I wasn't too sure about his owner. I tried to listen to his chest but a deep, rumbling soliloquy of contentment made that difficult.

"Darryl! Don't be silly!" Mrs. Dalrymple blushed as I looked up. "Inside joke," she explained.

I knew many people who had good rapport with animals but Mrs. Dalrymple was the first to share an off-colour joke with her cat. Continuing to examine Darryl, I noticed a small lump on his neck.

"How long has he had this?" I asked, parting the fur for his owner to see.

Mrs. Dalrymple thrust her head between mine and Darryl's. "Oh, my goodness!" she gasped. "He never mentioned anything to me about this!"

"Maybe he didn't want to worry you," I couldn't help adding.

"It must be new. I would have noticed it." Mrs. Dalrymple turned her distraught face towards me. "What are we going to do?"

"Well, it may be nothing," I replied, "but I think it would be best to remove the lump. Then we can send it to the lab for analysis."

"I see."

Mrs. Dalrymple gazed at her beloved. Her eyes were partly masked by lids that were losing the battle against gravity. Even so, I could see a faint shimmer on their surface. I handed her a box of tissue. She took one and dabbed delicately at each eye.

"What was that, dear?" Sniffling, she looked past me with a puzzled frown.

I shook my head. "I didn't say. . . ."

"Dr. McBride," Mrs. Dalrymple interrupted, "could you explain the procedure?"

"Of course," I answered in relief. This was something I was trained to handle. "First, we'll sedate Darryl using. . . ."

"No, no, dear. Talk to Darryl. He's the one having the surgery."

I glanced at my patient, who was preoccupied by a crack in the ceramic tile.

"Ah...Darryl?" I began, looking back at Mrs. Dalrymple.

"Down. Down," she ordered as if speaking to a dim-witted mutt. "It's less intimidating if you're on his level."

My knees cracked in protest as I knelt on the floor, eyeball to eyeball with my patient. After a brief discussion about anesthetic, Darryl grew bored and began swatting the coiled doorstop attached to the wall. It bounced up and down with satisfying *boings*. For Mrs. Dalrymple's benefit, I continued, describing the surgery and post-op recovery.

"Thank you," she breathed when I was done. "He's much more at ease now, don't you think?"

"Oh, yes," I agreed, folding my arms across my chest and nodding wisely. I gave Mrs. Dalrymple a brochure on helping cats adjust to a move. Fortunately many of the same guidelines applied to people as well as cats.

Bernie turned to me after Mrs. Dalrymple left. "Do you think she can talk to animals?"

I shrugged. "I dunno. She hears voices, that's for sure."

"Just like Uncle Seamus," Bernie shivered.

Bernie's Uncle Seamus was legendary at Ocean View Cat Hospital. According to Bernie, he had "the sight." Apparently, it ran in her mother's family. So did a fine tradition of distilling alcohol from grain.

"I wonder if she has any Irish blood?" Bernie mused.

I held my tongue. Ireland was, after all, the country that produced and marketed leprechauns. Psychic Irishwoman or misguided cat-lover, Mrs. Dalrymple had nonetheless booked Darryl's surgery for tomorrow. I wasn't sure she would even show up.

"There's something wrong with her," I told Hughie the following day. "I think she needs help. I don't know if she's just lonely or needs to talk to a professional."

"Well, Em, you're a vet. Help her by making her cat better."

I was just changing into my scrubs when I heard Bernie clapping her hands together to get everyone's attention.

"Girrrls! Girrrls! Look lively."

I tucked the rest of my hair under the surgical cap and stepped out of the bathroom. "What's wrong?"

"It's Darryl! The wee lad's escaped!" Bernie announced.

"Escaped? Escaped from where?"

"Here!" Bernie cried. "Mrs. Dalrymple was holding him, but he jumped out of her arms when the mailman came."

"But we have double doors. How did he get out?"

"Ach! The ignoramus!" Bernie fumed, referring to the mailman with whom she had an ongoing feud. His delivery of the mail was not linked to any particular time of day nor the correct address. "The outer door stuck on the grating and the gobshite was too lazy to close it!"

I didn't know what "gobshite" meant but I suspected it wasn't complimentary.

Tanya, Hilary, and I followed Bernie into the busy parking lot. We shared the two-storey building with several retail businesses on the lower level and eight doctors' offices upstairs. Even a friendly, outgoing cat like Darryl would be upset by the noise and traffic.

Mrs. Dalrymple was on her hands and knees, wedged between a red pick-up truck and a van. When a boisterous, blue-collar group clutching coffee and donuts returned to the truck, Darryl streaked across the parking lot and sought refuge under a black car.

"Oh dear!" she wailed. "He's just not listening. I'm never going to catch him."

"Of course you will!" Bernie reassured her. "We just have to work as a team. You girls," she ordered, pointing to Tanya and Hilary, "you go over to that cluster of cars and block his escape routes. I'm going to stop the traffic."

I joined Mrs. Dalrymple on the other side of the expensive-looking black sedan and peered underneath as she tried to strike up a conversation with Darryl. Bernie planted herself in the middle of the parking lot, feet spread and arms wide apart in a defiant gesture. No cars dared venture past.

"Lose a patient?"

I turned to find myself face to foot with a pair of Guccis. Squinting in the bright morning glare, I looked up. A tall man carrying a briefcase was silhouetted against the sun. Car keys dangled from his hand.

"Yes, actually," I stammered, lowering my behind and raising my head. "A cat."

"Can I help?"

"Um, well…could you go up there?" I pointed to the front of the car. "So he doesn't try to escape that way?"

"Sure."

The stranger placed his briefcase on the hood then lowered his lanky frame to the ground. Smiling at me from underneath the car, he waited as Mrs. Dalrymple tried to coax Darryl toward her. He was just within her grasp when a skateboarder rumbled past. Poor Darryl had an immediate change of heart. Rushing the parking lot's eight-foot-high fence, he disappeared into a backyard. Frenzied barking erupted and soon the whole street was in full cry as bored dogs took up the cause.

"Oh!" Mrs. Dalrymple collapsed against the van. "What am I going to do? I'm already late for work!"

"You go to work, dearie," Bernie soothed, draping her arm over Mrs. Dalrymple's shoulder as she walked her to the car. "Dr. McBride can't do surgery without her patient. She can look for Darryl," Bernie added, glancing back at me. Bernie no doubt felt a certain kinship with Mrs. Dalrymple.

Mrs. Dalrymple grabbed my hand. "Oh, thank you, Dr. McBride! Darryl likes you," she said. "He told me." Opening the door of her car, a relic from days when gas was cheap and vehicles were big, she wedged herself behind the steering wheel. Woman and machine disappeared in a cloud of blue smoke.

I stood at the edge of the parking lot as the crowd dispersed. Hilary and Tanya had already returned inside. Surgery may have been on hold, but there were a million other things I could be doing besides tracking down a talking cat who didn't want to have his lump removed even after I had explained the process in great detail.

"I have to go too. Sorry." I whirled around as the stranger belonging to the elegant car tapped me on the shoulder. "I hope things work out."

"Me too. Thanks for your help," I added.

"My pleasure," he replied, slipping into his car.

Convinced that Darryl would never show his face, I trudged up and down the street anyway, calling his name. A curious family of crows followed me from tree to tree, cawing raucously. Then I searched through several backyards, poking under bushes and peering under decks until someone threatened to call the police. I returned to Ocean View empty-handed. At noon, a gangly teenager sauntered into the hospital. His face was studded with pimples and piercings.

"Mom asked me to look for the cat," he mumbled with a sullen shrug.

"Oh, hi. I'm Dr. McBride."

"Nathan. Look, I only got ten minutes," he announced, popping a cigarette into his mouth.

"You can't smoke that in here, dear," Bernie told him.

Staring at Bernie, he removed the cigarette from his mouth in slow motion and dropped it into the box. "So, where's the cat?"

"Well, that's the problem," I replied, feeling my temperature rise. "We don't really know where the cat is."

Folding his arms across his chest, Nathan stared at me.

"I can show you where we last saw him," I offered. "We think he's hiding in a yard somewhere."

I took Nathan outside. Watching his insolent shuffle down the sidewalk, I vowed never to have children. Less than ten minutes later he reappeared, catless and reeking of cigarettes.

"Tell Mom I couldn't find him."

Without a backward glance, he pushed open the hospital doors and left.

Bernie looked at me. "No wonder his mother talks to animals."

Mrs. Dalrymple called several times that afternoon. Disappointed that no one had seen Darryl, she brightened up when I mentioned her son had stopped in at the hospital.

"Which one?" she asked.

Dear God. The woman had more than one?

"Nathan," I shuddered.

"That was nice of him. I don't see the boys much," she explained. "They live with their father."

After an awkward silence, I promised to call with any news. We had already posted signs in the neighbourhood and called the local shelters. Hopefully, someone would notice a stray cat in the area. I finished with my last appointment at five and was looking forward to a leisurely evening. I strapped on my bicycle helmet and was just leaving when Mrs. Dalrymple chugged into the parking lot. Even after she turned off the ignition, the car continued to sputter, somehow sensing that if it stopped now, it might never start again. She struggled to close the window which stubbornly refused to budge.

Spying me at the bike rack, she poked her head through the gaping hole. "Yoo-hoo, Dr. McBride! Has anyone seen Darryl?"

Key in hand, I shook my head. "No, I'm sorry. Nothing yet."

Mrs. Dalrymple thrust the car door open. Clutching a bag of cat treats, she squirmed past the steering wheel.

"It'll be dark soon," she said.

As I watched, she started down the sidewalk, a lonely figure in a shapeless beige overcoat, alternately shaking a bag of treats and calling Darryl's name. I dropped the bike lock key back into my pocket.

"Mrs. Dalrymple!" I called, running to catch up.

I joined her on the sidewalk. Taking the bag of treats from her outstretched hand, I shook it while she called Darryl's name. We searched both sides of the street, peering into backyards, scrambling under porches, knocking on doors. No one had seen a grey and white cat with a lime green collar. I glanced at my watch, wishing I was home soaking in the bathtub.

"I'm just going to try the next street," she said.

Ocean View Cat Hospital was situated on the south side of one of the busiest streets in Halifax. The north side was marked by apartment complexes, commercial real estate, and a high school. The south side was largely single-family dwellings. I hoped Darryl had the good sense to stay on the south side. Few cats could outsmart four lanes of traffic.

I followed Mrs. Dalrymple onto Mariah Crescent. A little girl hosting a tea party for her dolls had not seen Darryl but introduced us to all her guests.

"I'm Jessie. I'm four," she added, holding up three fingers. "Do you know Billy? He has the measles. I'm not allowed to play with him."

Mrs. Dalrymple grabbed my arm. "Look!" she pointed.

From the large bay window of Jessie's house, a long-haired tabby cat idly flicked her tail as she watched us.

"That cat knows something!" Mrs. Dalrymple hissed.

She turned back to Jessie. "Is that your cat in the window, darling?"

"Uh huh." Jessie poured some imaginary tea into a pink china cup and held it up to the teddy bear's mouth. When he had finished, she offered him a plate full of pebbles. "Biscuit?" she asked politely.

"Could I...could I talk to your cat?" Mrs. Dalrymple's voice held an edge of excitement.

Jessie looked up. "Can you talk to cats?" she asked, her eyes wide with wonder.

"Oh, yes," Mrs. Dalrymple assured her.

The screen door opened. "Jessie?" A young woman in grey sweatpants stood on the porch. "Supper's ready."

"Mommy!" Jessie pointed to Mrs. Dalrymple. "She talks to cats."

"And dogs," Mrs. Dalrymple added.

Jessie's mother eyed us suspiciously. "I already donate to the humane society."

"We're not looking for money," I explained.

"We're looking for my cat," Mrs. Dalrymple explained breathlessly. "And I think your cat might. . . ."

"I'm Dr. McBride," I said, interrupting Mrs. Dalrymple before she could elaborate on her conversational skills with other species. "I'm a vet at Ocean View Cat Hospital."

"Oh, yes," the woman smiled. "My friend Amy takes her cat there. What does your cat look like?" she asked Mrs. Dalrymple.

Mrs. Dalrymple took a deep breath. "Well, he's grey and white, short haired, with gorgeous green eyes. He has a shiny coat, very thick. I brush him every day," she added. "His name is Darryl, that's D-A-R-R-*Y*-L. He wears a lime green collar although he thinks it's a bit gaudy," she confessed. "He has a wonderful sense of humour. Oh, and he has a freckle in his right ear."

"He sounds lovely," Jessie's mother smiled, "but I'm sorry. I haven't seen him. Honey." She asked as her hand gently caressed the little girl's head, "Have you seen any new kitties in the neighbourhood?"

Jessie shook her head back and forth in an emphatic "no." Her pigtails flailed softly against each rosy cheek.

I thanked them and turned to leave.

"But Rachel did."

"Who's Rachel, dear?" Mrs. Dalrymple asked in a conversational tone that belied her sense of urgency. "One of your little friends?"

Jessie pointed to the window where the cat still watched us. "That's Rachel."

Mrs. Dalrymple clapped a hand over her mouth. "I knew it!"

she hissed.

Jessie's mom got down on her knees so that she was level with her daughter. "Honey, how do you know that Rachel saw this lady's cat?"

Jessie shrugged. "I dunno."

"Jessie…," her mother cautioned.

The little girl put a thumb in her mouth. "She told me."

"Jessie!" her mother scolded gently. "You know cats can't talk to people except in stories."

Beside me, I felt Mrs. Dalrymple stiffen.

"She's had a long day," Jessie's mom apologized. "and we really do need to have supper. I hope you find your cat. Come along, Jessie."

Jessie waved goodbye and raced up the steps into her house.

Mrs. Dalrymple waited until Jessie's mom had gone inside, then looked at me. "I have to talk to that cat."

"But…."

"I just need to get a little bit closer."

"Can't you tell from here?" I asked nervously, scanning the street.

"Dr. McBride," Mrs. Dalrymple shot me a withering glance. "I don't read lips."

While I waited on the sidewalk, Mrs. Dalrymple skirted around to the side of the house and stared at Rachel. The cat appeared preoccupied with her glorious white bib. I couldn't tell if she and Mrs. Dalrymple were engaged in a meaningful conversation or not. After a few moments, the cat disappeared from view and Mrs. Dalrymple joined me on the sidewalk.

"Well?" I asked.

"Cats can be so stubborn," she grumbled. "Not like dogs.

They'll tell you everything that's on their mind. I did find out that we should be looking near water."

"Near water?" I asked. "Couldn't she be any more specific?"

Mrs. Dalrymple sighed. "They were having baked salmon for supper. The cat was a little distracted."

Just then I heard someone calling my name and turned around. Jessie's mom was standing on the front porch waving. I wondered if she had seen Mrs. Dalrymple peering inside her window.

"Dr. McBride," she called out, "Jessie did see a cat that looked like Darryl. At her friend Billy's house. He has the measles," she explained to Mrs. Dalrymple, "and she knew she wasn't supposed to be there."

"Oh, well," Mrs. Dalrymple said graciously, "children will be children. Now where does this Billy live?"

Jessie's mom pointed down the street. "Three houses down. It's the big yellow one."

Without another word, Mrs. Dalrymple surged past me, her coat billowing in the breeze. Dead leaves and grass clippings fluttered in her wake. I thanked Jessie's mom and raced down the street. I caught up with Mrs. Dalrymple just as she rang the doorbell. An elderly man answered.

"Yes?"

"Excuse me, sir," she panted, "but have you seen this cat?" Mrs. Dalrymple thrust a picture of Darryl in his face as she gasped for air. It had been taken at Christmastime. Darryl, wearing a large red bow, was perched on a table beside a rather garish ceramic Santa Claus.

The man studied the photo. "Nooo...I don't believe so."

"But you must have!" Mrs. Dalrymple cried.

"Who's there, dad?" A woman, closer in age to Jessie's mom, came to the door. "Billy, stay inside," she ordered.

Mrs. Dalrymple composed herself. "I have reason to believe that you might have seen this cat."

Billy, who was tired of the measles, tired of being inside, and tired of being told what to do, pushed past his mother onto the porch.

"Hey, Mom! That's Rocky!" he announced.

"Rocky? Oh, no, dear," Mrs. Dalrymple assured him. "This is Darryl with a *Y*."

Billy's mother smiled indulgently. "The children call him Rocky. We thought he was a stray. We were going to take him to the shelter tomorrow."

"The shelter!" Mrs. Dalrymple gasped and grabbed the porch railing for support. "Where is he now?"

"My sister's playhouse," Billy made a face. "I wanted to keep him in my room but Mom said no."

"We thought he should stay outside in case he had fleas or something."

"Fleas?" Mrs. Dalrymple bristled.

"Thank you so much for taking care of him," I interrupted. "It was very kind of you. Do you think we could take him home now?"

Mrs. Dalrymple's head bobbed in mute appeal.

"Yes, of course. Just follow me."

Ignoring his mother's orders to go back inside, Billy raced ahead and opened the gate into a beautifully landscaped backyard. Its most prominent feature was a large, above-ground swimming pool.

I continued to stare at the pool, tripping on the flagstone

pathway that led to Darryl's temporary lodging.

"Oh, yes," Billy's mother acknowledged, "it's lovely having a pool, especially on those hot summer days."

I could only nod in agreement. A flowering vine cascaded over a trellis on one side of the playhouse. Marigolds bloomed in the window box. Directly above the window box, a familiar face peered out between the lace curtains.

"Oh!" Mrs. Dalrymple clapped a hand over her heart. "I'm coming, my precious!"

As Billy opened the door, Mrs. Dalrymple dropped to her knees and Darryl strolled into her waiting arms. She quickly snapped his leash in place then buried her face in his fur. After a moment, she struggled to her feet and tearfully thanked Billy's family. We left the way we had come.

I never saw Mrs. Dalrymple again. I called a few days later to reschedule Darryl's biopsy but the phone had been disconnected. I could only hope that the lump was a harmless cyst or a fatty deposit. Was Mrs. Dalrymple certifiable? Or was she a cat whisperer?

Those who know aren't talking...at least, not to me.

Chapter 20

"Dr. McBride? He's done it again," the refined British voice sighed. Elizabeth Dearborn was an elegant matchstick of a woman who jumped out of airplanes for fun. Her husband was a cardiologist and her daughter, Lisa, attended private school in Ontario. Sylvester was the four-legged family sadist. Mrs. Dearborn doted on him.

"It was the telephone repair man this time," she said in a voice that had resigned itself to Sylvester's peculiarities. It neither rose nor fell, but floated gently as if reading a bedtime story to a drowsy child.

"The poor man just turned his back for a moment," she continued. "I had to take him to the hospital."

"Has he been getting his medication?" I asked.

"I assume so. They gave him an injection and wrote out a prescription. A very nice gentleman, really. Do you know he has a mushroom farm in his basement? How lovely."

"I mean Sylvester."

"Oh, yes!" Mrs. Dearborn acknowledged. "Every night when Jack and I have our bourbon, Sylvester has his Valium."

Whatever evil thoughts Sylvester harboured about the rest of humanity, he was putty in Mrs. Dearborn's manicured hands. I pictured the three of them sprawled in front of the fire, swapping stories and popping hors d'oeuvres while servants hovered discreetly in the background.

"Let's try increasing his dosage by half a tablet," I suggested.

"If there's no improvement in a week, call me." In most cases, I would recommend letting a cat like Sylvester outside to shred trees instead of people, but Mrs. Dearborn lived three floors up in a condominium.

Two days later, Mrs. Dearborn called me again.

"Dr. McBride?"

"Yes?" I answered warily.

"I think Sylvester has that problem where pussies can't pee-pee."

I looked up at the ceiling tiles. Why me, Lord?

"Have you checked his litter box?" I asked Mrs. Dearborn.

"Oh, yes," she replied in a pastel voice.

"And there's nothing? Not even a little bit?" I asked. "Are you sure?"

"Oh, quite sure. There's been nothing for two days," she replied matter-of-factly.

Two days? That wasn't possible. "He must be peeing somewhere else," I assured Mrs. Dearborn.

"Where else would he go, Dr. McBride?" she asked innocently. "There's only one litter box."

"Sometimes they don't always use the box," I explained.

"You don't mean…," Mrs. Dearborn hesitated.

"I'm afraid I do."

"Oh dear."

"Let's not jump to conclusions," I continued. "He may be just fine."

Peeing outside the box is the darker side of feline behaviour. No self-respecting cat would commit such a heinous crime without good reason, although they think outside the box all the time. Besides urinary tract problems, certain medical conditions like arthritis can trigger the behaviour. Stress can also be a factor. Before bringing Sylvester to the hospital and stressing everyone, I suggested Mrs. Dearborn check her condo thoroughly.

When I returned at five for my evening shift, there was a note that Mrs. Dearborn had discovered a terrible smell on her husband's new golf bag. She wanted to bring the golf bag in for an expert opinion. As soon as she stepped through the doors of the hospital, I was able to confirm that a very expensive golf bag had been sprayed with cat urine.

"Oh, that's wonderful, isn't it, Dr. McBride?" she purred. "Now we know he isn't blocked."

It was indeed wonderful news, although I wasn't sure Dr. Dearborn would feel the same way.

"Oh, I'll just buy him a new one," Mrs. Dearborn smiled. "He'll never know the difference."

I advised that we should get a urine sample from Sylvester to make sure he wasn't developing cystitis from crystals or bacteria, although the latter was unlikely in a male cat. I gave her a collection kit so that she could get a sample of Sylvester's pee at home and bring it into the hospital for a urinalysis. The kit included non-absorbent plastic litter beads, a specimen container, and a syringe. Mrs. Dearborn pulled the syringe out of the bag and looked at it in horror.

"Oh, dear. Where do I put this?"

"Just replace his regular litter with the beads. Once he pees, you pull back the plunger on the syringe to suck up the urine, like a turkey baster. Then you squirt the sample into the collection bottle and bring it back to the hospital. Simple," I smiled. "The fresher, the better."

Mrs. Dearborn looked skeptical but agreed to give it a try.

"Do other people have pussies like Sylvester?" she asked.

Immediately I thought of Claude and a few others who enjoyed sampling my flesh.

"Because I think I must be a terrible cat mother for him to act the way he does," she continued sadly.

True, Sylvester walked a fine line between normal and schizophrenic, but I knew Mrs. Dearborn was a wonderful owner and told her so. "Cats are just like people," I assured her. "They have their own unique personalities and ways of looking at the world."

Mrs. Dearborn stared through the glass doors into the parking lot where her Mercedes waited. "Jack's away a lot," she said. "And Sylvester's such good company. He really is. But I'm not sure if he's happy."

After a moment, she turned back towards me, a bright smile pasted on her face. "Well, I must get to my aerobics class. Ta-ta."

It was several days before Sylvester co-operated. His urine sample arrived by taxi since Mrs. Dearborn had a prior commitment with the dentist. The driver stared glumly at the vial of amber liquid on the counter while Bernie signed his voucher.

A brief note from Mrs. Dearborn said she found the sample in the laundry basket this morning. In the treatment area Susan and Hilary were both busy so I ran the test myself. Both bacteria and crystals could irritate the bladder and make a cat so uncomfortable that he squatted anywhere. Some cats even went so far as to blame the litter box for their discomfort and refused to set foot inside it. We could dissolve the crystals with a special food while bacteria would respond to antibiotics. However, both the dipstick and the sediment analysis revealed urine any middle-aged cat could be proud of.

I was convinced that Sylvester's house-soiling was stress-related. I called Mrs. Dearborn to discuss a change of medication, outdoor walks on a leash, or perhaps even another cat for companionship. She listened attentively for a few moments then apologized for interrupting but did I know if a full house beat a flush? Her cultured voice seemed far away and her words slurred. I wondered if she had started in on the bourbon a bit early.

The hospital had recently started carrying a new line of catnip toys. Instead of the usual mix of fish and mice, we had ventured into produce: carrots, bananas and apples. I told Mrs. Dearborn that the apple she had ordered was in and she could pick it up when she came by for Sylvester's new medication. She thanked me and hung up.

It was several days before the issue of Sylvester's pee-pee raised its ugly head once again. Hughie strolled casually into the office and began flipping through a journal.

"So, Em…how are things?"

I looked up from the bowl of pasta I was immersed in. "Fine."

"No problems?"

"Nooo…no more than usual." I put down my bowl and eyed him suspiciously. "Why?"

"Well…," He closed his journal and laid it down on the desk. "It seems Mrs. Dearborn is a little upset."

"About what?"

"About your suggestion that he should be put down. What was it you called him? A bad apple?"

"What? I *never* said that!"

Hughie shrugged. "Well, it doesn't sound like something you would say. But he is a nutcase."

"Well, if Mrs. Dearborn said that I said that, she's a nutcase too! And actually, I think she'd been drinking the day that I called. She probably doesn't remember what I said!"

"Well," Hughie acknowledged, "she wouldn't be the first client to toss one back before noon. I'll call her back, explain it was all a misunderstanding and go over your treatment plan."

I would be delighted if Hughie called her back but this was my case and I wanted to set the record straight. After I finished my morning appointments, I sat down at the desk and picked up the phone. I glanced at the clock. It was twelve-thirty. Chances were good that Mrs. Dearborn had already been into the liquor cabinet. I considered calling the first thing the following morning but that was no guarantee either. My Uncle Carl used to wash down his bacon and eggs with orange juice fortified by vodka.

Sighing, I dialed Mrs. Dearborn's number. It was picked up on the first ring but no one spoke.

"Mrs. Dearborn?" my voice echoed in the void. "Is that you?"

"Yeah-es," came the tremulous reply. Her voice had that same far-away, distracted quality I had noticed before.

"This is Dr. McBride."

"Oh yeah-es."

"I'm calling about Sylvester."

"Yeah-es?"

"I wanted to clear up any confusion about our phone conversation the other day."

"When are you coming to tea, dear?" Mrs. Dearborn asked.

"Well…um…not today. But maybe sometime. I'm calling to…."

"Was your mother's name Isabel? Or was it Frances? No, Isabel. I used to know an Isabel McBride. Oh, she was the devil," Mrs. Dearborn chuckled. "How she teased the boys! I remember one time. . . ."

"Mother Dearborn?" I heard a woman's voice. "Who are you talking to?"

"No one!" Mrs. Dearborn hollered. She waited a moment then whispered into the phone, "Do you play poker? I'm just dying for a good game of poker."

"Eleanor!" The voice was nearer and more insistent.

"Elizabeth's coming!" Mrs. Dearborn hissed. "She threw the cat off the balcony this morning. Cheerio, dear."

Amidst muffled background noises, someone picked up the phone. "Who is this, please?" I noticed the same well-bred British accent, the same phrasing, but the voice was slightly different.

"Mrs. Dearborn?" I asked. "Elizabeth Dearborn?"

"Yeah-es?"

"It's Dr. McBride."

"Oh yeah-es. Mother Dearborn told me you called. After you said he should be put down, I. . . ."

"But that's just it!" I rushed to correct her. "I didn't. . . ."

I was interrupted by the peal of a doorbell.

"Will you excuse me a moment, dear? That will be the afternoon shift."

From somewhere nearby, Mrs. Dearborn senior was refusing to eat tuna fish casserole. "Tell her, Elizabeth! Tell her! It tastes like she concocted it in the loo! And I refuse to have a bath today."

I heard the sound of a slamming door followed by silence.

"Dr. McBride?" Mrs. Dearborn picked up the phone. "I've done a terrible thing."

I tensed, remembering the other Mrs. Dearborn's comment about the balcony.

"Mother Dearborn is such a handful. Quite squirrelly, really, when she's off her medication," Mrs. Dearborn sighed. "She normally stays with my brother-in-law but he's collecting rocks in Africa for three weeks." Her tone implied he was not only daft but thoughtless.

"They're both incontinent, you know," she whispered.

"Your brother-in-law?"

"No, dear," Mrs. Dearborn said patiently. "Sylvester and Mother Dearborn."

"But Mrs. Dearborn, I would never suggest a cat be put down just because he was peeing somewhere he shouldn't. There are things we can do to fix that. I mean, you wouldn't put Mother Dearborn down just because she's incontinent. Right?"

When Mrs. Dearborn didn't answer right away, I wondered if she was giving the idea some serious thought.

"I know Sylvester would be a happier pussy if he got outside to play and meet some friends," she said finally. "So I…I put him in a picnic basket and lowered him to the ground," she finished, her voice trembling.

"I see."

"I couldn't very well lower Mother Dearborn off the balcony," she giggled nervously.

"No, I suppose not."

Mrs. Dearborn hesitated. In a sad, small voice, she asked, "Do you think he'll come back, Dr. McBride?"

Mrs. Dearborn's condominium was nestled on the shores of Halifax's Northwest Arm, a spectacular inlet of the ocean. The expansive grounds were graced by towering pines and flowering shrubs. A variety of birds and consequently a number of cats considered the place paradise.

"Hopefully," I replied.

I knew Mrs. Dearborn loved her cat and had acted out of desperation but Sylvester had never been outside his condo. I had no doubt he could protect himself against feline trespassers but there were many other urban dangers for an unsuspecting apartment cat. And how would Sylvester ever find his way back up to the third floor?

The next time I saw Mrs. Dearborn was several weeks later on Channel 10. The local affiliate ran a live, half-hour community program called "Pix at Six." A pair of obnoxiously cheerful co-hosts conducted interviews, cooked with Maritime flair, and in between, reveled in feeble jokes. It was one of Mom's favourite programs.

"Emily, come here!" she ordered from the living room. "They're going to talk about cats!"

Peanut butter sandwich in one hand and a glass of milk in the other, I plopped in front of the TV.

"And what do you do with a feisty feline if you live on the third floor of a condominium?" one of the co-hosts asked breathlessly. "Well, Mrs. Elizabeth Dearborn has the answer."

From the grounds of the condominium, the film crew zoomed in on a smiling Mrs. Dearborn. She waved from her balcony then began lowering the picnic basket like Rapunzel unfurling her hair. The camera followed the basket's descent to the ground. And there, waiting patiently for his ride up to the third floor and the usual tuna snack en route, sat Sylvester Dearborn. The interview continued back inside the apartment.

"He's a much happier pussy," Mrs. Dearborn explained to the television audience as she as she cuddled the big, grey tabby. And indeed, he seemed much more tolerant of the human race, purring politely throughout the interviewer's questions.

"He was very stressed as an apartment cat and did naughty things. I think he just needed to burn off some extra calories." Mrs. Dearborn smiled as Sylvester rubbed against her face. "I myself jump out of airplanes," she added brightly.

Chapter 21

THE SOUND OF HEARTY male laughter shook the walls of my exam room. In the next room, Hughie was busily charming Jesus Rodriguez, the property manager. Jesus must have been adopted. He was a blonde, blue-eyed tower of muscle and sinew from a small fishing community on Nova Scotia's south shore. Not a drop of Latino blood coursed through his veins.

Even in the coolest weather, Jesus preferred his sleeveless T-shirts. So did our female staff. Jesus was the man who got things done, a wily negotiator who was just as comfortable pouring concrete as designing his own personal investment portfolio. He had completed a second marriage and was working on a third when Hughie's five-year lease renewal came due.

"Yeah," his voice boomed, "my ex, the darlin', was supposed to return all my CDs last week. But she's into the *craft* scene." He paused, waiting for Hughie to ask the inevitable.

"Can't Remember A F----- Thing!" Jesus roared in delight.

Ms. Pratt's eyes opened wide. I apologized for the thin walls and wondered silently why she continued to bring her cat to us. Only a few short months ago, one of my clients had called her "dear" and then confided that his cat had no balls.

Evelyn Pratt's favourite colour was brown. Her entire wardrobe was built upon this theme except for a flashy turquoise ring that dominated her right hand. After thirty-odd years with the Halifax school board as a teacher-librarian, Ms. Pratt had recently retired. Now her cat Emily (named after Brontë, not McBride) was lethargic and refusing to eat. We decided to run some blood tests and rehydrate her with fluids. Clutching Emily, Ms. Pratt padded softly behind me as I led the way to the isolation ward.

We settled Emily into a kennel. As Ms. Pratt adjusted her tartan blanket and arranged an assortment of crocheted mice, a tiny white paw batted her leg from below. Startled, she looked down. The occupant of kennel number three looked up with big, blue-grey eyes.

"Meet Phyllis," I smiled.

"Oh, my!" Ms. Pratt reached for the outstretched paw then shrank back as she read the "Touching Spreads Disease" sign. Evelyn Pratt had great respect for the written word.

Several weeks ago, a client on her way to work had noticed Phyllis wandering, injured and bewildered, in the middle of a city boulevard. She jammed on the brakes in rush-hour traffic and leapt out of the car, ignoring the angry chorus of horns. Grabbing Phyllis, she drove to the hospital. Already late, she called her boss and told him she was bloated and had cramps. He encouraged her to take the morning off.

Phyllis' left front foot had been horribly mutilated. In what is termed a "degloving" injury, all the skin had been torn away, exposing raw infected tissue. With three cats of her own, the kindly soul couldn't take Phyllis home so I told her we would look after Phyllis until she could be adopted. We had been applying honey to the affected area daily, then bandaging the foot. The antibacterial and disinfectant properties of honey encouraged the growth of new, healthy skin.

As the days passed, Phyllis' foot got better and her belly got bigger. Hughie clung to the faint hope it was worms, but X-rays revealed a happy jumble of miniature skeletons inside. We all were excited about the impending births, but a hospital ward was no place for kittens. The immune systems of young animals are not fully developed, making them more susceptible to disease.

Kneeling, Ms. Pratt chatted with Phyllis. I looked up just as Hughie tore past the window with Jesus in tow. They were probably heading into surgery, where an ominous water stain on the ceiling tiles was spreading daily. Jesus tipped his blue ball cap and blew me a kiss.

"Will she be all right?" Ms. Pratt asked, on her hands and knees.

"I think so," I replied. "Her paw is healing well."

"But it would be better for the kittens if they weren't exposed to all these germs," Ms. Pratt glanced accusingly around the room.

"Well, at least it's better than the street," I sighed dramatically. It occurred to me that the retired Ms. Pratt could provide an excellent home for our latest orphan.

"Yes, I suppose." Ms. Pratt's forehead rippled in a thoughtful frown. Straightening her sparse frame, she rose from the floor just as Jesus winked and blew another kiss on his return trip. Something akin to horror crossed his face as he quickly looked away.

"Oh, for heaven's sake," Ms. Pratt grumbled. "That man just winked at me."

She waited until Hughie and Jesus had vanished around a corner and then opened the isolation door.

"Does he work here?" she shuddered.

"He's one of the property managers. Don't worry," I assured her, "he winks at everyone."

"Humph!" she sniffed.

"He can be a little rough around the edges but he's a good guy to know if your toilet's plugged," I joked.

Ms. Pratt raised her eyebrows. Her toilet had probably never plugged. Gathering her coat and purse, she wished me a good day and left for the literacy council, where she volunteered twice a week.

Several hours later, Emily vomited a cigar-shaped fur ball. She sniffed it with detachment, then turning her back, devoured a plate of food. This was followed by a head-to-tail sponge bath. Cats are equipped with their own loofah in the form of a bristled tongue, a kind of self-spa. Sick cats do not groom themselves nor do they eat full plates of food.

Ms. Pratt was delighted to hear the good news. "May I take her home this evening?" she asked.

"Well, her bloodwork was normal but I'd like to keep her overnight, just to be sure. I've given her some furball remedy which she quite likes. It's tuna flavoured," I added. "If there's no more vomiting and she continues to eat well, we can send her home tomorrow. Is that OK with you?"

"Ms. Pratt?" I repeated when she didn't answer. "Is that OK?"

"Oh, yes!" she replied. "It's just that...well...I was thinking."

Here it comes, I thought. She wants her records transferred. Between Jesus and Cecil, the poor woman could take it no longer.

"I would like to take Phyllis home too," Ms. Pratt announced.

"Really?"

"Just until the kittens are weaned," she added hastily. "Because the hospital environment is not the best place for them."

Hughie would be thrilled. Phyllis' care had already cost him hundreds of dollars and would likely reach over a thousand before the newcomers were ready to be adopted. I murmured words of encouragement.

"And I have a large house with lots of room. They could have the spare bedroom. It's a lovely dusty rose with a large bay window and an ensuite bathroom. Oh, and a walk-in closet too. I almost forgot," Ms. Pratt babbled in a most un-Pratt-like manner.

"Now, there is the issue of Gloria," she said thoughtfully.

Uh-oh. There was always a Gloria.

"She's my half-cousin from Musquodoboit," Ms. Pratt explained. "She sleeps in that room when she comes up once a month to have her feet done. She doesn't really like cats. But she can sleep in the living room pull-out. What do you think?" Ms. Pratt paused.

I didn't want to be the one responsible for ousting Cousin Gloria from her birthright, but Phyllis did need a home.

Without waiting for me to answer, Ms. Pratt continued. "I've been researching the care of pregnant and nursing cats. I feel I'm prepared and could provide an excellent home. And of course I would make sure the kittens went to only good people."

Ms. Pratt was volunteering to look after pregnancy, parturition and parenting. Cousin Gloria could sleep in a pup tent outdoors for all I cared.

"Of course, this all depends upon Emily," Ms. Pratt said thoughtfully.

"Yes, of course," I breathed.

"Then it's settled. I'll come by tomorrow. At seven o'clock," she added.

I had just hung up the phone when Hughie rounded the corner, clutching a bottle of pills.

"Guess what?" I chirped. Without waiting for his answer, I launched into a detailed account of my conversation with Ms.

Pratt.

"That's great," he said with a faint smile, then passed me the bottle. "Can you read this? I can't find my glasses."

The writing was small but legible. "For the temporary relief of menstrual cramps...," I looked up with a grin.

"Keep reading."

"...muscle spasms and tension headaches. Adult dosage: 1–2 caplets every 4 hours. Do not exceed 6 tablets daily."

"Thanks," Hughie snatched the bottle from my hand. Twisting off the cap, he popped two pills and chased them down with a cup of stale coffee. "That print's a lot smaller than it used to be."

"Do you have a headache?" I asked.

"Well I don't have menstrual cramps!" Hughie grumbled. Sighing, he added, "It's Jesus. He wants to raise the rent five dollars a square foot."

"Wow!" I sympathized. "What are you going to do?"

Hughie muttered something unintelligible then grabbed the bottle and swallowed two more pills.

The following day, Ms. Pratt arrived promptly at 7:00 P.M. with a gangly teenager in tow.

"This is Charles," Ms. Pratt announced, formally introducing me to the tall, stooped boy in a Chicago Bulls jersey. Charles stared at the floor and mumbled a response. As was the current style, his frayed blue jeans sported several gaping holes, most noticeably in the knees and one on the backside. A green ball cap turned backwards sat snugly on his head.

"Charles wants to be a vet, don't you, Charles?" his aunt prompted.

"Uh-huh." Charles had found a crack in the tile and was tracing its outline with the toe of his unlaced Nikes.

"Maybe you could volunteer here after school," Ms. Pratt added, as Charles drifted towards the display of cat toys.

Charles didn't look like the volunteering type but you never could tell. Caring for animals sometimes brought out the best in kids like Charles. I watched as he lifted the lid on the jar of catnip toys and inhaled deeply.

"Charles!" Ms. Pratt barked. "Come along."

Charles dutifully shuffled along behind us to the isolation ward. When Emily caught sight of her owner, she rolled on her head and somersaulted against the bars.

"My! She looks wonderful!" Ms. Pratt's pale complexion grew gloriously pink. She scooped Emily into her arms and after a flurry of kisses gently placed the little cat inside the carrier. Rummaging in her purse, she produced a set of keys and dangled them in front of her nephew.

"To the car, Charles."

Cat carrier in one hand and car keys in the other, Charles departed. He took a wrong turn into the storage room and re-appeared a few minutes later, blinking. Ms. Pratt caught his eye and pointed down the hall. As he strolled through the treatment area, she shook her head.

"Now then," she continued, opening a small, blue appointment book. "I've scheduled Phyllis' bandage changes for every third day at 5:00 P.M." She clicked her pen. "When are the babies due?"

"I would guess roughly two to three weeks."

"Guess?" Ms. Pratt looked up from her book.

"It's an educated guess," I ventured with a smile.

Ms. Pratt continued to stare. Guessing was clearly not an option.

"Well," I began, feeling like an awkward teenager with braces, pimples, and Ms. Pratt for homeroom. "We based that on her appearance and the size of the fetuses, since we don't know exactly when she mated. In fact," I added, gaining confidence, "it could have been over a period of several days with different toms. Female cats in heat are quite amorous and. . . ."

"Yes. Well. That's fine then." Ms. Pratt snapped her little book shut and bent down to collect the impatient Phyllis. "She'll be fine, won't she?"

"Oh, yes!" I replied airily. No more guessing for me. "Cats make wonderful mothers. They know exactly what to do. Besides, you can always call us if you have any questions."

Ms. Pratt nodded in approval then glanced at her watch. "Where *is* that boy?" she frowned.

Charles could be stalled anywhere along the route. Tired of waiting, Ms. Pratt picked up Phyllis' case of high protein food. I followed behind with Phyllis in a spare carrier. We found Charles in reception, studying his fingernails and stealing glances at Tanya.

"Is Emily in the car?" his aunt asked as she struggled with the case of food.

"Yeah."

Ms. Pratt tapped her foot. We waited.

"Manners, Charles!" she cried at last. "The door?"

"Oh, right." Charles thrust his bulk against the door and held the car keys out to his aunt.

"You may drive," she announced.

A slow grin spread across Charles' face, exposing a retaining wall of chrome. If nothing else, one day he would have a perfect smile. Leaping into the driver's seat, he inserted the key in the ignition and started the car. Unleashed by Charles' size twelves, the normally sedate, brown sedan whooped with enthusiasm. Rap music made a brief appearance but was quickly replaced by the mellow tones of the CBC. Once Ms. Pratt had secured herself behind a seatbelt, I put Phyllis' carrier in her lap. Under his aunt's watchful eye, Charles slowly backed up the car and crawled out of the parking lot.

By the second bandage change, Ms. Pratt had decided to adopt Phyllis and rename her Charlotte. She had kept the two cats separated the first night until she could stand it no longer. Emily refused to budge from her post at the door to the guest bedroom. Charlotte howled incessantly despite the dusty rose walls, the bay window and the walk-in closet. At 3:00 A.M., wide awake, Ms. Pratt threw open the door and stood ready with the plant mister, an effective weapon for disrupting cat-to-cat combat. She needn't have worried. The Brontë sisters toured the house then curled up together on Ms. Pratt's queen-size bed.

"Well, if she's going to keep Charlotte, we'll spay her at no charge once the kittens are weaned." Hughie offered. "It's the least we can do."

Ms. Pratt called Saturday morning. The first kitten, a large black male, had been born an hour earlier. Charlotte had dutifully washed him and purred as the kitten nursed. But she seemed restless and left him for long intervals. I assured Ms. Pratt that sometimes several hours passed before another kitten emerged and that it wasn't unusual for Mom to take leisurely excursions between births.

By early afternoon, however, no one was passing out cigars. Charlotte had apparently decided one kitten was plenty and showed no interest in producing any more.

Hughie took the call. I was up to my elbows in an abscess/castration combination. Tired of feline turf wars and the ensuing vet bills, Mr. Jamison wanted them "cut off and thrown away" at the same time as I repaired the abscess. Still, I hoped to leave by closing time at 2:00. One of my friends from vet school was getting married at four.

"Is she straining?" Hughie asked. "Does she seem distressed?"

"I…I don't think so. Dr. McBride said everything would go just fine!" Ms. Pratt whined.

Hughie glanced at me. "Well, Charlotte may just need a little boost of oxytocin to start those contractions," he suggested. "I can come by once we close."

At five minutes to two, Lyn MacDonald called. Sparky, her overweight grey tabby, had spent most of his morning in the litter box.

"Why do they wait until the last minute?" Hughie moaned, taking off his jacket. Saturday clinics were exhausting. By now, we had both worked six hours without a break. Sparky's bladder was full and getting fuller. He would need to be anesthetized immediately and his bladder flushed.

"Em, can you go to Evelyn Pratt's house? That'll be a quick injection and off you go to the wedding. I'll look after Sparky."

I jumped at the chance. Ms. Pratt lived nearby and oxytocin was quick-acting. I was clearly getting the better deal. Hilary packed the house call bag while I changed into a fresh pair of scrubs.

Ms. Pratt met me at the door of her carefully maintained home. A curious Charlotte trotted down the stairs, her swollen belly swaying with each step.

"Oh!" Ms. Pratt cried, ringing her hands. "I just know all

those babies are dead."

Charlotte purred and rubbed figure eights through my legs. She didn't show any outward signs of stress. "Where's the kitten she had this morning?" I asked, reaching down to pat Charlotte.

"Upstairs. Emily's babysitting."

Charlotte followed us up to the third floor where Emily was sitting in the basket with the mewling kitten.

"Charlotte's been nursing him on and off but whenever she leaves, Emily jumps right in," Ms. Pratt explained.

I picked up the baby, who squealed in protest. Unconcerned, Charlotte polished off the rest of her lunch and then waddled over to a window. She batted at a fly that buzzed within her reach.

"He looks great," I grinned. "Healthy and strong." I returned the kitten to the basket whereupon Emily immediately began washing him.

"Now, mama, let's have a look at you."

While Ms. Pratt held the squirming Charlotte, I inserted the tip of my gloved baby finger into her vagina. She appeared to be fully dilated. I reached into the house call bag and drew up the oxytocin. The purring Charlotte didn't even notice the injection.

"What now?" Ms. Pratt asked.

"We wait," I smiled. "It won't take long."

When the first injection appeared to have no effect, I repeated it fifteen minutes later. Conversation lagged then drew to a standstill as the two of us stared at Charlotte's belly. At 2:45, I called the hospital and told Susan to get the surgery ready for a C-section. We eased Charlotte and her baby into a carrier, then sped back to the hospital. Ms. Pratt decided to stay home with Emily and a tumbler full of sherry. Things were not going as she had planned, nor as I had predicted.

Back at the hospital, things were not going well either. Apparently, Sparky MacDonald was the owner of the penis from hell; an oddly twisted appendage that thwarted Hughie's best efforts.

"For Chrissakes!" Hughie fumed. "What kind of penis is this? It's like a god-damned corkscrew!" Dipping the catheter into more lubricant, he tried again only to be met by failure.

"Damn," he snorted. Beads of perspiration dotted his forehead. He had been trying to thread the catheter for over ten minutes in a procedure which normally required one or two attempts. The sensitive tissue would be starting to swell, further decreasing the chance of success. If Hughie couldn't clear the obstruction and drain the urine, Sparky would die. He stopped for a moment and took a deep breath as he stretched his cramped back and shoulder muscles.

Then he picked up the catheter once more and, adding a dollop of lubricant, began threading the flexible tube along its convoluted route. He was finally rewarded with a steady stream of urine. He began flushing the bladder to get rid of the sand-like crystals while I waited for the anesthetic machine. Anxious to avoid another confrontation with Sparky's penis, he left a temporary catheter in place. Urine would drain into a collection bag through a narrow tube. Hughie finally turned off the anesthetic machine and waited for Sparky to wake up. I glanced at my watch. It was 3:45.

"Don't you have a wedding to go to?"

I shook my head. "Yeah, but I've got the C-section. That's OK. I can make the reception."

"Em, go. I'm on a roll." Hughie alternately gnawed on a peanut butter sandwich and made notes in Sparky's medical file.

"Tanya's coming in to help," he added. "We'll be fine. Go!"

I thanked him and fled to the church in my Tweety and Sylvester scrubs. The back pews were all taken so I slipped in beside an elderly couple mid-way up the aisle. Sunlight poured through the stained glass windows and pooled on the hardwood floors in muted mosaics of colour. The air was warm and stagnant as the crowd waited in hushed anticipation. I removed my coat and laid it on the pew. In a floral arbor at the front of the church, an organist caressed the keys with a light touch. I leaned back and felt myself beginning to drift until a gloved hand reached over and grabbed my leg.

"Dear," she whispered, "I just wanted to tell you how much I love your outfit. You young people are so creative."

This observation had to be repeated several times for her husband, who was evidently hard of hearing. Soon the entire pew was focused on my wedding attire. Mercifully, Marsha, the bride, appeared at the door in a cloud of white lace and organza. The organ picked up the pace and I was forgotten.

By the time I returned Monday morning, Hughie had still not recovered from his medical marathon.

"Have a nice weekend, Dr. McBride?" he croaked, shuffling past.

"Uh-huh," I managed, still recovering from my own marathon. Sometime after midnight, I apparently performed "I Got You, Babe" barefoot on stage with Marsha's brother. This was followed in quick succession by "Big Girls Don't Cry" which, from all reports, brought the house down. I woke up at Marsha's parents' house Sunday afternoon, still in my scrubs with feet the colour of the Sydney tar ponds. A wedding napkin was pinned to my shoulder with the name "Jason" and a phone number scrawled in black ink. That would require some discreet investigation.

According to Susan, the surgery went well, but the kittens had been in rough shape. After such a long wait, they were stressed. Their own fecal material had leaked into the amniotic sac, dangerously contaminating the fluid. The anesthetic had depressed them further, causing erratic heartbeats and only occasional breathing. But, Susan reported happily, they were all doing fine now and Ms. Pratt had decided to keep two of the kittens. Why Charlotte was able to deliver only one naturally was a mystery as none of the remaining four were particularly large or breached.

Charlotte and her entourage arrived right on schedule Tuesday evening for the bandage change. The damaged foot was healing well and I decided to keep the bandage off. Ms. Pratt had been unable to decide on which two kittens; consequently, she was keeping all five. While a crowd gathered to admire the babies, Charles hovered in the background, swaying to the beat that leaked from his earphones.

"I don't discourage him. It's Bach. Well, Bach as interpreted by The Metal Bunnies," she explained, rolling her eyes. The rolling came to an abrupt stop when she spied a burly man with blonde curls and dark roots.

"Jesus? Jesus Rodriguez?" she demanded.

Startled, Jesus took a step backward. "Mrs. Pratt? How…how are you?"

"It's *Ms.* Pratt, Jesus. You never could get that straight."

"Yes, ma'am."

"What in the name of God have you done with your hair, Jesus?"

The crowd's attention subtly shifted.

"Well, I…well, you know, it's the style right now, Ms. Pratt," he stuttered, fingering his tool belt.

"Humph."

Jesus edged his way to the back of the crowd. As promised, he had returned to replace the damaged ceiling tiles in surgery and finalize the lease agreement.

"Did you ever get your Grade Ten, Jesus?" Ms. Pratt called out.

"Yes, ma'am…I graduated Grade 12. Night school."

"Well, good for you, Jesus! That took gumption."

Jesus nodded and smiled nervously.

"What about that nice girl you got…?"

"We got married," Jesus replied hastily, without mentioning the subsequent divorce, remarriage, two children, one dog, second divorce, and upcoming engagement.

"I see. And what do you do now, Jesus?" Ms. Pratt was relentless.

"I…um…well, I have my real estate license. And I do some consulting. I have my own company."

"Good for you, Jesus. Excellent! I always said you had a lot of potential if you'd just leave the girls alone and concentrate on your studies."

"Thank you, ma'am. Nice to see you again." He reached for the doorknob.

"By the way, Jesus?"

"Yes, ma'am?"

"Have I seen you in this hospital before? In a blue ball cap?"

Jesus shook his head vigorously. "No, I don't think so, Ms. Pratt. Maybe my brother Victor. He does odd jobs for me."

"Yes…perhaps," Ms. Pratt replied in a thoughtful voice as Jesus fled through the door.

Anxious to get back behind the wheel of his aunt's car, Charles picked up the carrier. Ms. Pratt thanked everyone then turned to her nephew.

"Come along, Charles," she said, "and for heaven's sake, don't shuffle."

Outpatient clinic was hectic as usual. In between appointments, I spied Hughie on the ladder in surgery.

"Where's Jesus?" I asked, dodging the bits of ceiling tile that rained down on me. "I thought he was going to replace these."

Hughie grunted something unintelligible as he struggled to fit a tile in place. When it finally settled into position, he clambered down the ladder. Brushing bits of tile out of his hair, he smiled.

"Well, Em, it seems Jesus was in a bit of a hurry to leave tonight. He agreed to a reasonable rent increase and I agreed to replace the ceiling tiles."

Whistling cheerfully, he picked up the next tile and headed back up the ladder.

Chapter 22

Hughie rapped impatiently on the bathroom door. "Em! What are you doing in there? I have to be back for two."

He paced up and down the hall while I changed out of my scrubs, removed all traces of mascara and tied my hair back in a ponytail. Searching through my purse, I found the lip balm and applied a thick layer. Instead of our usual lunch on Friday at Cecil's, Hughie wanted to go mid-week instead. A ride in Hughie's Jeep any day of the week required certain precautions.

"Are you ready?" he asked when I emerged from the bathroom.

"I just have to check on Hiram."

Hiram was an unsettling Persian-Siamese mix with bulbous eyes and a high-pitched scream that he unleashed at random. I adjusted the drip rate on his IV line while Hughie jangled his car keys and sighed dramatically.

"OK. Where's the Jeep?" I asked, looking around the parking lot.

"What Jeep?" Hughie raised his arm and a brand new car blinked its lights and unlocked its doors in silent invitation.

Bending at the waist, Hughie opened the door for me with a flourish. This was a marked departure from his normal routine of jumping in the driver's side and kicking the passenger door open.

I stared in awe at the glistening interior, not yet dulled by dog hair or fast food, and lowered myself into the luxurious leather seat. The door closed with finely engineered precision. Hughie slipped into the driver's side, adjusted his seat for maximum comfort and donned a pair of sunglasses. He turned on the radio then pulled out of the parking lot with uncustomary restraint.

Passengers in the Jeep always had to stay alert. But wrapped in comfort and secure in the warranty of a new car, I leaned back and closed my eyes, inhaling its sparkling fresh scent. For the first time in a year, I was sorry the ride to Cecil's pub was so short.

Hughie glowed. He was charming and expansive throughout the meal. He talked about growing up in Cape Breton and his dream to become a veterinarian. He mentioned how pleased he was with my work, even suggesting a raise and the possibility of partnership down the road.

"New girlfriend?" Cecil winked, noting Hughie's high spirits.

"New car," I answered with a grin.

"Even better!" Cecil slapped Hughie on the back. The two launched into a discussion on torque, engine size, and fuel efficiency that left me yawning.

"Ce-cil!" The two-syllable command sent Cecil scurrying to the bar where a lineup had formed. Mrs. Cecil, a robust fisherman's daughter from Big Tickle, Newfoundland, towered over her husband by at least a foot.

"Move it, big boy!" she ordered, swatting him with a dishtowel. As she waddled past, Cecil untied her apron then watched with admiration as she bent over to pick it up.

Hughie leaned back in his chair with a beatific smile. After a moment, he glanced at his watch.

"Well, I guess we should be getting back to work." Picking up the check, he rose from the booth. "My treat," he added, goodwill flowing from every pore.

It was a leisurely stroll to the car parked a few blocks away on a quiet side street. Hughie was reluctant to park near the high school until I convinced him it was safer than the busy street that ran past Cecil's. The September morning had started crisply, but by early afternoon people were shedding their layers in favour of T-shirts and sandals. Hughie rolled up his shirt sleeves and slung his jacket over his shoulder.

"Em, when was the last time you took any vacation? I think...," Hughie's voice trailed off as we approached the new car. A long jagged scratch extended the entire length of the passenger side. Hughie ran his finger along the ugly scar.

"Apparently this was not such a good place to park," he remarked.

There was no mention of the raise on the long, quiet drive back to work.

The following morning I noticed a familiar, rusty face in the parking lot. Dull and surly, it glared at me through a cracked headlight. Hughie was just as dull and surly as his transportation. Susan kept her eyes glued to *Veterinary Technician* as Hughie rummaged through the drawers, banging them shut in frustration.

"What are you looking for?" I asked.

"Eye ointment. It's never where it's supposed to be!"

Wordlessly, I opened a box on the counter and handed Hughie a tube of Pentamycetin. He grumbled his thanks then, turning quickly, crashed against the stainless steel treatment table. Gripping the tube, he limped up the hallway, muttering to himself.

"Dr. McBride?" Hilary interrupted. "Your nine o'clock is here."

I took the chart and glanced through the medical history.

There was little to read. The cat was apparently a stray and had been discovered only last night.

As I entered the room, a tall, well-dressed man rose to his feet. "Hi. Steve Shaunessy from the parking lot."

I reached for his outstretched hand. "Yes, I remember. How are you?"

"Oh, fine," he smiled, shaking my hand. "Tell me, did you ever find the missing cat?"

"We did. Long story with some interesting twists," I grinned. "Happy ending, though."

"Good. Good. . . ."

The smile faded from Mr. Shaunessy's face. Releasing his grip on my hand, he reached for the box on the floor and gently placed it on the examining table.

"This little fellow arrived at my barn late last night. He's in pretty rough shape. I haven't named him yet," he added.

When I saw the emaciated, pathetic creature inside, I knew why. Except for a few random patches on his legs and tail, he had no fur. A thin layer of skin was stuck to his skeleton. Too weak to stand, the little cat raised his head in a silent meow that stabbed at my heart. He sputtered and gagged as mucous from a severe respiratory infection clogged his airways. Every breath was a struggle.

"Oh, poor baby," I whispered.

"He arrived in the trailer with my new horse, all the way from Texas," Mr. Shaunessy explained. "Can we help him? I mean, I'd like to try if you think there's a chance."

For a moment, I could only stare at the little animal stretched out before me, just another cast-off of human society. Some animals were blessed with loving owners, and some knew only abuse at human hands. Luck was all that separated the two.

Rather than move the cat, I took a pair of scissors from the drawer and cut down the four sides of the box. He watched me but made no effort to move as I listened to his heart and lungs. I turned to Mr. Shaunessy.

"The first thing we should do is test for him feline leukemia and AIDS."

"AIDS?" Mr. Shaunessy looked up.

"We just need a drop of blood," I explained. "If the result is negative, then I'd like to start him on an IV drip right away. He's severely dehydrated and malnourished." I lifted a pale gum flap revealing an abscessed tooth and a broken fang. It looked like he had been hit in the face.

"That must be painful," Mr. Shaunessy grimaced.

I nodded. "He's probably unable to eat. We'll treat the infection with antibiotics for now, but when he's stronger he'll need dental work."

The rectal thermometer beeped. I paused in my examination to remove it and record the temperature. Not unexpectedly, the cat had a raging fever.

"And these lesions," I continued. "I don't know what's causing them. She could have a fungal infection or possibly an allergy. I'd like to take a skin scraping and see if we culture anything."

Ignoring the ugly red sores that scoured her face, Mr. Shaunessy continued to rub the small ears. "She?"

I nodded. "A little girl."

The cat lifted her head and leaned into his gentle touch. "How old?"

"Less than a year," I answered.

Mr. Shaunessy shook his head. The clock in my exam room

ticked quietly.

"What if she's positive?" he asked at last.

I hesitated. "Then the kindest choice would be euthanasia."

Mr. Shaunessy's hand lingered on the small body. Amidst the rattle in her chest, a new sound emerged, irregular and broken, but unmistakable.

"She came a long way looking for a better life," Mr. Shaunessy said softly as he continued to pat the little cat. "Please. Do whatever you can."

With a final glance at the pathetic little creature in the box, he picked up his briefcase and turned to leave.

"Dr. McBride?" He paused at the door. "Her name is Allison. It was my mother's name," he added. "It means 'light of the sun.'"

I looked down at the box in my arms and nodded. "It's a good name."

Mr. Shaunessy smiled wistfully then left. I carried little Allison back to the treatment area where Susan and Hilary drew blood for the test. Her veins were tiny and it took several attempts before they were successful.

Susan removed the needle from the syringe and added three drops of Allison's blood to a special vial. Turning it upside down a few times to mix the reagents in the tube with the blood sample, she then transferred the contents to the "well," a small depression in the test kit. Blood flowed from the well across a membrane to four white circles at the other end. Two were controls. The other two were test sites, one for leukemia and one for AIDS. If either or both turned blue, there was no hope of recovery.

Ten minutes can seem like an eternity. It was the number of minutes required for a chemical reaction that would determine if a single stray cat would have a fighting chance at life or would be humanely euthanized. Hilary quietly folded laundry while I hovered nearby, waiting for the tell-tale blue tinge of a positive result. It never came. When the rattle of the egg timer shattered the ten minutes of silence, the circles were still unbelievably, incredibly white.

"All right!" I grinned. "Let's get to work!"

By mid-morning, Allison was resting on a thick pile of afghans in the isolation ward. Her IV line kept kinking so we were forced to keep her front leg straight with a temporary splint. Life-sustaining fluids, vitamins, and antibiotics coursed through her veins while she slept.

Before I left for lunch, I called the Shaunessy home with an update. The phone rang seven times. I was just about to hang up when a voice answered breathlessly, "Hey, man. Whazzup?"

"Uh…Mr. Shaunessy?" I struggled to be heard over Randy Travis.

"Nope. This is Tony," a cheerful voice answered.

"Would Mr. Shaunessy be there?"

"You mean Stevie?"

"Steve, yes," I replied. "It's Dr. McBride calling."

"Oh, right! The cat doctor! Stevie said you'd be calling. He had to go to an appointment. Just a sec…."

Randy Travis faded to a whisper and we resumed our conversation. I could hear odd snuffling sounds in the background.

"Sorry 'bout that. I'm in the barn. Me 'n' the horses like country music. Steve? Not so keen. I take advantage when he's away," Tony chuckled. "So…what's up, doc?" he added, in his best Bugs Bunny voice.

I explained the results of the combo test.

"That's awesome!" Tony declared. "She's one tough little cat to get this far. Stevie's really fallen for her.... Hey!" Tony covered the receiver but I could still hear his muffled voice. "Harold, quit eatin' Naomi's oats, ya daft old fart."

"Sorry 'bout that," he apologized. "He's got his own oats right in front of 'im. Don't matter. They got brains the size of peanuts but Stevie loves 'em too. I'll tell him to call ya when he gets home. Thanks, doc."

Steve called the hospital that night, elated. I cautioned him that we weren't out of the woods yet. Allison still hadn't touched any food. If she didn't eat overnight, we would force-feed her in the morning. I didn't know how long she had gone without food, but extended failure to eat can cause liver damage. I had taken some skin scrapings as well but it would be a couple of weeks before we would get any results. In the meantime, I planned on trying her with a hypoallergenic diet.

Mr. Shaunessy was quiet. "I have a feeling she's going to be OK."

In spite of the odds stacked against her, I shared Mr. Shaunessy's faith in Allison for reasons I couldn't quite explain. All animals are unique. Like us, their personalities are shaped by a combination of genetics and experience. But Allison possessed an inner strength that had kept her alive when others would have died.

Although weak, she did seem a bit brighter the following morning. Her eyes followed Susan in the isolation ward as she prepared breakfasts, cleaned litter pans and gave medication to patients convinced they didn't need any.

"Any luck?" I asked, noting three plates of food in Allison's kennel.

Susan shook her head. "She sniffed at them, that's all. Should

I try her on something else?"

Ocean View Cat Hospital carried three types of hypoallergenic food. Doctor Richard Johnson carried a fourth. Hughie was fond of referring to him as Dr. Dick-Dick.

"No. I'll go to Johnson's to pick up a few tins of venison and rice," I announced.

Susan lost her grip on the laundry basket. Hunched over the anesthetic log, Hughie looked up, his mouth wide open. A dark stain spread across the counter where Hilary had overfilled the iodine prep bottle. Only Tanya, humming along with her headphones in the surgical ward, was oblivious.

"I could order some food in," Susan offered at last, breaking the silence.

"That would take too long."

"What about Dr. Prince in Bedford?" Hilary suggested.

"Johnson's closer."

I had heard the rumours about Johnson but always figured they were a bit exaggerated, especially the one about his hair transplant. Speculation about the source of his oddly textured, curly hair ran wild at staff parties. From clients we learned of the disparaging things he said about our practice. In all fairness, he said disparaging things about everyone. He tottered a fine line but had never been reprimanded by the veterinary association because he had been practicing since the dawn of time. This afforded him a certain status among his younger peers.

"Well, Em. I see you've made up your mind. Good luck." Hughie shook my hand gravely. "We'll never forget you."

Johnson's hospital occupied a crumbling stone building shaped like a tombstone. I hoped to borrow a few tins from his receptionist and leave but Johnson was lying in wait.

"Ah, Emily. You're looking particularly lovely today," he remarked, rubbing his hands together.

"Richard," I nodded, glancing down. Johnson barely scratched 5' 6". He whipped out a plastic bag from behind his back and dangled it in front of me.

"You wanted some feline hypoallergenic food?"

"Yes, thanks," I replied, reaching.

"What's it for?" he asked, pulling the bag just out of my grasp.

"A client," I smiled, reaching forward again and grabbing the bag.

Johnson snorted. "Steve Shaunessy's cat?" He stared at me with little piggy eyes.

"How did you know?"

"Ah…I know a lot of things, Dr. McBride," Johnson smirked. "Make sure you run up a big bill. The guy's loaded."

I stepped back a few feet and studied the curly thatch of white hair on the top of Johnson's head.

"Besides…," Johnson lowered his voice and looked around. He needn't have bothered. The waiting room was empty and behind a glass partition, his gum-gnawing receptionist was buried in a glossy magazine.

"Guy's a queer. His type gives me the creeps. I used to see his horses but I won't go out there anymore." Johnson shuddered then glanced at his watch.

"Hilda!" he barked. "Those X-rays done?"

Clutching ten tins of cat food, I mumbled my thanks then gratefully stepped outside into the sunshine. When I got back to the hospital, Hughie was scrubbing for surgery. I felt like jumping into the sink and scouring away the slime from my visit to the dark side.

"How did it go?" he asked.

I shook my head. "Don't ask. Got my food though!" I held the bag up triumphantly.

Hughie nodded, whistling a happy tune as he scrubbed. His mood had improved dramatically since yesterday.

"What're you doing?" I asked, changing the subject. "I didn't think there were any surgeries today."

"Remember little Mimi Warner with the crushed tail from yesterday?"

I nodded. "Yeah, I thought they didn't want to pay for the surgery."

Hughie grabbed the sterile towel and patted his arms dry, then slipped into the surgical gown. Behind him, I tied the strings of the gown together while he snapped on a pair of sterile latex gloves. When he turned round, his eyes were crinkled in a broad smile above the face mask.

"Well, Em, seems Billy Warner and I are both repairmen. He works on car bodies and I work on cat bodies." Holding his sterile arms above his waist, Hughie pushed the swinging surgery door open with his foot.

"Allrighty, then, what have we got, Susan?" His cheerful voice faded as the surgery door closed behind him.

"Dr. McBride?" Hilary poked her head around the corner. "Come see."

I followed Hilary to the isolation ward where Allison was polishing off a plate of food. Her raspy tongue scoured the plate clean, but just to make sure, she sniffed it thoroughly. Hilary and I shared a smile. She had arrived at work long before we opened, just to spend time with Allison before the demands of a new day took her to other patients, other responsibilities.

"Her fever's broken too," Hilary whispered, not wanting to break the spell. Unable to stand on her own yet, Allison had been lying down while she ate. Exhausted from the effort of eating, she closed her eyes and slept. Lingering for a few moments, I watched her chest rise and fall. Her breathing was raspy and mucous clogged her nose, but she had eaten on her own! With enthusiasm! Her ears twitched, as if somewhere deep within her brain, she heard my thoughts. I covered her with an afghan and tip-toed out of the room. Thank God for Dr. Dick-Dick.

In the week that followed, Allison continued to do well. We unhooked the IV line and monitored her progress closely. She ate well but starvation had caused her intestinal tract to shrivel and weaken. For several days, explosive diarrhea sent the staff scurrying to open windows and light candles. We rejoiced when one morning, Susan discovered a well-formed bowel movement lying proudly uncovered in Allison's litter pan. Her skin lesions were improving and the antibiotic had reduced the pain in her mouth.

After a quick trip to Toronto, Mr. Shaunessy arrived Saturday afternoon to take Allison home. His flight had been delayed and his luggage lost, but he was jubilant. I lifted Allison out of the kennel, cradling her like a baby. The first time I held her in my arms, I had cried. Today she was a full pound heavier as she gazed into my face and purred.

"You've worked a miracle," Mr. Shaunessy murmured.

"Not me," I smiled, shaking my head. "Allison did this…with a little help. She's a very special cat."

"I know," Mr. Shaunessy said softly.

I carried Allison out to the car. Mr. Shaunessy removed his cardigan and arranged it on the passenger seat. Allison was still quite weak and content to lie on the soft, warm sweater. I stood off to the side as Mr. Shaunessy bent down to pat her. Arching her scrawny neck, she rubbed his face in return. After a few moments, he stood up and gently closed the door.

"Dr. McBride." He turned to look at me. "I have AIDS."

I took a breath, trying to keep my voice level and professional, as if I ran into this kind of situation everyday.

"Well, there are certain precautions you should take then. It's very important that you don't get scratched or bitten. And make sure you wear rubber gloves when you change the litter pan, too."

Mr. Shaunessy nodded. "Thanks. But I know that. What I meant was...she's come through so much. Am I a risk to her?"

I looked at Steve Shaunessy standing tall in the late afternoon sun. A warm breeze rippled his shirt and sent leaves scurrying past. Behind him, bright sunlight bounced off Hughie's brand new car, parked proudly in its reserved location. No trace remained of the long, disfiguring scar.

"No," I said at last. "AIDS occurs in lots of species but each virus is specific to that species."

Mr. Shaunessy took a deep breath. "Thank you, Dr. McBride," he said, shaking my hand. "Thank you so much."

He opened the car door. "Let's go home, Allison."

I watched them leave. There was so much I wanted to say but in the end, I just smiled and waved goodbye. Our pets give us far more than we give them. We provide food, shelter, toys and a warm lap. They give us the opportunity to love selflessly.

Back inside, Bernie began turning off the lights. One by one, the staff left for the day. Only Hughie and I remained. I checked on a couple of inpatients then called their owners with updates. By the time I was ready to leave, Hughie and Sullivan were heading out for a romp in the woods. Emerging from the darkened hospital, we blinked in the brightness of a beautiful September afternoon.

Hughie filled his lungs. "Wow! What a day."

Sully wagged his tail as he sensed the possibilities. It was a day to dig in the dirt for bugs and eat them fast before anyone hollered "No!", a day to jump over logs even if you didn't know what was on the other side.

"Do you need a lift, Em?" he asked, locking the hospital doors.

I looked around the nearly deserted parking lot. In one corner, blushing-pink blossoms of a late-flowering hydrangea brushed against a high wooden fence. A cat strolled across its narrow ledge, unconcerned, then disappeared into the yard below.

"Thanks, but I think I'll walk. It's a beautiful day."

Hughie tooted the horn and waved as he drove away. "Let's talk about that raise next week. It's been a year!"

In the passenger seat, Sully stood with his front feet on the arm rest, his head poking out through the partially open window. He barked in excitement as the wind whipped his fur and tipped his ears back. He was the fastest dog in the universe.

I unzipped my jacket and cast it over my shoulder. It was a day for leaping over logs.

The End

CPSIA information can be obtained at www.ICGtesting.com
Printed in the USA
LVOW081121201211

260303LV00001B/93/P